I0612172

Sicilian Refuge

Titles by Keith Weaver

An Uncompromising Place
Un endroit sans compromis
The Recipe Cops
Balsam Sirens
Mr. Drumlin's Orchard
Walking with Albert

Sicilian Refuge

Keith Weaver

IGUANA

Copyright @ 2019 Keith Weaver
Published by Iguana Books
720 Bathurst Street, Suite 303
Toronto, ON M5S 2R4

All rights reserved. No part of this publication may be reproduced, stored in a
retrieval system or transmitted, in any form or by any means, electronic,
mechanical, recording or otherwise (except brief passages for purposes of review)
without the prior permission of the author.

Publisher: Meghan Behse
Editor: Paula Chiaros
Front cover image: Photo by Victoria Chen on Unsplash
Front cover design: Daniella Postavsky

ISBN 978-1-77180-337-3 (paperback)
ISBN 978-1-77180-338-0 (epub)
ISBN 978-1-77180-339-7 (Kindle)

This is an original print edition of *Sicilian Refuge*.

For Roberto Zingales, with gratitude

Brief Notes on a Mystery

On March 4, 1861, a man named Ippolito Nievo boarded the steamer *Ercole* in Palermo, which sailed that day for Naples. The *Ercole* never arrived. It was presumed lost in the Tyrrhenian Sea, taking all passengers to the bottom.

No trace was ever recovered of Nievo or what he took with him on the ship.

Nievo was a member of Garibaldi's Thousand, about a thousand untrained and untried people who accompanied Garibaldi from Genoa to Marsala in Sicily. Garibaldi's objective was to drive the French from Sicily and the southern half of the Italian peninsula, known then as the Kingdom of the Two Sicilies. That they succeeded came as a surprise to many, and was due to a number of factors, not least of which was Garibaldi's superb generalship.

Nievo was an important member of Garibaldi's senior officers, being the man in charge of the finances for the expedition. The purpose of his trip to Naples was to discuss those finances, which is why he carried the account books with him when he boarded the *Ercole*.

Under other circumstances, the loss of the *Ercole* might have gone unremarked by history. But at the time of his presumed death, Nievo was not yet thirty years old. At that young age, he had already produced a respectable quantity of poetry, and his one novel, *Confessioni di un Italiano* (Confessions of an Italian) went on to become a classic of Italian literature. As a result of Garibaldi's immense charisma, the success of the military campaign, and Nievo's prominence then and later as a man of Italian letters, and because of the mystery that swirls around his last voyage, the name Ippolito Nievo has acquired practically mythic status in Italy.

I have added two fictional details to Nievo's story. Those details drive most of the action in the tale you are about to read.

One

It was cold. Something smelled of ginger.

Images of Chinese lanterns and chopsticks swayed oddly before him, but then the pain cut in as an atonal interjection or a misread score played by a panicked novice musician.

I'm on the ground, he thought. But there was something funny going on. *Am I imagining this? Can't be. It looks so real.* And then panic. A large black boot swung toward his face. He winced, bracing for the impact, but nothing happened. *What's going on? Must have missed.* He had seen the boot, but he was aware that he was alone. His initial puzzlement was turning to confusion, then to an awakening fear. The boot swung at him again. He attempted to move out of its path, and then hot pain seared through him once more. But the boot had missed him. *What's happening?*

Now he knew, somehow, that he really was alone. His face was painful, swollen, and he realized that he was lying on his right side. *My teeth!* A cautious probe by his tongue found no gaps or sharp edges. His sense of place and time was returning. It was night. A light shone dimly from somewhere to the right, behind him. He moved his left hand over the ground. Rounded pattern. Gritty. Cobbles. Cautiously, he raised his hand to his face. Something sticky on his left cheek. *Oh God! Surely I haven't lain in some dog shit!*

Blood. It was blood. And then he knew what had happened. Three young punks had attacked him. He had to get up and away in case they returned. His left hand went to his pocket. No wallet. *Shit!*

It took him about three minutes to rise to a sitting position on the ground. Right side insanely sore, deep breaths impossible, maybe one or two cracked ribs. And the huge lump high on his right cheek. It was obvious that he had also taken one to the gonads, but it wasn't completely debilitating, so he must have turned slightly or got a leg in the way to deflect the blow partially. And they had taken his wallet.

No. He remembered now seeing the wallet on his desk. But they had evidently taken whatever money he had had on him. Didn't matter. It was just money.

Using the support offered by a nearby bicycle rack, he was able to pull himself up and stood, leaning against the wall of a building. For a few moments, he drifted on waves of nausea. He looked at his watch, but the face was shattered, the hour hand was gone, and the watch had stopped. A church bell sounded in the distance, and he counted the chimes. Nine o'clock. The street was deserted. Near the bicycle rack lay an aluminum take-out tray, contents only partly eaten, the container tossed or dropped and the congealed remnants scattered near it. The smell of ginger. He looked away, riding out another wave of nausea. He checked his pockets again. No keys. Just a handkerchief.

By now, most of the mental fog had cleared. He was in Karlsruhe. That much he could recall. He was here doing a project. The work was going well. Just that afternoon, he had spent four hours in the university library after attending a two hour tutorial in conversational German over the lunch period. The immediate past was now flooding back in, filling a vacuum fringed by tatters of confusion.

He staggered forward. He had gone out for – milk. That was it. Milk. *Milch.*

To a small shop a couple of hundred metres from his flat. Didn't remember getting there. But he did remember Angelika. Earlier that evening, she had come to see him. That's why he had left his wallet and keys behind when he went out in a rush, away only a few minutes, to get mi–

She's still there. Still at his place.

He took a quick look around. Maybe his money had just fallen out of his pockets. Nothing on the cobbles around him except a few grubby stubs of paper and something that looked like his bus pass. He leaned down carefully, "gingerly" he thought, in a sudden access of dark humour. He picked up the pass, had to wait a moment for the street to stop spinning, and saw that the pass belonged to someone called Sieghard Lehmann. Absent mindedly he shoved it in a pocket.

His mental state returned to normal fairly quickly, but he was puzzled and a bit intrigued at the sense of unreality, of novelty, that came over him as he realized where he was, why he was there. It was almost like entering a short stretch of real-life experience but suddenly sensing that it paralleled exactly a dream from some time ago, or it might even be that the dream had returned now in full detail, having been completely forgotten for who knows how long. In fact, it was a bit like how he imagined it might feel to live through a short clip of someone else's life.

But that sense faded as quickly and as irretrievably as a real dream does on awakening, and within another couple of minutes, he felt at home with the notion that he really was in Karlsruhe, in streets he knew and could recognize without effort.

It took him about ten minutes to return to his flat, staggering at first, then walking slowly. He lived in a reasonable student lodging, probably a bit better than most, and the door latch was released a few seconds after he had pressed the buzzer for RC.

She was sitting in the small kitchen, reading a magazine, and didn't look up right away when he entered. When she did look up at him, smiling, her face collapsed into a mask of shock.

"Ryan! Oh my God! What happened?" She rose from her chair and rushed over to have a closer look.

"I was mugged."

"In Karlsruhe?"

"Yeah, well, it's a big city."

"But–"

He moved away, entered the small bathroom, and began dabbing a wet facecloth at his cheek after he had examined his image closely for a few seconds. No other cuts or bruises. This wasn't the first time he had heard of street violence in Karlsruhe, but it was the first time it had touched him. He walked through to the sitting area and parked himself in a large chair. A dull throb had now engulfed his head. Angelika had maintained a solicitous flow of questions and comments. Did he report it to the police? Should he be seeing a doctor? Did he have a supply of iodine? Where did he keep his BandAids?

But an intense desire for quiet and solitude had settled over him. He answered Angelika's questions but then added that he was tired and woozy and wanted to lie down. With Angelika's help, he rose from the chair, made his way to the bedroom, and lay down on his bed. Angelika said she would stay a while in the sitting area in case he needed anything. He nodded.

His head pounded out a beat that shattered any thoughts even as they formed, leaving a feeling of jigsaw puzzle pieces floating in space, colliding randomly in an annoying clatter.

He awoke some time later realizing that his mouth was full of foul-tasting cotton wool. The light was still burning in the hallway. It was 2:15 a.m. Angelika would have gone home long ago. Only a vestige of his headache remained. There was stiffness in his side and back. It felt as though his right cheek was pumped up and when he looked in the bathroom mirror it was evident that his eye was swollen almost shut. The evening had been a train wreck. He decided to forage in the kitchen for something soothing and filling . . . but not just yet. He sat in his kitchen, wanting just to be still for another quarter hour, to interrogate his body, see which pieces complained. A short to-do list formed in his mind: book an appointment at the university health clinic and get himself checked over; buy a new watch; get some milk, of course; revise his schedule to increase his daily study time for German from one hour to two; follow up the two intriguing references he had uncovered that afternoon at the library.

His thoughts turned to Angelika. For Ryan, a vague feeling of unease had developed concerning their three-week acquaintance. It wasn't just the very odd way they had got to know each other, an experience that had some puzzling and still unexplained aspects, or that he had fallen into an easy acquaintanceship with her, even though he was not looking for female company and had decided to steer clear of any sort of commitment. It wasn't just his sense that Angelika would have readily gone to bed with him if he had picked the right moment and made a move or that she had made none herself, that she seemed happy to stand to one side and wait. It was a bit of all of these.

He was convinced that the events that had brought him to Karlsruhe were also playing into what seemed like the most significant thing that had happened yet in his life. Against this hugely positive background there was an increasingly ominous and shadowy sense that something, somewhere, was not right.

Two

He must have gone back to bed and fallen asleep once more because now he was stretched out, head on pillow, trying to rise. Again. Even though he did so carefully and slowly, the action brought howls of complaint from his right side, his back, and his groin. None of them was a paralysing shooting pain, however, so he carried on and stumbled to the kitchen once he was steady on his feet.

Four o'clock in the morning. A nice bowl of muesli, he thought, but he had not been successful in getting milk. Well, maybe there was just enough milk left to mix with a bit of water, since he had no desire to venture out again into the night, where at this hour there would be no place open that sold milk.

A quick look in the fridge, hoping against hope – and there was a half litre of milk. Angelika must have brought it from her place after he had gone to lie down the first time. He prepared a small bowl of muesli, then thought about things as he sat and munched it. The night huddled against his kitchen window, peering in like a hungry supplicant and, oddly, reminding him of the path that led him to his present place and moment, a path that he could follow back to a time earlier in Toronto. Only two months ago, he reflected. But it felt almost like a lifetime. His mind drifted back . . .

It was mid-May. He was still living with his parents in Toronto, three and a half months after he had quietly and ignominiously dropped out of his course at the university. Before any possibility had arisen of him being in Karlsruhe or anywhere except Toronto. And he was living the vaguely dissatisfying reality of jolting along an increasingly bumpy life road.

It shouldn't be like this, the recurrent thought nagged him once more. The opportunities were there, waiting to be picked. And he knew it was down to him to pick them. He also had the deep feeling that any of those opportunities, if taken, would have returned purpose and optimism to his life. And yet here he was. Rudderless. Adrift academically, he had allowed his existence to wander into a state of pointless carnality involving his latest conquest, the promiscuous and he sensed, opportunistic, Diana. His life had become one of profound dissatisfaction.

But two things had loomed, things that were going to be watched by his parents, things that should have demanded his own serious attention: his upcoming birthday and the approach of a new academic year.

Twenty years old, in less than three months. He knew exactly what that meant – renewed scrutiny by his parents.

By his mother. His extraordinary mother, at least to him. And he suspected to many other people as well. Medium height, slim, elegant, high cheek bones betraying her Czech family background, golden-blond hair now slightly subdued by hints of ingrown grey. Ryan regarded her now, and always, as a stunner. Even her name, Michaela, had always seemed exotic to him, although now she went by the shorter Mika. The picture was completed by grey-blue eyes, a delicate nose, fine expressive lips, a smile that could shatter diamonds, and faint humour lines around her eyes that she made no attempt to conceal. But perhaps most young men had this rose-tinted view of their mothers.

His mother had been devastated – her word – by Ryan's lapse into what she probably considered a state of inexplicable irresponsibility. But behind it all, really, were her complex feelings about him. Her real and deep motherly love. He felt there was something more: a need, a craving, to feel pride in an accomplished and successful son, and distress that his present path would leave that need unfulfilled.

Then there was his father. James Chandler was a rather different kettle of fish. Ryan appreciated his father's patience, his comment that one or maybe two false starts were excusable, his self-control. Ryan was pretty sure that he had now used up all the slack his father had given him and that he had to get his house in order very quickly.

On that May morning, in Toronto, uttering a groan of low-level anxiety, concern, and desire for the luxury of procrastination, he climbed out of bed and headed for the shower.

There, he worked out the details of his day. His life was not completely dissolute, even though it could justifiably be called aimless, random. He busied himself in a slate of charitable functions that kept him occupied for more than half the day, every day. But all that was just filler. In no way could it be called an occupation, far less a career or anything having a discernible future worthy of the name, and he wouldn't dare try to float such a sham past either of his parents. Showered, shaved, and dressed, he went through to the family kitchen and breakfast room to have the first meal of the day.

His mother greeted him cheerfully. "Good morning, Ryan. What would you like?"

"Good morning, mother. I think just toast and juice, please."

His father was examining a report at a small desk near the window away from the breakfast table. He set it down, came to the breakfast table, and clapped a hand lightly on Ryan's shoulder.

"Good morning", he said, as he sat down, unfolded his napkin, and smiled at Ryan's mother as she placed a plate of eggs and bacon before him. "Will you have some time later this afternoon?" he asked Ryan. "There's a project I want to discuss with you that I'd like your help on and I think it will be interesting." His fork hovered halfway to his mouth as he waited for an answer.

"Yes, of course", Ryan said. "How much time will I need?"

"Oh, not more than an hour, I think. I have two conferences in the office this morning and a lunch meeting, but I'll be spending the afternoon working here. Would three o'clock suit you?"

"Yes. Fine", Ryan replied. "Do I need to prepare anything?"

"No. It will be essentially a planning session, so just come with an open mind."

Breakfast was congenial. After about twenty minutes, Ryan looked at his watch, said he had to get moving, and rose from the table. "See you at three, Dad."

They both smiled and acknowledged his departure.

A faint alarm bell warned him that the meeting with his father signalled trouble ahead, but he chose simply to suppress the thought, to live with present fears rather than open the can of far more ominous future imaginings.

Three

James Chandler was a very successful corporate lawyer. He was always deliberate in approaching any situation, and he could bring to bear subtlety and delicacy to whatever level was required.

Whenever Ryan thought of his father, many images came to mind. He remembered especially his father's passion for organ music and the organ lessons he had worked at assiduously for years. Whenever thoughts of music came to mind, Ryan recalled the stunning performance his father had given when he was allowed to play the organ in Timothy Eaton church that one time. And while James Chandler was a complex, extremely determined man wielding a razor-sharp mind, he somehow managed to prevent this causing him to browbeat, buffalo, or intimidate people. He always found ways of dealing with people at levels that didn't make them unnecessarily uncomfortable, and he always found a way to get what he wanted in a manner that was calm and didn't leave the other party feeling that they had been cut off at the knees.

Ryan thought about all this as he worked his way through his tasks at the food bank. A half-assed plan for his life formed in his mind, although it was largely shrouded in the fog of imprecision, the haze of nebulous outline, and the insecure grasp of faltering commitment. Some of these shameful dog-ears in his plan were straightened out during the morning. By noon, he had something that he could at least claim was a framework, although he expected that it could be reduced pretty much to mental rubble by just a few of his father's well-placed logical incisions, then reconstructed in a form that Ryan could not yet foresee. Not stopping for lunch, he worked until two o'clock, then left for the meeting with his father.

But when he arrived at his father's den just before three o'clock, there was a note taped to the open door: *Conf. call. Back 3:20. Sorry.*

Ryan felt apprehensive, not only because he had no idea what form or which direction the meeting would take but also because he would be entering this meeting as one who had allowed things to drift to the point where he had relinquished all personal initiative, and the outcome would be beyond his control. He knew that the meeting would be civil; it always was that.

He took a seat at the large table surrounded by five comfortable reading chairs. He looked around the room and smiled at the many good memories it raised for him. It was large, all the walls having floor-to-ceiling bookshelves. His father's desk sat to one side, but most of the room was unencumbered, allowing the attractive oak floor to radiate its warmth. Rising from his chair, Ryan walked toward a familiar section of the book shelves. He recognized the wide selection of classics ranged in front of him. He had spent a good deal of time here when he was younger, and on rainy days he still had a deep urge to go into the den, curl up with a book, and listen to the quiet, civilized whispering of the rain outside. Idly, he pulled several books from their slots, savoured their texture and the distinctive smell that rose from them, opened them at random, and smiled at the occasional familiar passage.

Returning to the table, he opened the file he had brought with him. It contained notes he had written in preparation for the meeting, ideas for his future. These were not just meaningless scribbles, not notions that would crumble at the first of his father's questions. Rather, they were what he felt could be called a strategy, a proposed life strategy for Ryan Waddington Chandler. But, even so, he knew that they represented nothing that his father would accept as a "plan". It was a start. But his eye was drawn back again to the books, to old friends.

"Sorry, Ryan. Had to take that call."

Ryan looked up. His father crossed to his desk, dropped a notebook, picked up a file, walked to the table, and took a seat beside him. And then right off the bat, he caught Ryan off guard.

"I wanted to let you know that your mother and I have decided to sell the house."

"Sell the – what? Why?" What did this have to do with Ryan's life? Perhaps nothing. Perhaps he had completely misread the situation. But, better to withhold judgment. "Have I misunderstood completely? Is that what we're meeting about?"

"No. I'm sorry", his father said. "I should have found a better lead-in. But now that we're on the topic, let's continue. You probably have some questions."

Yes, indeed. There were questions that rose up instantly. Were his parents selling his abode out from beneath him as a way of forcing him to take charge of his own life? Surely not. That was completely out of character for his father. "Well, yes", Ryan said when he found his voice. "Where are we – or rather, where are *you* moving to? And this seems sudden, at least to me. Is there a problem?"

Ryan's father nodded in understanding. "First of all, it's always *we* the three of us, not just *we* your mother and me. And no, there's no problem. This is not something imminent. We'll be deciding on the schedule; it isn't being imposed onto us. But let me lay it all out for you in some order.

"Your mother and I have talked about this for several months, and we've decided to take advantage of the fact that I'll be travelling more, and piggy-back more holidays onto those trips. We're looking at condominiums. There are several that offer the floor area we want and good terrace space so that we can have at least a semblance of being outdoors."

"But the garden?" Ryan began. "Mother has always had a garden . . ."

"That's true. But you might not have noticed that she's leaving more and more of that work to the landscape people. She's more interested in just enjoying the garden now. One of the units we've been looking at has a large terrace, half open and half enclosed but fitted with sliding doors and screens for the summer. Your mother got quite excited about the possibilities."

"What sort of arrangements? I mean, how should I–"

"You're probably worried or upset that we haven't consulted you, but this is not a fait accompli that you'll have to accept. We've made no firm plans. But to be quite blunt, your mother and I want to craft our own future going forward, and I expect that you will want to do the same, independent of us. At some point, our futures are going to diverge, and your future is going to be a lot longer than ours."

They had reached the segue.

"So that brings us to what I wanted to talk to you about. But understand, I didn't ask you here to force you to do anything. You must be aware that I'm concerned about your – let's call it temporary lack of direction – but that's not what I want to discuss either."

His father pulled a few sheets from the file that he had brought with him. "You know I've travelled to Europe three times this year already. What you probably don't know is that I've been asked to help set up and run a new programme involving four universities and three firms, ours being one of those firms. We can get into the details of that later. Have you heard of IAESTE?"

"No", Ryan answered, not at all sure where this was heading.

"It's an international programme for student exchanges. It was set up in 1948 to try to help promote understanding among countries after the calamity of the Second World War. I've been involved in the IAESTE Canada committee now for about five years. We've been looking at something a bit different over the past few years."

Ryan's father placed a single sheet on the table. On it were one paragraph of text and two diagrams.

"We're looking at something more ambitious than just student exchanges. The idea is for students to work on projects that are more challenging, that have larger scopes and take longer to complete. But more than being just work projects, they would aim to give students a deeper understanding of another national culture."

As he spoke, Ryan's father pointed to the diagrams, and he paused here to see whether Ryan had any questions.

"We went through a lot of paperwork and formalities, but in the end everyone recognized that we need a convincing field test of the concept."

Another pause.

"That's where you come in, Ryan."

"Me?"

"Yes. I would like you to be the guinea pig for this project."

"But . . . What? How? I mean, I don't understand what you're asking. Do I have a choice?"

"Ryan, surely you know that you always have a choice."

"Well, sure, yes. But which country? When? For how long? How is the project to be selected?"

Ryan's father just looked at him steadily for several seconds. Speculatively? Just collecting his thoughts? Hoping for a response?

"You remember high school? How you sailed through those courses, took the top prizes more than once for your essays and reports. Then you went off to the University of Toronto. There wasn't a prouder man than me in all the city, but I hadn't realized then just how badly I had let you down."

Ryan's face registered genuine surprise. "You've never let me down. It's me who has let you down."

But Ryan's father was shaking his head.

"No, I did. I was the one who pushed and set high standards. And you always met them. It's true that I never beat or lectured or shamed or harangued you. The pressure I applied, I'm ashamed to say, was far more subtle. I expected you to leap from secondary school to university without a backward glance, but I expected you to do it all on your own, that there'd be no wrinkles, no bumps in the road. So now, I want to offer you a chance at something different."

"Just like that?" Ryan said. "Drop everything? Well, drop what little there is and just flit off somewhere to do a project I have no idea about?"

"No", Ryan's father said calmly. "Not like that. I've become convinced that this could be a life-changer for the right sort of young person. I'm also convinced that there's probably nobody better placed than you to put it through a trial. In fact, I believe in this so strongly that I'm prepared to promise the committee to fund the trial myself – if you choose to be the guinea pig, that is. But, let's be clear. You can refuse without any comeback. So, now, can we at least spend some time talking about it?"

Ryan spent almost three minutes cooling down. He had to give his father a hearing. He couldn't just assume that it was all a cheap trick to try to jog him, cynically, out of his current lifestyle. In some surprise, Ryan realized that the resistance he was sensing in himself was just a reluctance to face change.

So they talked. For more than two hours they talked. Ryan agreed to think about it. But even before he left the den at well past five thirty, he could feel a twinge of interest, a flutter of excitement, and deep inside himself, something was urging him to agree. That he was about to embark on something that would unfold in Germany and immerse him in topics on which his present knowledge was zero, that was all in the unknown future.

Four

Thinking about and preparing for a big change is quite different from actually making a big change.

There were many discussions. Even as he worked to get his mind around the basic idea and then to flesh it out and begin background preparations, Ryan was aware of his own burgeoning interest in and enthusiasm for the project. He worked hard on that preparation, and in very little time, he had taken complete and personal ownership.

But the larger significance of what he was undertaking began to dawn on him only during the overnight flight to Frankfurt. The realization that he was venturing into something relatively unknown was confirmed later at Frankfurt airport when he was searching for the railway station, fumbling to buy rail tickets, to find the right train, and to do all this in settings that were not familiar. All this was in sharp contrast to what now seemed the relaxed and casual confidence with which he had approached his research for this project, back in Toronto.

Get used to it Chandler, his Inner Voice instructed sternly. *There's no stopping and there's no going back.*

Karlsruhe was Ryan's ultimate destination because his research in Toronto, which had defined the project that would occupy him for months to come, had identified a nineteenth-century event in that city associated with what turned out to be a minor turning point for the science of chemistry.

The Hotel Baden was a small establishment tucked out of sight near the main marketplace in Karlsruhe. The ridiculous intensity of his relief when he finally found the place indicated how badly his inner self wanted to grab any firm handhold, no matter how tenuous or even how illusory. And the Hotel Baden was only a temporary spot until he could find himself student accommodation for up to the next eight to ten months.

His mood during that first night in the hotel was a mixture of elation and trepidation. Like an astronaut on the way to the moon, being the repository of a scarcely believable amount of kinetic energy and now largely in the hands of huge competing gravitational forces, the die had been cast – there was no turning back, and he simply had to get on with it.

But soon, Ryan settled into what became a continuation of his advance preparations. Once he had set himself upon a path, he found that tasks were lining up almost of their own accord and crying out to be done. He had homed in on a project, centred on a technical meeting that had taken place here in Karlsruhe in 1860.

Five

As it happened, it took Ryan only four days to find his own place in Karlsruhe. It was a decent flat, in about the middle range of student accommodation. It was quiet, everything appeared to work, and he now had to make it his home. He undertook his relocation from the hotel with that same feeling of mild turmoil that had come over him periodically since he had decided to enter into this venture. There was interest in doing something different, no question. But there was also concern that this new reality, whatever it was, would turn out to be something that was so unexpected in so many ways that he would never find a way out of it. Some of it was a natural resistance to change, but some of it was a concern that what he was leaving behind was the real thing, and his project would lead him down a path to illusion, a hall of intellectual mirrors, a trackless psychological wilderness, and that getting back to the reality he knew could be a route strewn in dangers. The more he thought about this, the more he realized that it was the very vagueness of his situation that was the most disturbing.

His first night in his flat was not much more than an exchange of the strangeness of his hotel room for the strangeness of his permanent lodgings. He walked around and took stock of things. The furniture was a bit shabby, but it was solid. There was no air conditioning, but he would just have to put up with the heat of summer and early autumn. He might need simply to suffer through any heat in the following year, depending on how long it took to reach the end of his project. There was a bedroom, not large but adequate, a smallish bathroom – into a tight corner of which a shower cubicle had been squeezed next to a bathtub that looked as though it could have been a contemporary of old Karl Wilhelm himself, a large living, dining, and working area, and a small but nicely fitted kitchen. The place had an air of Prussian stiffness and reserve.

But places have personalities, and he wanted to get off on the right foot. So he spoke to his new flat in the language he expected it to understand.

"Guten Tag. Ich bin nun dein Einwohner."

Having thus introduced himself – *Hello. I'm now your new resident* – to his new abode, Ryan felt as though relations between them began to thaw a little almost immediately, and he put this down to the crash course in German he had completed the day before he boarded the plane to Frankfurt. For two weeks, his instructor at the Goethe Institute in Toronto had driven him eight hours a day, and then at the end of each day had given him three hours of homework, and although this had left deep linguistic welts, it had also equipped him to get by surprisingly well while emitting a very limited number of howlers.

The research he had done for his project in Canada filled two large accountant's cases, and these were the first items he unpacked from the shipping trunks that had been delivered to the home of Professor Hartmann at the Karlsruhe Institute of Technology, or KIT. Hartmann was Ryan's local contact for both everyday matters and research questions, and it was clear after only a few minutes into their first meeting – not much more than ten minutes of social contact – that, although Hartmann was at least thirty years his senior and appeared to warm slowly, they would get along. Ryan had hired a large SUV-type taxi to retrieve the trunks from Hartmann's home. It took two days for him to settle into his new rented flat, and on the third day he had spread out files across his desk and dived into them where he had left off in Toronto. The familiarity of the research material, the sense of becoming settled, and a few days of strolling in his new city caused a feeling of comfort, easiness, and purpose to push aside the initial sense of dream and illusion that had engulfed him.

Ryan thought about the planning for the project. His living and work arrangements had been designed to be transparent and to make it easy to confirm that the work he documented was indeed his own. He had begun keeping a diary, something that he considered essential in order to be able to claim ownership over everything. An initial meeting had been scheduled with Hartmann. Ryan would then be left for a few weeks to get into a new working routine. Then there would be regular biweekly meetings after that with Hartmann so that there would be a record of some structured, independent academic oversight. His meetings with his parents, particularly his father, would be few; in fact, he had only one such meeting over the entire scheduled duration of the project.

Ryan set to work. In the space of just a few days, the entire project had taken on a different feel. Things began falling into place naturally. He was in Karlsruhe mode. There were differences, of course. That he had expected. But the reality was outstripping the expectation. More easily than he expected, he was becoming used to life in Germany. This was made simpler by the sheer amount of psychic energy he was directing at his project. There was no time to fret over things not being the same as back in Toronto.

As it is right now, he thought, closing his laptop and rubbing his eyes.

"Six o'clock", Ryan mumbled, looking at his watch. Spurred by a grumpy rumbling stomach, he assembled his notes for the day, filed them into folders, and prepared to venture out into a mild Karlsruhe evening in search of dinner and relaxation.

Throngs of people, many in their twenties and thirties, surged through the streets. Ryan strolled not quite aimlessly, pleased at how comfortable he was feeling in his new German surroundings, how much of the snatches of conversation drifting past him he could follow. Wearing light-weight jeans, a short-sleeved cotton shirt, and a pale-blue jacket slung over his shoulder, he was essentially unrecognisable from others his age. The only slight difference was that, unlike many Germans, none of his clothing displayed any English words.

At the end of a twenty-minute stroll, he was in Ludwigsplatz, an area almost completely covered by outdoor seating. Conversation filled the air, spilling into the streets and pedestrian alleys from the many tables. He found an unoccupied space and seated himself so that he had the most inclusive view of the streams of people passing.

"Speisekarte?"

"Bitte", he managed to return before the young man, evidently his server, had moved out of earshot. The menu, the *Speisekarte*, had been lobbed onto the table in front of Ryan, not in an unfriendly way, as the young man passed.

"Zum Trinken?" The question came at him as the same server made another pass.

"Ein Pils. Null komma fünf."

Within a few minutes, the young man placed a large glass of beer in front of Ryan and nodded acknowledgement without slowing down to Ryan's request for a *Jägerschnitzel*. The evening was fine, warm but not humid. A light breeze wafted past him, the beer was cold and good, and Ryan noted the civilized surroundings he found himself in. There was the architecture: strong, distinctive, meeting a consistent standard, and making its own solid, slightly reserved, Germanic statement. There was the comfortable atmosphere of people at ease in surroundings that blended effortlessly into the virtues of a summer evening. Most of all, there was the complete lack of unpleasantly blaring music – the bane of far too many communal spaces in North America – as though the lack of such music would leave the air ominously brittle and devoid of life or scare people off in anechoic near-panic.

Ryan's meal arrived and his hunger set him to work on it immediately. Twenty minutes later, he waved for another beer and sat back in that halo glow generated by the knowledge that at least here and now, life was truly good.

"Sind hier Plätze frei?"

Ryan waved in welcome, indicating that the other seats at the table were free. There were three of them, young women, all in late teens to early twenties. It was the most forward of the three who had spoken. She had a deep summer tan that made her blue eyes and medium-length sandy hair stand out even more, and she and her two friends took seats, falling back into the conversation he had heard as they had approached his table. Ryan glanced at the three of them several times, but focussed on a quiet nursing of his beer, idly examining the streetscape around him and doing desultory vocabulary exercises triggered by words and phrases that drifted to him through the evening. As the remaining beer volume headed toward zero, Ryan glanced at his watch, judging that there would be more than enough time for another glass of something before he strolled home.

"I will guess that you are not German."

Ryan surfaced from a reverie in German that had something to do with *Steinpilze*, for reasons he could not retrieve. When he turned to look at where the question had come from, he realized that he and the tanned young woman were the only two at the table. She wore a speculative expression and smiled knowingly.

"Where did your friends go?" Ryan asked in German, imitating the Bonn accent of his instructor at the Goethe Institute in Toronto, something he had worked on carefully during his time with Stefan.

Her smile transformed itself into an expression of mild surprise.

Ryan maintained a pleasant but neutral expression, looked directly at the young woman for a few seconds, then took a sip of beer.

"Plötzlich so beredsam?" he said, asking in German idiom if the cat had got her tongue.

The young woman reached quickly for her handbag. "I–I'm sorry", she stumbled in German. "Excuse me." And she began to rise.

"No. It's me who is sorry", Ryan said quickly in English. "I apologize. Please, stay and have a drink."

She sat down again slowly.

"I want to switch to wine", Ryan said, looking around for a server. "What would you like?" He waved twice at passing wait staff, to no avail. The young woman raised a hand, and a server appeared instantly out of nowhere. *So ist das Leben*. Such is life, when it comes to young women being able to attract a waiter's attention. She asked for two glasses of riesling, and some lamp genie placed them on the table almost instantly.

By now she had recovered. "Are you Canadian?" she asked, to end a gap in the conversation that was becoming too long.

"I'm much more likely to be American. Why ask if I'm Canadian?"

"Maybe I'm tired of meeting Americans and wish for a change."

"Yes, I am Canadian. And judging by your accent, you're from Karlsruhe or somewhere nearby." Ryan was taking a chance here – he had no real idea how to recognize a Karlsruhe accent. But he had a friendly suspicion about this young woman.

Her gaze now became openly curious. "Yes, I was raised in Karlsruhe. My family moved away six years ago when my father became a professor at Stuttgart. I came back to go to KIT."

They both regarded their wine, then Ryan said, "Zum Wohl!" and raised his glass. They sipped and then watched their surroundings for a few moments. Ryan broke the silence, introduced himself, related a little of his background, and in response to her questions, he filled in details on when he had come to Karlsruhe and described the project he was working on in vague "history of chemistry" terms.

Then he asked her about herself. She was not very forthcoming at first. He soon found out that she was studying physics but had spent a lot of time lately thinking about her future and wasn't sure she had made the right academic choice.

Ryan made reassuring noises, modifying something expressed often by his father in telling her that a degree was just a beginning, and that while it would be a poor choice to study physics if one wanted to be a lawyer, there were few dead ends in education, and that in the general world out there, nobody really cared about what degree you got or where you got it after you had about five successful working years behind you.

She nodded, pondering this, evidently not ready to believe it without some further thought.

"But I'll need to be able to call you something other than *you*", Ryan said.

This caught her off guard, and she had to think about it for a few seconds before she understood.

A smile spread quickly across her face. "Yes, of course. Angelika", the young woman replied.

They talked some more about Germany and Canada, until Ryan made getting-ready-to-leave noises. They paid and she looked at him directly and said, "Okay. See you around."

On the way home, Ryan reflected that normally he would expect such an encounter to end there. But in Angelika's case, he knew things were different.

Not because he had any feelings for her or was particularly intrigued.

But because he knew that she wanted something.

Six

Professor Doktor Ingenieur Gustav Hartmann let it be known to Ryan right away that he wanted to be called Gus. After an initial 'Welcome to Karlsruhe' meeting with Hartmann and a 'my door is always open' statement, they arranged to have their first formal project meeting a month later. During that time, Ryan had settled fully into his new flat, met Angelika, and done sufficient work on his project to make a review meeting with Hartmann worthwhile.

Now, in the third week of September, he and Hartmann were together in Hartmann's office for their first project meeting. Ryan took a few seconds to take in the man and his setting.

Professor Hartmann appeared to be in his fifties, was grey-haired, had a somewhat jolly face, and at what Ryan judged to be about five feet ten inches, he was a little shorter than Ryan. His hair probably had once been blond, to match his fair skin and washed out blue eyes. Hartmann had a mobile but serious face, didn't smile much, and seemed to need his hands being occupied, by fiddling with a pen, fingering papers, or just gripping the edge of his desk. His office, in part of the KIT science complex, was neat, but all the shelves on two walls were solid papers, reports, and books. He was at ease, his blue eyes engaged Ryan confidently, and on this occasion he toyed continuously with a pen.

"I got used to the informality a few years ago during my sabbatical at Cornell", he said, "and I rather liked the change from what is required here."

Ryan had brought a large armful of files, and he was interested to see how the discussion would go, still having no inkling on Hartmann's level of interest or his approach in dealing with students.

"I was hoping, Dr. Hartmann – sorry, Gus – that at the end of this meeting we could reach agreement on the direction and scope of my work and some basis for reviewing progress regularly."

Hartmann nodded, and Ryan noted the mild approval in his expression.

"We can certainly aim at that", Hartmann began. "But I was hoping that we could start by having you walk through what you want to achieve in general terms."

Ryan allowed his perplexity to show. "But we've already agreed on formal objectives."

"Yes, we have", Hartmann replied, "but that was a long-distance agreement over words on a page. You and I need to have a common working understanding of just what those words mean. So, if you could take a few moments and describe in your own terms what you hope to do . . ."

Ryan collected his thoughts and began soon feeling a sense of surprise at how easily the narrative was coming to him. As he spoke, Hartmann jotted a few notes on his pad but otherwise focussed on Ryan.

"So", Ryan concluded, "I hope that at the end of my term here, I'll be able to produce a short account of what the 1860 conference achieved, how the delegates reached that result, and the background against which they worked."

Hartmann looked up from his notes. "I have some idea from your project documents on what you're trying to do. I have to confess my interest in this project. But I'm curious. That 1860 conference must be almost completely obscure for anyone but historians of chemical science. What led you to it as a topic?"

Ryan smiled and leaned forward. "Well, it was the first ever international scientific conference. It was intended to bring order to the problem of atomic weights, where there was no agreement at that point. And that lack of agreement caused endless problems and arguments. I was intrigued to see that in the decades leading up to the conference, there were still hints of alchemy in the air. But mostly, I think, I was attracted by the interesting range of personalities involved. And, in the background, I wanted something that would stretch me."

Hartmann flipped through some papers in his file.

"You certainly seem to have succeeded there, Mr. Chandler. A student of English and philosophy, I see. A huge jump from there to the history of nineteenth-century chemistry. Most interesting."

Hartmann closed his file and looked up at Ryan, appearing to change intellectual gears.

"What background material have you consulted thus far?" he asked.

Ryan nodded. "There are the usual scientific surveys by Jaffe, Read, Partington, and Levere. I've also consulted the large work by Thorndike. And I've spent quite a bit of time on the books by Rocke, Principe, Moran, and Newman."

Hartmann nodded in approval. "You're evidently aware that various aspects of the Karlsruhe conference have been documented many times. What do you feel you can add?"

Ryan took this as an academic challenge, not as a negative comment or a dismissal.

"This has all got to do with worldview", Ryan began. "When we look back at 1860, we can do so in many ways. Each of those ways involves a context, and each context will be somewhat different, and possibly greatly different, from all the others. But that all existed against a common background. I want to document that common background. And that's really more a question of social history than chemistry. That's what I hope to add."

Hartmann had leaned forward. "And what do you see as the main elements of that context?"

"Well, first, it's very difficult to see things the way someone in the past saw them because we know many things that were still hidden from them. There were social, scientific, and historical aspects as backdrops to the things that those people knew. But many of them were groping toward a new understanding, and some of them were better at that than others. Williamson for example, seemed to have been very good at it."

Ryan leaned forward in his seat, now comfortable with his topic. Hartmann sat back in his chair, smiling faintly, hearing material he was long familiar with but appearing to enjoy having it come from a student who had such an unusual background to be undertaking work like this. He nodded a couple of times, encouragingly, as Ryan spoke.

"On practically all fronts", Ryan continued, "physics was making enormous strides during that period. Just twelve years earlier,

Europe had seen the year of revolution, 1848. The centre of gravity for both chemical research and mathematics had very recently begun shifting from France to Germany. The Second Empire had been declared in France less than ten years previously. The Franco-Prussian War was just ten years in the future. Even closer were the events that led to Italian unification, and some of those events were already underway as the conference took place. There were strong and weak figures at the heads of various empires and countries. It was a time of great change on a number of fronts. Plus the nature of chemistry itself had just undergone an enormous conceptual change. The last major elements of alchemy were gone. Things were becoming much more quantitative."

At that point, Ryan stopped rather abruptly and felt himself blushing.

"I'm sorry, Gus. This is the student pretending to inform the professor."

Hartmann smiled broadly and chuckled. "Not at all Mr. Chandler, Enthusiasm is always welcome. But you must be aware that you've covered a lot of ground in just a few sentences. I assume, I hope, that you aren't expecting to go into all that in any detail."

"Ah, no", Ryan mumbled, recovering from his ongoing blush. "I'll stick to the conference, the conferees. Even then, I expect it won't be easy. I'll need to work like a dog, and I'm afraid I'll need to rely on you fairly heavily for guidance."

Hartmann nodded then leaned forward, signalling a change in the focus of the meeting.

"When I studied the prospectus for your work, I was hoping that you would move in this direction. But now let's talk about some specifics." They then spent a few minutes going over the outline Ryan had prepared for his final report. Hartmann suggested some changes and additions, and they formulated a set of standing items that could be used for periodic reviews.

Then Ryan was back outside in the golden light of late August. Students flowed past on foot and on bicycles. The combination of the quiet regal mood, which seemed to hover over Karlsruhe, and the positive interview lifted Ryan's spirits.

Although he felt a renewed urge to rush back to his flat and get to work, he decided that could wait. It was time for a mini-celebration and a bite to eat. He walked through the grounds of KIT, crossed Kaiserstrasse, and made his way toward Kapellenstrasse. His objective was the pub called Der Vogelbräu, where the beer and food were good and the ambience very hard to beat.

Ryan made his way to the beer garden. The place was about half full, and he found an empty table pleasantly shaded by overhead vines and took a seat. He ordered a large Pils and a salad plate, then just allowed himself to be carried along by the babble of conversation, punctuated regularly by peals of laughter from nearby tables.

Ryan's beer and food arrived, and he was ready for both of them. Unexpectedly, he was gripped by his surroundings: the colours and aromas of the food and beer in front of him; the relaxed and civilized feeling of what was going on around him; the lack of offensively loud amplified music; the natural, leafy, outdoor ambience; but mostly by the stunning surprise of feeling at home in a place, a culture, and a language that he had known almost nothing of just three months before.

And he realized that this was his father's doing, that his father had manoeuvred him into his present situation, knowing full well what the impact would be. The stray thought, inserting itself yet again, that he had been wasting his time up to now, that it had taken him far too long to get his ass in gear, brought a smile to his face.

"You crafty old bugger!" Ryan said, more loudly than he had intended.

"Who? Me?"

Ryan's reverie ended in a gentle thud, and he turned to look at the smiling face of a sandy-haired youth about his age.

"Oh! No!" Ryan said hastily, once he had returned from his mild out-of-body experience. "I was just talking to myself."

"Germany does that to people. Something you'll need to watch if you plan on staying here any length of time." His table companion spoke English fluently, but through the light accent there was something that Ryan had noticed many times now: the slightly clipped delivery, the pure vowels, and the disciplined syllabic stresses that flowed harmoniously and rhythmically in German but lent a slight pizzicato when carried over to English.

A tall glass of beer arrived for the smiling German sitting beside Ryan. He lifted it immediately in salute, waited until Ryan did the same, then clinked his glass against Ryan's saying "Zum Wohl!"

A quarter of their beers vanished, and the glasses clunked down again on the table in a satisfying Wagnerian ring of victory. Valkyries vanquished. Rheingold recovered.

"I'm Wolfgang, but call me Rick."

"Rick? As in Casablanca?"

"Hey? What?"

"What's wrong with Wolfgang?"

"Too much Germanic baggage."

"Why Rick?"

"My second name is Friedrich. I don't really like either of my names."

This seemed to be going nowhere in particular, so Ryan introduced himself.

"Great name!"

"No, not really. It just describes a little king who provisions ships."

Rick's food arrived, and they both settled into the job of eating. But conversation continued as the occasion of empty mouths allowed. Ryan asked if Rick was studying at KIT and was offered the reply that he was enrolled. The vague response from Ryan to the counterpart question, that he was "working on a special project at KIT", seemed to satisfy Rick's curiosity.

"Your English is good", Ryan said, as he was catching the eye of their server after draining his glass. "Where did you learn it?"

"Just here and there. No fancy courses."

"I wish I spoke German that well", Ryan offered, in German.

"Ah! You catch me off guard", Rick replied also in German. "I thought you must be American, but the ones I've met seem to speak only English."

"Yes, well. Many of them mangle English too."

Rick thought this was hilarious and it kept him chuckling until two more glasses of beer landed authoritatively in front of them.

Conversation drifted through their pasts, covered Ryan's previous three months, and inevitably turned to football. In due course, Ryan looked at his watch and was astonished to see that it was almost five o'clock.

"Places to go?"

"I'm on a schedule."

"Aren't we all! Time gobbles everything."

That slowed Ryan down, and Rick had to explain the proverb, and German proverbs generally, and he realized that yet another vast field of practical learning awaited his attention.

"Let's do this again", Rick said. "How about tomorrow night?"

"Suits me", Ryan replied in genuine enthusiasm. "Same place?"

"Nah. We'll try somewhere different. Let's meet at your place, say at six o'clock."

"You don't know where I live."

"Not yet. But I will when you tell me."

By then Ryan had had some cards printed, and he flashed one to Rick, who dropped one of his own on the table.

There was a friendly row about who would pay, but in the end Ryan won. As they spilled out into Kapellenstrasse, they were all smiles, two freshly minted friends, both looking forward to whatever that had to offer.

The afternoon had been one of mild euphoria and surprise, and as Ryan wandered homeward, he thought about his project but even more about the new world in which his father had conspired for him to land. He took a leisurely way home along Kaiserstrasse, making a side trip to look again at Jochen Gerz's placards on the edge of the Schlossplatz and stopping for what had quickly become one of his favourite desserts: *heisse Himbeeren*.

A new and appealing dimension had expanded into his intellectual world, brushing aside a number of items not firmly rooted. One of these items had been something puzzling he had noticed in Hartmann's office.

Its image was now submerged. But it hadn't gone.

It was at work.

Like the worm in Blake's poem.

Seven

Ryan and Rick got together at the end of the next day. And it was a welcome change for Ryan after a day of slogging over the biographies of chemists and wading through correspondence from more than a hundred and sixty years ago in which bad-tempered researchers seemed to take more joy in slagging each other than in actually explaining what they had been doing and what they had found. He had also now filled in the details of two timelines: one extending over a period from 1790 to 1900, the second stretching from 1830 to 1870. These two timelines covered the lives and careers of most of the big-name chemists whose work affected, or was affected by, the 1860 Karlsruhe conference. And he had compiled more detailed profiles of seven men: Gay-Lussac, Ampère, Mendeleev, Meyer, Berzelius, Cannizzaro, and Avogadro.

Ryan wondered how the organizers of the conference ever could have thought that this group of headstrong men would end up agreeing on even everyday things – what to eat, what the weather was like, whether various books by Dickens, Balzac, and Manzoni were really all that good – let alone the existence of atoms and molecules, or even a common scheme for atomic weights. From the accounts Ryan had read of it, pretty much from the moment the conference began, it looked as though it was doomed to failure.

"How are tricks?"

Rick was attracted, for some reason, to slang greetings in English.

"Fine."

They shook hands, and Rick slapped Ryan playfully on the shoulder, which brought an involuntary wince.

"Oh! Sorry man", Rick said. "Problem with your shoulder?"

Ryan tried to divert the discussion, but eventually the story came out about Ryan being mugged a little more than a week earlier.

He related the whole business in a relaxed way, even laughing over it, and showed Rick the bus pass he had found at the scene.

"I'm not sure why I kept it. It's not important."

"What do you mean, not important?" Rick said in some heat. "Did you try to find this guy?"

"No. I've no reason to be sure he was even one of the muggers. Besides, I've got better things to do with my time." He shrugged off the whole matter, but Rick quietly pocketed the bus pass.

They enjoyed another stellar evening. Rick led Ryan through a warren of small streets and alleyways, ending up in a quiet courtyard where about fifteen tables were set up, most of them occupied by groups of people in subdued conversation. Rick dodged questions on how his studies were going, but said that he was working on a paper.

"It's not something I have to do. In fact, nobody knows that I'm doing it. But I think it will help get me through my course nicely."

Under a bit more questioning, Rick indicated that what he was working on hinged on the idea of *error* and how people in the nineteenth century reached conclusions about something being an error in a social context.

"Bit complicated, isn't it?" Ryan observed.

"It's hellish complicated", Rick said. "People tended to take stands on things being absolutes, especially the notions of truth and error, when what they really were expressing were just approximations or best judgments. I was particularly tickled by the eighty things that Pius IX identified in his ludicrous 'Syllabus of Errors.'"

"What? More papal bull?"

It took a few minutes for Rick to overcome his convulsive laughter. "That's what I like about English", he said, wiping tears from his cheeks.

"Do you think much has changed?" Ryan asked.

"About bullshit? Oh yeah! There's a lot more of it around now."

"No", Ryan said, starting again. "I meant in terms of how people look at truth and error."

"In what way?"

"Well, don't you think that people still yearn for absolutes?"

Rick was all smiles. "Yearn! That's a good word. I have to use it more! But you're right. People still hope for absolutes, but as well as more bullshit, there's also a lot more solid information available now than there was a hundred and fifty years ago. If they want to be taken seriously today, people have to avoid running afoul of hard facts, which means they need to know what facts are out there."

Ryan was doubtful about all this and sensed a good friendly argument in the offing.

"Are you sure?" Ryan asked in what he hoped was a challenging way. "Doesn't that sort of statement apply only to areas where everyone feels bound by a code of telling it like it is? Areas like science and the disciplines that apply science?"

"No. There are plenty of indicators showing that people in general are disposed toward the truth."

Time for a feint.

"Well, but that's a problem for you because you're using the word *truth* in an undefined context. Something might be true in a colloquial sense. But it might turn out not to be true at all when more rigour is brought to bear."

Ryan didn't expect Rick to parry ineffectually in sixte.

"I'm not sure just what you mean."

Deft move into a fleche.

"Suppose someone says to me that it's raining cats and dogs. Pretending to be literal-minded, I ask him to clarify. He says it's coming down by the bucketful. I keep on questioning him, and eventually he allows that it's a light drizzle, not likely to accumulate more than about a centimetre in twenty-four hours."

Rick took refuge in retreat. "So. All you've done is make his statement more precise."

"No. I've done more than that", Ryan said. "I've forced him to shift from a vague to a more specific metaphor. But even more important, I've moved him into an area where, if I want, I can now push him more strongly on what's black and what's white versus what's grey. The more forcefully I push, the smaller his black and white areas will become. I can show him that he's in an area that's mostly, and perhaps essentially completely, grey. In the end, I should be able to get him to express himself in terms of categories like knowns, uncertainties, unknowns–"

"You're not going to quote Donald Rumsfeld at me, are you?"

"Don't knock it. He was trying to express something important. He just happened to be talking to a group of people who had no interest in science or rhetoric, didn't know their ass from their elbow in either area, and in any case were just looking for a cheap score."

"I'm not sure where this is going. It seems to have nothing to do with the case I was making."

"It has everything to do with it", Ryan replied. "People are extraordinary in that they can make fine judgments without the benefit of a lot of scientific apparatus. They always have been able to do this, and they still can today. But some odd things can happen. The idea of a *fact* can be hard to define, even today, but more so in the past, and the material that facts come from can be internally contradictory."

Rick's scepticism seemed to be fading.

"The more facts there are", Ryan continued, "the greater the amounts of time and effort that are needed to get one's head around it all, and the harder it can be to use the right fact in the right context. And we all know that facts can be misused in various ways."

"Sounds like this is becoming one big confusion", Rick commented drily.

"Yes", Ryan said. "It could do that. But behind it all, there's that huge background canvas called *worldview*, or some similar name. Worldview usually brings in a large load of baggage: misconceptions, preconceptions, unquestioned assumptions, cherished beliefs, dogma, the presence of groups not averse to using coercion. The further one gets away from the hard sciences, the larger and richer this background canvas can be."

"Doesn't that just make things worse?" Rick objected.

"No. And the main reason for that is that worldviews can change. Suddenly. It took the Roman Church three hundred years to admit that Galileo had it right and they had it wrong. That's a bit of a pathological case, but it does show that, even there, a time came when the writing on the wall trumped the fiercest dogma."

Rick was now nodding. "I'm guessing this is where you start talking about your project."

"You've got it", Ryan said. "What I've learned over the past few months is that there's a background canvas even in science. This is one of the things I'm having to look into in my work on the 1860 chemistry conference. But what's changed today – at least I think it's new – is the nature of bullshit. Not too long ago, I came across a little booklet by a Princeton academic, Harry Frankfurt. Quite readable, and he nailed all this very nicely."

"Most interesting, Dr. Chandler", Rick said after a short pause.

Ryan blushed sheepishly, realizing suddenly just how much he had held the floor.

"Sorry. Didn't mean to turn into a pompous prick. But yes, an understanding of what's meant by worldview in a specific time and at a specific place seems to be important for my project."

Rick looked at him in an odd expression of sardonic speculation.

"You wouldn't like to write a twenty-thousand word essay for me, would you? And I need to get more information from you on this thing by Harry Frankfurt."

"No, I'm too busy writing my own stuff, but I'll pass on my copy of Frankfurt's essay." Short pause here. "And I can see the value to both of us in talking about this a bit more."

By then, they both realized that a budding casual friendship had quietly expanded into a more intellectual engagement. The fact that this change was sealed by the shared consumption of three more beers only underscored the importance of beer as a valuable means of unlocking the metaphorical cabinet.

Each of them took something away from this meeting. In Ryan's case, it was the recollection of a pleasant verbal joust. For Rick, the takeaway was a task that he needed to carry out quietly on behalf of his new friend. He wouldn't realize until much later just how incendiary the findings from that task would become.

Eight

The following week, Ryan put his head down and pushed forward on his project. The work was going well, smoothly, and the weeks flew by. His periodic reviews with Hartmann were going well. Hartmann saw a project that was unfolding as it should and required little corrective action from him. In fact, he noted to Ryan a couple of times that the work was adding clarity to a number of areas that suffered from long-standing vagueness and was possibly even reporting some original research.

This generally positive direction of his work was complemented by the awareness that engaging and unexpected social elements were linking up to Ryan's life in Karlsruhe. It had been only a few days earlier that Ryan returned in late afternoon to his flat to find Angelika waiting for him outside.

"Hi, Ryan", she said, smiling.

"Hi", he said in reply, feeling the smile on his own face. "What's up?"

"Nothing much."

"Have you eaten?" he asked.

"No."

"Well, come in while I drop my things. Then we can go off somewhere and have dinner. Okay?"

There were quite a few places near Ryan's flat, they picked one, and soon were seated before some solid German food.

After a few moments, Angelika set down her knife and fork and looked at Ryan.

"You puzzle me a bit. I would expect you to go for French or Italian cuisine. Yet here you are", and she gestured toward Ryan's plate of *maultaschen.*

"I don't need to force myself here", he said through a broad smile. "German food is good. I really enjoy it." Ryan went back to his meal, but when he looked up again a few seconds later, he noticed that Angelika was still looking at him somewhat speculatively. They smiled at each other and resumed eating.

Their casual meetings continued. After that dinner, and several other informal pub evenings, Ryan became aware that they had slipped into something that wasn't quite a routine, but also wasn't simply a series of random meetings. Without giving it a lot of thought, he welcomed this connection to Angelika, being well aware that he was a non-German slipping into a German way of living.

A change occurred the day that Ryan invited her to his flat, they had prepared and eaten dinner together, and then had chatted until she said she had to get back and do more studying. After she left, Ryan spent some time reflecting. Angelika was an acquaintance, nothing more, and they had in common only their age and being students at the same institution. But he had to admit that it was a comfortable and relaxed acquaintanceship. She was always pleasant, and Ryan examined only idly his mild curiosity at why she was persisting in keeping their connection alive. She was open and frank in a way that he had come to be familiar with among young Germans since his arrival in Karlsruhe. She had a good sense of humour, something that always appealed to Ryan, she tolerated his fractured German and encouraged him as he improved it, and there was every sign that she was interested in him as a person and, perhaps, was also attracted physically. He enjoyed her company, probably more than he was prepared to admit, but wasn't interested in trying to move things to another dimension, in part because of the need to focus on his work, in part for reasons he hadn't examined. Maybe she found her course boring. Maybe he represented some sort of novelty value to her. In any event, he fully expected the relationship, whatever it was, would soon fizzle, he would realize one day that he hadn't seen her or heard anything from her for a couple of weeks, and that would be the undramatic end of it.

Looming larger in Ryan's work were his discussions with Rick. What had started off as a beer friendship soon became more an extended and wide-scope intellectual joust. And the main area of focus was Ryan's project.

Rick demonstrated a sharp intellect that could roam in comfort over large areas, and he quickly became a perfect sounding board for Ryan's ideas.

"Doesn't that bother you?" Rick asked, as he set down his glass of beer. The venue on this occasion was not another pub but the kitchen in Ryan's flat, where Ryan had offered to treat Rick to a scratch meal and a five-litre keg of Bitburger.

"What? Not having a good grounding in chemistry? Well, I do have to work for every crumb, but because of my relative chemical ignorance, I can see the world in a way that's probably closer to how the attendees at that conference saw it. I don't have a lot of modern chemical baggage that I have to try to ignore. All the people at that conference were indeed eminent scientists, and I'm very much aware that my own chemical ignorance hardly puts me on a level equal to theirs."

"So how do you deal with all that? In a practical sense, I mean?"

"Well", Ryan began, "it means that I'm pretty much condemned to a lot of ongoing hard work. But I did try to get a working background before I came here. I even hired a graduate student to put me through a crash course in chemistry."

"That must have been interesting!"

"It was brutal. He stretched me to the limit. But in the end I think he helped me gain a basic level of chemical familiarity. At least there was somebody there to ask. Overall it saved me a lot of time and frustration."

"Do you still come up against stuff that stops you short?"

"All the time. One of the things that my graduate student helped me do was compile a list of topics, terms, major experiments, important papers, things that defined significant new signposts after 1860. That's turned out to be an enormous help. I still consult that list every day. Well, I call it a list, but it's a ninety-page booklet."

"So he constructed that booklet for you?"

"No way! He helped me compile a list of things, then pointed me toward some sources, and told me to get on with it."

"So", Rick began, "you came here with–"

"I came here with my head spinning, a list of about eighty sources that I could use to get started, a very rough first outline, an initial three-page statement of what I was trying to accomplish, and my graduate student's chemical cheat sheet, my vade mecum."

"Wow! Seems like rather light armour."

Ryan nodded vigorously.

"During my first two weeks here, not a day went by when I said to myself that this was all ridiculous, that I had no idea what I had taken on, and that I should just pack up everything and head back home."

"And what stopped you?"

There was a long pause here. Ryan looked around the room, the kitchen in his own flat in Karlsruhe, thought about the campus, the pubs he had come to know, the spoken and written German all around him, the young man before him who would have been an unapproachable foreigner a few months ago but was now a friend. He reflected on how this had somehow all become familiar and understandable, a new beginning. And then he thought of the wreckage of his life in Toronto.

"I've never liked quitting, and I think that's what made me so miserable and lost in space when I dropped out of university. When I was preparing to come to Karlsruhe, the couple of months I spent reading and thinking, I remember the exhilaration of taking on something much bigger than me, and I don't want to lose that again."

"Still", Rick said through a wry smile. "All that champagne! All that sex!"

"I'm not sure it was a good idea telling you about all that."

"Relax man! I'm not getting at you."

"What then?"

Rick suddenly looked distracted.

"I can't . . . I'm having trouble . . . Am I coming down with something?" he said, apparently in some alarm, shaking his head.

"Are you all right?" Ryan asked, concern now evident on his face.

Rick's features cleared suddenly.

"No, of course I'm not all right! My beer glass is empty!"

"Okay", Ryan said, relaxing. "I get it. Stop taking yourself so seriously, Chandler!"

The evening went on for another two hours. Their talk ranged over several areas, but somehow always came back to Ryan's project. There was also a healthy strand of ribaldry that made its way into the exchange. But when it came to Ryan's project, it was inevitable perhaps that Rick asked questions and Ryan tried to give short and to-the-point answers.

"Tell me a bit about alchemy", Rick asked at one point. "I'm supposing it was more than just a bunch of crazed hermits boiling vats of urine in dark caves."

Ryan was surprised at how much he actually knew on the topic, and how readily it came out when he had to explain it in everyday terms to another person.

"So, a lot of this stuff just fell by the wayside, because–"

"Because of lots of reasons. But over a period of time, a mood seems to have come across many people, a mood that said that because we could see physical changes occurring under specific conditions, and because these were reproducible, there had to be something more than just *ex cathedra* explanations."

"Ex what?" Rick asked.

"Ah. Sorry. It means 'backed by an authority that can't be challenged.'"

Rick was obviously filing that one away.

"So the old alchemical outlook just collapsed?" Rick asked.

"A lot of the ideas lost their power to convince, but the alchemical worldview was far from being unique, and it certainly wasn't constant over time. It did collapse, but it would be a mistake to think that on one day there was something at centre stage called *alchemy* and the next day it was something called *chemistry* that had the limelight. Alchemical ideas dissipated slowly, in bits and pieces, but some of them hung around for a long time. You could see the influence of alchemy on chemistry well into the eighteenth century, if you knew where to look and what to look for."

"Ah!" Rick said looking off into space.

"That was one interesting thing my graduate student told me, that it's surprising how many people have a basic idea that science just turns up fully formed."

"As opposed to?"

"As opposed to having to be formed and reformed painfully. Just think of caloric, phlogiston, and the huge long philosophical struggle over the existence of atoms. It wasn't that people were stupid. It was just that something was only barely visible through the mist. Some people saw one pattern. Others saw a different pattern."

Rick looked directly at Ryan for a moment.

"This is all gripping stuff, Ryan. Important in its own way. But a horrible distraction from beer and football. And you'll need to explain this caloric and phlogiston to me one day."

Ryan looked very sheepish. "Sorry, man. Why the hell didn't you stop me?"

"What?" Rick said in mock dismay. "And impede the flow of intellectual progress?"

"Yeah! Yeah! I get it . . ."

They were both smiling now.

"Well, no. You don't really get it", Rick said.

Ryan's smile faded. He looked at Rick in what he felt later must have appeared to be imbecilic puzzlement.

"Beer, Ryan! Where's the fucking beer?"

And they both broke out laughing.

***

After that evening with Rick, Ryan put his head down for the best part of a week. The amount of material was massive, but he found that he had a better feeling about it all as time went on. What he would have found baffling and overwhelming a month earlier was now a challenge he accepted.

The concept of worldview revealed just how many tentacles it possessed. But he felt that he was wrestling the thing to the mat, piece by piece.

It was a Thursday, in the early evening. Ryan left the library later than usual and started home. He had planned to stay much later but had come across several items that he wanted to read in the comfort and absolute quiet of his living area. As he strolled across the

Schlosspark, he pulled out the pages he'd copied at the library and leafed through them. They were letters, and they recorded impressions of some of the conferees several days after the sessions had been completed. Ryan had found a letter written by Lothar Meyer, one of the youngest participants at the meeting, and it was clear that he had been particularly impressed by a document circulated by one of the Italian delegates, Stanislao Cannizzaro.

It wasn't easy picking his way through the German, and he was surprised when he looked up and saw that he was within a few minutes of his flat. But the material was absorbing, and Ryan slowed his walking pace even more as he read. He climbed the steps of his building, still immersed in reading the letters. As he entered the flat, now moving very slowly and trying to disentangle a particularly involved flourish of German phrasing, he sensed, more than being consciously aware of, the sound of papers being shuffled. Nose stuck in his photocopies, he finished a long paragraph, and then saw Angelika through the doorway that led into his large living area and work space. He moved into the room and was about to say hello when he realized that Angelika was reading through his files. There had been eight or nine bulging file folders arranged on his desk, but now they were open and spread out. A deliberate search was underway.

"Angelika?"

She jerked upright. A false smile appeared on her face, but it didn't quite cover the underlying expression of embarrassment and panic.

"I'm, I just, I thought I would tidy up your files."

"They don't need tidying. What are you looking for?"

"Nothing. I-I'm–"

In two long strides, Ryan was at the desk and grabbed Angelika's hand as she quickly tried to cover a notepad.

"You're making notes from my files. What the hell is going on?"

"I-I'm sorry. I should never have come here. I must leave."

She reached for her large handbag, but Ryan gripped the strap and pulled it roughly away from her. "Tell me what you've been doing here!"

"Please. I must go. Please forgive me."

Ryan looked down at the notepad. The headings for his report had all been copied out, and there were many annotations in German.

"How long have you been spying on me? What are you looking for?"

Without waiting for an answer, he opened her handbag. "Do you have any of my stuff in here?" He looked quickly through her handbag but could see nothing untoward.

Angelika was now in tears, but Ryan was too angry to be affected by that.

"It's not what you think", she said in a tremulous voice.

"You don't know what I think! But you have no good reason to be snooping through my papers!"

"Please. Won't you let me explain?"

"No! Leave!"

Ryan sat on the bed after Angelika had left. Anger, sadness, and deflation mingled in the remnants of a ruined evening. But he couldn't just leave this matter dangling, and he made a call to see if he could get to the bottom of it.

Nine

The day after he had thrown a tearful Angelika out of his flat, Ryan mounted a fierce attack on his studies. By three o'clock that afternoon, after a frenzy of typing on his laptop, he had drafted another thirty pages of his end product. He stopped, went out, had a sausage and a beer, then returned to his flat. At six thirty, red-eyed from almost eleven hours of intense writing, reading, and note-taking, he washed his face in cold water and then looked over the many points he had noted needing further work.

There were a couple of dozen details that would result in minor rewrites of various paragraphs in his opus, but the main item was a page of notes on two particular men: Cannizzaro and Piria. It was not just Cannizzaro's youth and drive that had caught Ryan's attention but also the signs of his patriotic fire, something Cannizzaro shared with Piria, a brilliant chemist and one of Cannizzaro's mentors. Some initial online digging on these two revealed what appeared to be a large amount of interconnected material. An aside about Piria tickled Ryan, the fact that he had been born in Scilla on the Italian mainland just opposite the tip of Sicily and at the northern entrance to the Straits of Messina, this location being associated with the Greek myth of Scylla and Charybdis. Very little of this would be of immediate relevance to his end product document, but it was background that Ryan couldn't resist. It was Cannizzaro's prominent role in helping make the conference ultimately a success that had Ryan's attention.

Unshaven and losing the autonomic argument being mounted on behalf of an empty stomach, Ryan decided to throw in the towel for the day. He was just thinking about dinner when his phone vibrated. It was a text from Rick: *Time to eat you old hermit. Lots to discuss. Meet me at Sockenschuss.*

In a final defiant gesture to a stomach now crowing over its victory, Ryan paused to jot down a few last ideas for searches he would do the next day on Cannizzaro and Piria. Then, checking that he had enough cash, he grabbed a light jacket and sent a return text to Rick as he left the building.

Sockenschuss was a well-known hangout in Karlsruhe, and when he arrived there he wasn't surprised to see Rick waiting at the entrance. After their usual greeting and ritual jostling, Rick inclined his head toward the heaving pub.

"It's too busy. We won't be able to talk in there. Probably won't even find a place to sit. There's a better spot not far away."

Ryan knew enough not to argue, and he followed Rick up Ettlinger Strasse and then off into a succession of side streets. On the grounds that nowhere in central Karlsruhe is very far from anywhere else, what Rick had said was true, strictly speaking. Still, it needed almost twenty-five minutes of brisk walking to bring them to the Bierakademie. All the way, Rick babbled on about his course, his professors, his fellow students, and just about everything else that bore any relation to his studies. By the time two large glasses were thumped down in front of them, the siren calls of the beer left them both helpless.

Ryan downed a quarter of the beer before him, gave the universal life-is-good sigh that is prompted by the first alcohol at the end of a long day, and looked at Rick.

"So. Your studies are going well, then."

"What? Did I say that?"

"So. Your studies are not going well, then."

Rick dug in his pocket and dropped a card on the table between them.

"Remember that?" he asked.

It took Ryan only a few seconds to remember the bus pass he had found in the street where he had been attacked.

"What about it?"

"I know where he lives."

Ryan stared at Rick in complete puzzlement.

"Why does this matter? What do you expect me to say?"

"I don't really expect you to say anything. I know you don't want to go after him. Not like me, who would want to beat out of him why he, and probably a gang of his friends, came after you. I'm not going to try to convince you to do that. But I think you should know that he lives in the same building as Angelika."

They both gazed into what seemed a very long silence.

"It's a coincidence that I'm just going to dismiss", Ryan said at length.

"That's an intelligent way of sidestepping the whole matter, if it's such that it can be sidestepped", Rick replied. "But I recall a useful comment you made to me some time ago, that every action has the potential for an upside and a downside. And I include here the idea of *inaction* as part of the concept *action*. At least you and I should talk about it."

"Okay. Let's talk about it. I'll go first. Angelika and I met and she hung around for a while. I'm not sure why. Then – you know what happened – I caught her and threw her out of my flat. I haven't heard from her since, and I don't expect to see her again. End of story."

"That's about what I expected you to say", Rick responded, in a voice that appeared to be laden by the wisdom of the ages. "One event, such as you being mugged by a bunch of thugs, could be random. Another event, you as a stranger to Karlsruhe, having no prior connections to the place, becoming involved with a woman who just happened to come across you, who pursues you. *Then* you're mugged by our thugs. Those two things taken together might just be coincidental. But is it a good idea just to brush off that possibility? Add to that a situation where someone who might have been one of the muggers lives not far from your lady friend. Now we have what can reasonably be called a pattern. I'm asking you not to ignore this."

This was all expressed so patiently and deliberately, that rather than becoming irritable, Ryan sat considering it for a moment.

"All right. Maybe we have a pattern. My inclination is still to ignore it."

"And wait for the next 'coincidence'? For a guy undertaking the kind of project you're working on, in its way very worldly and pragmatic, you baffle me, Ryan. Why would you not want to shine a light into this dark corner, if only to show that there's nobody there?"

"Mainly because I think it all would be just a waste of time. The only thing I would expect to find is indignation, denials, and probably some rough language."

"That might well happen. But you might find something else."

"Like what?"

"Like an explanation. Like a desire to make amends, a desire not let a bad situation go unresolved."

"Well, obviously, you're talking about Angelika."

"Yes. From what you've told me about her, it seems to me that, somehow, she was led off into the weeds. You said that the night you interrupted her snooping she wanted to explain. Probably she still does. And she might be encouraged in that if she felt that the temperature had come down on your side."

"You're suggesting that I should approach her?"

"Yes."

"And suggest to her that maybe I acted too rashly?"

"Yes."

"You're nuts, Rick."

"No. Look. I'm not suggesting that you need to debase yourself. All you need to do is make an opening. Remember, you're not trying to win her back or engage in any other chivalric nonsense. What you should be trying to do is determine whether there's any common element between her actions and the mugging. If there is, you need to find out what it is. Chances are it hasn't gone away, and it's probably just waiting for you to go to sleep again."

Despite his resistance, Ryan felt himself being swayed by Rick's logic.

"Come on, man. You know enough about women to be able to read Angelika. I haven't met her, but from what you say, she's far from being a witch."

They talked about it some more, and Ryan finally decided that he would give it a go. In terms of his own paradigm, there was a considerable upside and no discernible downside.

Ryan pulled out his cellphone, thought for a few moments, then sent Angelika a text.

"Noch zwei Biere?" Their server had arrived and refocussed them both onto matters demanding immediate attention. A moment later, two more large full glasses signalled the end of relationship discussions.

Later, as he walked home, Ryan received a message back from Angelika. Through wording that expressed hedging and hesitation, the meaning was clear enough. She wanted to talk.

But it was late. Ryan tapped on his phone: *Can I call you tomorrow?*

His expectations were low to non-existent. As it turned out, they would be exceeded in a way and by a margin that he could not have foreseen.

Ten

At just after eight o'clock the next morning, Ryan called Angelika.

"I'll come right to the point", he said. "I feel badly about how our last meeting ended and . . . I'd like to talk about it. Can we meet in the Weinstube in the Botanical Garden sometime today?"

There was a silence here, and Ryan half expected, in a mixture of relief and disappointment, that she would say no.

"Okay. I can be there at four o'clock."

"Good. I'll see you then."

Something told Ryan that this whole lark quite possibly could be a waste of time and maybe even counter-productive. But he tried to put himself in Angelika's shoes and imagined how she might feel if it played out in different ways. If she really did want to explain what she had been doing that night, it could mean one of two things: either there was something he had misunderstood entirely or it would be some sort of confession on her part. If it was the former, he would have to make some serious amends. If it was the latter, he would need to make it as easy and painless for her as possible. Alternatively, she might just try to explain away the whole matter. If what she presented to him turned out to be either a smokescreen or an attempt to brush it all off without any real explanation, he would simply express his regret and break off the relationship as gently as possible. But, to his surprise, he found himself hoping that it wouldn't come to that. He mulled over the possibilities for about an hour, resolved to be at the Weinstube by three thirty, then shelved the matter and returned to his project.

By noon, Ryan had compiled initial files on Cannizzaro and Piria, and had identified another four books that he felt would be essential to read or at least look into. One of these stood out above all the others, and he decided to locate a copy in the KIT library on his way to meet Angelika. Throughout the morning, his thoughts had kept circling back to her, and he found this odd, interesting, puzzling. He had ended relations with many young women, and in each case this had been a straightforward business. In each case, an attraction, an interest, an infatuation had run its course, and ending it was just a natural and necessary matter. Some of these young women had remained friendly acquaintances, well, a few at least. Most had disappeared angrily into the smoke of burnt bridges. In his own mind, he felt that he was making heavy weather over the possibility of ending his liaison with Angelika, and this he found baffling. Was she somehow different from all the others? He couldn't see how or why. Was their situation different in some basic way? Not at all. Had he changed? To his own surprise, Ryan found that he stumbled in trying to find a quick and simple answer to this last question. In fact, that the notion of "quick and simple" should come to mind almost automatically left him perplexed and uncomfortable. Indeed, the exercise of thinking back over how he had parted from a number of the young women in his life, given his privileged life situation, raised a troubled feeling within him. Was it the change between then and now that was causing him to respond differently? He was now distanced from his privileged status back in Toronto. Was that causing him to look at people, at young women, differently?

The generally unsettling nature of this line of thought made it easy and expedient for him to tuck it away, place his notebook and the files on Cannizzaro and Piria in his briefcase, and head off to the campus. He settled at one of the library's computer terminals to look for the books he had noted.

He felt that the time he spent in the library that day was productive – to what extent and in which manner it was productive he wouldn't know until later. He had come across a small trove of papers that looked good; they had been digitized but they were all in Italian, and he didn't hold out a lot of hope of finding English translations. One of these papers contained a reference to a monograph by Piria, and to Ryan's surprise, the catalogue said there was a copy in the KIT library. He located it on the bottom shelf of a gloomy corner, and one that was little used judging by the dust that had settled there. Several other books near it were on the same topic and he looked through them all. One of them, a slim monograph by someone whose name was unfamiliar looked of only marginal interest. But then he found something else. Just inside the back cover of the book was a sheaf of notes, folded and tucked away. The paper was old, brittle, and the notes probably hadn't been looked at by anyone in a long, long time. Ryan decided that some care was needed, and an examination of the notes became a task for later.

He checked out the three volumes, then settled down once again to thinking about sections of his report. The time passed quickly, and just after three o'clock, he packed up his things and started making his way toward the meeting with Angelika.

Arriving at the Weinstube about a half hour ahead of the meeting time, Ryan found a table outside, as isolated as possible from the central clutch of tables. He pulled the books from his briefcase, intending to give them a cursory assessment, and began leafing through the first one. *The Atom in the History of Human Thought* had at least the potential to be the perfect soporific, but once he had dipped into it, he changed his mind quickly. Here was a lot of material that he sensed right away would be useful, an intelligent commentary moving effortlessly across science, philosophy, and religion. He was drawn almost immediately into that section of the book dealing with the nineteenth century.

"Hello, Ryan."

He looked up, startled, to see Angelika smiling pleasantly but hesitantly.

Ryan closed the book and rose from his chair.

"Hi, Angelika. Please. Have a seat. How are you? No, please sit on this side, next to me."

The ritual of becoming settled was more drawn out than usual, and the tension on both sides was evident.

"What would you like to drink?" Ryan said, at the same time catching the eye of a nearby server.

A half litre of riesling and a bottle of sparkling water were ordered, and as the server went off to get them, Angelika asked Ryan how his work was going. This gave him the opportunity to describe his visit to the library that day and to show her the book he had been flipping through when she arrived.

"It's going well", he concluded. "My report is nearly three-quarters written in first draft."

"Does that mean that your stay here in Karlsruhe will soon be over?" she asked in a tone that he was not able to interpret.

"No. There's still a lot of to do. I expect all that will take at least another four or five months."

Angelika seemed as though she was about to say something, but then looked away.

Ryan regarded Angelika for a moment, looked down at his hands, then raised his eyes again. "But we need to clear the air, Angelika."

She nodded, sighed, and looked down at the table.

Ryan reached out and took one of her hands.

"What happened, Angelika?"

She became tearful almost immediately. "I was stupid", she said simply, letting go Ryan's hand and reaching into her handbag for a tissue.

Ryan just waited, aware that he was unexpectedly in a state of some internal turmoil. It wasn't just because of the tears. It was a feeling of sympathy, and he knew that this feeling was the result of what he saw before him: someone who was genuinely confused, angry at herself, and remorseful.

Angelika dried her eyes for a time that was slightly too long and continued looking down at the table.

Ryan took her hand once more. "I'm not angry at you. Not any more. I just want to know. I want us to move on. Whatever that will mean."

She looked up at him, any embarrassment at being seen in an uncomplimentary state long since jettisoned.

"It seemed like an adventure. I didn't expect that anyone would be hurt. What was I thinking?"

"An adventure?" Ryan said, more as an expression of puzzlement than a question. "You mean that you were looking for something in my notes?"

Angelika nodded and looked down. She began drying her eyes again, and when she looked up at him once more, she was weeping freely.

"Oh, I'm so sorry!" she burst out. "I was supposed to look for something that they could use to discredit your report, your work. Then I could just disappear and not have anything more to do with you. But it didn't work out like that!"

This was a new twist. "They? Who is *they*?"

"I don't know. Someone contacted me, a woman. She gave me information about you. Then that night when you went to Ludwigsplatz they told me I should go and find you, become friends. It sounded exciting, and when I agreed, she sent me, or somebody sent me, fifteen hundred euros in an envelope. I'm so ashamed! I'm an idiot! I've behaved like a stupid, scheming, little girl!"

"How did you know who to look for?"

"They sent me a picture", she said, still dabbing at her eyes.

"A picture? Do you still have it?"

"Yes."

Angelika rummaged briefly in her handbag, then came up with two small stiff pieces of cardboard held together by a rubber band. The picture was between them. Ryan wondered at a hardcopy print, in this day of things electronic, until he realized that nobody could trace the origins of hardcopy. There seemed to be nothing distinctive about the picture, but when he looked at it more closely, he realized two things. In the image, he was wearing a shirt that he had bought just before leaving Toronto, and the only place he had worn it was Karlsruhe. Behind him in the picture were three trees, pollarded in a manner that one never would find in Toronto. The picture had been taken in Karlsruhe.

"I'm still not angry at you, Angelika, but I need to know more about who these people are and what they had in mind. When did they contact you? Has all the contact been by telephone? Do you have any idea at all who this woman might be?"

Angelika had calmed down a bit, and Ryan reached out and took her hands.

"I know that I was harsh with you when I found you in my flat. I was angry. But I thought about it for a long time afterwards, and I realized that I needed to get your side of the story before I started making nasty assumptions. So, believe me, I really do want to understand, and I'm not angry." And he smiled at her encouragingly.

Angelika returned a faint smile then let out something between a sob and a laugh.

There was a delay here. He and Angelika were both in turmoil, but Ryan sensed that they were turning a corner, that something positive was emerging. The day was warm. The sky was cloudless. And Ryan noticed the sun glinting off the wine in their glasses, one of those minor and mundane details that stay with one somehow, something he felt he would remember.

Ryan squeezed her hands then let one go in order to top up their glasses. "Just start from the beginning and tell me what happened. Try not to worry about how you feel or how you think I might feel."

"The night I met you in Ludwigsplatz, I thought I was some kind of superspy. The woman who convinced me to get into this mess had talked to me the first time about a week earlier. She told me that a number of foreign students were working at KIT under circumstances that were out of the ordinary, and there was a suspicion that some of those students were operating in a way that would reflect badly on KIT. She said that normally the university would just intervene directly and get the information it needed, but in this case, some of the students had high-profile overseas support, and the university wanted to be very careful. What I was being asked to do was a sort of fact finding. It sounded different and a bit exciting, and when I said I would help, she was very pleased and said she would be in touch later on what they wanted me to do."

"Did you ask who she was?" Ryan interjected.

"I did. She said that it was better that the whole thing be done quietly during this first phase. She said that she and I would get together later."

Ryan nodded, even though he found the whole thing hard to believe and wasn't really sure why Angelika would be taken in like this. He took a sip of wine and inclined his head toward Angelika's glass, but she just shook her head.

"You surprised me that night in Ludwigsplatz when you spoke some German, and there was something about you that made me want to see you again. I didn't hear anything more from the woman for quite a while, and in the meantime I kept seeing you."

Angelika took a sip of her wine.

"A few days before . . . before that night in your flat" – and here her chin began to quiver – "the woman called me again and said that I was to get as many details as I could about your project, but without you finding out. I must have hesitated because she reminded me that I had taken her money and that this sort of behaviour might reflect badly on a student if the university authorities were to find out. I decided at that point that I would finish what she wanted me to do, and that would be the end of the whole shitty thing."

Another short pause.

"Well, you know what happened next. You found me looking through your papers." Angelika broke down again.

Ryan took both her hands again and smiled at her when she looked up.

"Have you sent her any of the information you got from my files?"

"No. All the notes I took were left at your place."

"Has the woman called you again?"

"Yes. Twice. Asking what the situation is. I've told her that I haven't had an opportunity to find what she wanted. She said that I needed to hurry up."

Angelika fiddled with the wrinkled corpse that had once been a tissue.

"What are you going to do?" she asked.

"Well, I'm not going to tell you to get lost", Ryan said decisively. "Someone is using you to get at me, in some way and for some reason. I want to know who they are and what they want."

He squeezed Angelika's hands. "Will you help me?"

Tears were running down Angelika's face again, but she didn't bother trying to dry them. "Why would you want my help?"

Another hand squeeze. "Because we're on the same side now. Because you had the guts to turn up here today. Because I want to grind someone's face in the mud."

Angelika's expression was not readable behind the puffy eyes and the smeared make-up.

"But", Ryan began in a more matter-of-fact tone, "why don't you go and freshen up, then I'll walk you home."

Angelika smiled faintly again, a fleeting expression crossed her face, giving away her thought – *I must look a mess* – and she rose from the table.

Five minutes later, she returned looking three hundred percent better. Ryan had poured out the rest of the wine, he gestured her to take a seat again, then raised his glass. "Here's to sunshine."

They drained their glasses, Ryan paid, and then they began walking toward the Schlossplatz. When they reached the street named Zirkel, Ryan turned right, then stopped to look at Angelika, who had hesitated.

She looked to the left, in the direction where she lived.

"I thought we would go to my place and have something to eat."

She hesitated again, but then turned right with Ryan. Her expression was impossible to read.

It was six o'clock by the time they entered Ryan's flat.

"I have some *fiakergulasch* and *spätzle* in the fridge and enough things to make a good salad. Would that do?"

It turned out that it would do very nicely, and it took Ryan only a few minutes to heat the gulash and the spätzle and to toss the salad. He turned on his radio, selected HR1 at low volume, and opened a bottle of nice riesling.

"Time to eat", he said, leading her to his small table. As they ate, he switched to German, said that she would have to put up with his crap accent, his crap grammar, and his crap vocabulary, and deliberately made a couple of stupid mistakes that brought a suppressed giggle from Angelika. He talked about his time in Karlsruhe and what he had learned, and expanded on some of the historical aspects of his project. By the time they had finished their food, Angelika had relaxed noticeably, even though there was still something wistful about her expression.

Ryan cleared away the plates, apologized at having nothing for dessert, but then placed two modest glasses of a very good apricot schnapps on the table. "So", he said, raising his glass theatrically, "here's to getting to the bottom of all this shit!"

Angelika looked like she was about to say something, but then evidently decided against it. Ryan said not to worry just now about how they would get to the bottom of the shit, that he had a plan, that the whole nasty business had already occupied too much of their day. He held up his empty glass, gazed at it and licked his lips in appreciation, and mumbled something about really liking this stuff.

Angelika placed her empty glass lightly on the table and looked at her watch.

"It's getting late", Ryan said, rising and carrying the two empty glasses to the sink. Angelika rose as well, looked around for her handbag, and made those motions, automatically but unenthusiastically, that signal preparing to leave.

Ryan placed his hands on her shoulders. "There'll be plenty of time for studying later", he said.

There was no resistance or hesitation as they drifted toward Ryan's bedroom. She did not want to be alone.

After an initial tearful release, Angelika fell into the natural embrace of an evening of long, deep, and hungry love-making, as the gathering dusk enveloped them in friendly and demure anonymity.

Eleven

The tidal fingers of first light had just begun to feel their way along the beach of a new day when Ryan awoke. Saturday morning.

The image that greeted him was the swell of a woman's hips under the sheets. This was a familiar sight for Ryan, but somehow, that morning, it was new and fresh. As he listened to Angelika's regular breathing, he considered the previous evening and felt certain that a discussion of it would arise at some point, although he fully expected that it would unfold in a roundabout manner. The fact that he actually looked forward to this came to him as a surprise.

He rose quietly from the bed, collected watch, clothes, and shoes, pushed the door to the bedroom shut gently, and went off to have a shower. Then he went out for the morning's bread rolls and made coffee when he returned. As he laid out things for breakfast, he could hear Angelika stirring. She appeared briefly in a T-shirt, said good morning, and re-appeared fifteen minutes later showered and dressed. Ryan noticed that Angelika looked slightly nervous or disoriented, and he supposed that waking up in someone else's bed was not something she was used to. He jollied the conversation along during their breakfast and Angelika relaxed noticeably. The remains of breakfast can suddenly become desolate and depressing if one sits around them too long, and well before they could find themselves gazing at bread crumbs and coffee dregs and wondering what to say, Ryan began clearing away the dishes and said that he would walk her home. She smiled, said in a soft voice something about feeling very low yesterday and thanks for understanding. Ryan nodded in acknowledgement, and they left.

Twenty minutes later, in front of Angelika's building, Ryan hugged Angelika lightly and suggested that maybe they could get together for coffee in a day or two, and then, by way of a "so long for now", he started listing off some of the things he had to do during the rest of the morning. Angelika waved and smiled as Ryan backed slowly down the street, still logging chores and tasks on his fingers, and he thought that her expression bore traces of surprise, relief, intrigue, or maybe all three.

Ryan would spend more time thinking about their situation, but not just now, since he had to meet Rick. There were things to do. Although it was past eight thirty, it was a bleary, almost incoherent Rick who responded to Ryan's telephone call.

"Wha? What time is it?" Rick mumbled in sleep-hobbled German. "Shit, Ryan! It's the middle of the night!"

"Come on Rick. A couple of litres of beer will put you right in no time."

The groan that came back to Ryan over the phone carried all the indelicate nuances of light nausea, a percussive head, and a mouth full of mould scrapings from long abandoned garbage bins.

"I'll be right over, Rick. Don't go anywhere."

"Maa, ouagchh! Fuck!" And then the line went dead.

When Ryan knocked on Rick's door, the creature who answered had eyes that looked like two piss holes in the snow, but he also smelled of soap, deodorant, and orange juice, and probably had swallowed a dangerous amount of Tylenol.

"Come on in", the creature offered gamely. "Coffee?"

"No. No time for that. We're going out. Things to do." Ryan hustled Rick out into the hallway. After Rick executed a comical routine – trying to fit a blurry key into a lock that wouldn't stop swaying – and after a brief field test of the whole walking and balancing mechanism, they were soon outside.

"Where we going?"

"Well, I think we should just walk around a bit, allow some time for your electrolyte balance to re-establish itself so you don't short-circuit to death on some lamp post."

Rick's love of impromptu English street idiom brought a fleeting smile to his face, his more typical chuckling and chortling in response to situations like this presumably having been vetoed by a stomach still uncertain about being able to retain its contents.

"Then I want to talk about finding out who's trying to torpedo me."

"Torpedo you?"

"Somebody tried to coerce Angelika into passing on details of my project. I don't know who or why, but I suspect that my mugging a couple of weeks back had something to do with it. I'm hoping we can put our heads together and come up with a plan to figure out what's going on."

"So you think there's a link between Angelika and the street gang after all?"

"No. Angelika is just caught in the middle. I'm convinced of that. But I suspect that my mugging and the play to involve Angelika come from a common source. It's just a guess, but I think the mugging was intended to intimidate me, and that they hoped that when Angelika came along, she would look more like a friend. You know, someone I could turn to."

Rick went silent, but Ryan could tell from his expression that Rick was getting his mind around the problem. They walked for about twenty minutes, exchanging ideas at long intervals.

"I have to go in here", Ryan said.

"What? An internet café? Why not use your own computer at home?"

"Just to be extra sure that nobody is eavesdropping."

"Wow! This really is becoming interesting!"

Ryan went inside, sent his e-mail, then rejoined Rick, who had decided he wanted a bite of breakfast. The choice of sausage on a bun with hot mustard seemed risky in Rick's state, but looked good, so Ryan ordered one as well.

They munched happily as they walked along, and by the time they had finished and dumped their paper napkins in a waste bin, they had entered the KIT campus. They walked on for a few minutes in silence, stopping finally at a bench secluded among trees and well away from any walkway.

Rick looked almost half-human now and, mentally, was firing on all cylinders. He craned his neck, scanning the trees above and around them.

"What are you looking at?" Ryan asked.

"Not at. *For.*"

"Okay. What are you looking for?"

"Eavesdroppers", Rick said, deadpan, "or maybe *leaves*droppers." And then burst into a chuckle at his own joke. Ryan let the juvenile chortling and gurgling die down, but admitted to himself that he wouldn't be able to do something like that in German. Not yet.

Rick settled down, stared at his hands for a good thirty seconds, then turned to look directly at Ryan. "Don't take this wrong, but can you trust Angelika?"

"Yesterday, she spilled the beans about what led up to me finding her snooping among my papers. She wasn't happy with herself at all. I think she really does regret becoming mixed up in all this."

"Spilled the beans?" Rick said, looking puzzled. Then his face cleared. And through a giggle it was evident he was storing away the expression for use in the near future.

"We need a place to start", Rick said after a long spell of pondering. "Do you have any suspicion at all what might be driving this, where it might be coming from?"

Ryan had spent some time thinking along these lines, but he hesitated before replying.

"I can think of only three basic reasons why this would be happening. First, I pose a threat to somebody. Second, I've been mistaken for somebody else. Third, for some reason somebody doesn't want my project to succeed or even to be finished."

Ryan gazed into the distance, and Rick waited for him to resume.

"Take the first of these", Ryan began. "Any threat might arise from within the academy here or it might be that I've come across something or come close to something that somebody else feels is valuable and wants reserved for themselves."

Rick nodded in noncommittal acknowledgement.

"Being mistaken for someone else is a stretch, I think, and there would need to be something more behind it. But there are people who have enemies or competitors they fear, and there really are some weird cats out there. Besides, this is Germany, after all."

"What's that supposed to mean?" Rick bridled, but Ryan just smirked and ploughed ahead.

"Someone not wanting my project to succeed has to be driven by a purely personal agenda, I think."

"What kind of agenda?" Rick probed.

"Could be several things. Someone just picking a scab. Some sort of settling of scores. An old hatred or antipathy. A relationship gone sour. Don't know."

"That's a lot of possibilities", Rick said doubtfully.

"Yes. But we don't need to get into an endless game of scenario building and testing. We just need to follow the evidence."

"What evidence?"

"We need to find out what Angelika knows, and she might not be completely aware of what that is. We need to determine whether the guys who duffed me up fit into all this."

Rick had begun nodding. "The first of those is up to you", he said. "I'll look after the second."

They stood there for thirty seconds or so, each adrift in his own thoughts.

"Come on", Rick said in sudden decisiveness.

"What are we doing?"

"You'll see", Rick said and struck off purposefully across the campus, leaving Ryan either just to stand there or to follow him.

Twelve

Rick stood in the middle of Ryan's flat with a small black box held out before him. Ryan, looking slightly bemused, nodded at the thing. "What exactly is that?"

"It's a scanner", Rick said. "For bugs." He began walking through the room, holding the scanner up occasionally. Ryan followed him. "Where did you get that thing anyway?" he asked.

"Let's just say, I've always had a long interest in electronics . . . and a suspicious mind."

In the end, their efforts found nothing. Indicating . . . perhaps whoever was behind this couldn't place bugs or felt it wasn't necessary.

Following that exercise, they sat working their way through Ryan's supply of Bitburger as they hashed out a plan.

As levels dropped in their first glasses of beer, they reviewed what they knew to that point. Second glasses of beer came and went as they talked.

A third glass of beer was just celebration, no particular reason required.

On Sunday morning, Ryan called Angelika, asking if they could meet for mid-morning coffee. It was a lovely morning, and they agreed on a well-known Karlsruhe coffee house, Café Pan. The place was moderately busy, but they got coffee and some Kuchen and found a fairly quiet table. Ryan was pumped up by recent success in his project, and Angelika looked like a killer in tight black jeans and a multi-coloured sweatshirt bearing the words *Life's too short to drink bad wine*. In English, of course. But as they talked, Ryan realized something.

Angelika's shame of a few days previously had turned to anger. She now wanted to find out what she had been dragged into and why. Ryan asked more about the woman who had called her, convincing her to get into this caper. Angelika related the whole story, right from the top, and it sounded like she told him everything she knew. They finished the coffee and Kuchen and agreed on a plan.

That afternoon, at two thirty, they got together in the Bierakademie once more. It was quiet, there was plenty of space, and they were left alone. Rick was a bit stand-offish, so Ryan did much of the talking. It was clear that Angelika wanted into the club. She was very open about what had happened. Over the course of a half hour, Rick's hard exterior softened, but only a little. They didn't decide anything, but Ryan felt that Angelika's concern was eased somewhat. They parted at just after four o'clock, and Ryan went home to tackle his reading.

Late that night, he got a call. It was from Ted Burrows, a former high school classmate.

"Hey, Ryan! How's it going? I saw Diana yesterday. Man, is she pissed!"

"Hi, Ted. How did you get my number?"

"Hey, man! Like, we're buds! Can't I call you?"

"Well, it's almost midnight here."

"Wow! Hey, sorry man! Guess I wasn't thinking!"

Not much has changed there, Ryan thought, and was immediately alarmed at the strength of his negative reaction, but his concern was throttled back when Ted just charged on.

"Hey, can we get together? My old man promised me, like, a trip. Where are you, man?"

"I'm in the middle of a big project, Ted. Sure, I'd like to see you, but I can't just drop everything, not even for a few days."

The discussion moved on, raising Ted's inevitable disappointment and a somewhat sullen reaction to Ryan's lack of immediate enthusiasm, and they ended the call on a promise from Ryan to call Ted back as soon as he could. But even before they had finished, Ryan decided that he would get a new cellphone number. The question that bounced around uncomfortably inside his head for half an hour afterwards was *Did I, do I, really come across like that too?*

Monday morning was the date for another regular meeting with Hartmann. It was another bright day, now in late November. The meetings with Hartmann had settled into a comfortable and almost welcome routine since Hartmann's ongoing response to Ryan's work was uniformly positive.

There were the usual pleasant formalities, but then Hartmann jumped right in.

"I've been thinking about your project, Ryan. I have to say that I've become concerned."

Coming after five very positive meetings, this was a lightning strike from a blue sky.

"Concerned? About what? There hasn't been any real change at all since our last meeting."

Hartmann ignored this. "Over the past week, I have looked back over your project, and I believe now that it isn't proceeding in the best direction. I'd like to talk to you about some adjustments."

"This is a complete surprise. Can you give me a better idea why I'm not moving in the best direction and what a new direction might be?"

"We'll come to that. But I'd like just to review–"

"No. Please Professor. Just tell me straight up what the problem is."

Ryan noticed now that Hartmann was showing some discomfort, when he had been entirely at ease in all the previous meetings.

"Call me Gus. Please", Hartmann said, fearing that he was handling this not well, and trying to move back the old informal setting. "I need to explain–"

"No. I think we need to move to a more formal level, Professor. What is the problem?"

"I'll ask you kindly not to interrupt me again. I'm responsible to the university for the quality of the work of students assigned to me. You are one of those students, admittedly in an out-of-the-ordinary context. But you are nonetheless still a student and I am your adviser. And my judgment now is that your work needs to be redirected." Hartmann was now noticeably agitated.

"Let me ask you once again, Professor. What is wrong? What's changed? If you point to something substantive that we've both missed, I can accept that. But I can't accept being asked to make what I have to assume is a fundamental change without knowing the reason."

"We have–"

"I wasn't finished, Professor. We've had five meetings that I've found very useful. I've copied you on the notes I made from those meetings. There wasn't a hint in any of them that I might be heading down a wrong path. Not a hint."

Hartmann had begun to go red in the face, but Ryan felt that there was no turning back now.

"Mr. Chandler. I have responsibilities. To my faculty and to the university. One of those responsibilities is to advise students so that they can deliver their best. That's what I've been trying to do for you, so I really have to insist that we terminate this arguing and get down to the business of redirecting your work."

Ryan sat there, glaring at Hartmann, and trying to damp down the anger rising within him.

"I can't accept this, Professor. You want me to redirect my work, but you're not telling me why. What is it that is suddenly wrong with my project? Please tell me what the problem is."

"For goodness sake, Mr. Chandler, you don't even know what it is I'm suggesting! But I must tell you that if you refuse to follow my advice, then I will have to recommend to the university to terminate your project."

"Go ahead and do what you must do, Professor. But I know that this project was approved at a level higher than yours, and I won't hesitate to appeal to that level."

"This is outrageous, Mr. Chandler! Who do you think you are?"

"I'm just an average guy, even though I might be attempting something that's far from average. I'm determined to see this project through, and I'll be interested to see how others react when they review the notes from our previous meetings and have to reconcile those notes to this sudden demand to change a research direction that's been satisfactory up to now."

"Although I'm offended by your threat, Mr. Chandler, your notes have no standing. You could have written them all last night as far as anyone else is concerned. So I wouldn't put a lot of store in an appeal."

"On the contrary, Professor, my notes do have standing. Everything I've produced in this project, including the notes from our meetings, has been logged in a server in Toronto, since, as you know, I have no access to university computing space here. That server places date and time stamps on everything."

Ryan looked at an implacable Hartmann through a swirl of conflicting feelings. It was clear that there was no going back, but he now began wondering whether there was any way forward. He knew that he would need to document this meeting as soon as he left Hartmann's office, that this documentation had to be rigorously factual, and that Hartmann would need to be sent a copy of it. And he knew that his father would need to be informed immediately, that there would be disappointment on that front, and he didn't know how things would unfold from here. Perhaps they wouldn't. Perhaps the whole effort would just collapse. But his father was not the sort of person to agree to folding tents and stealing meekly into the night, and it came to him as something of a jolt that he was his father's son.

Ryan expressed his regrets to a stony-faced Hartmann and then excused himself. Once outside the building, he called Rick.

"What's up?"

"I just called to say goodbye."

"What? Hey, whoa, slow down, man! Goodbye? What do you mean goodbye?"

"My meeting with Hartmann just crashed and burned. Looks like my project might be finished. If so, I'll be leaving Karlsruhe soon."

"You're angry, man. And anger fucks up one's ability to think straight. But there's one really good antidote for anger. I'll meet you at your place in twenty minutes."

"What–", Ryan began, but the connection was gone.

The walk home was fifteen minutes of self-recrimination. Why did he let the meeting with Hartmann go off the rails so badly? Why didn't he give Hartmann more slack to offer his explanation, whatever it might have been? Had the whole disaster been mostly his own fault? By the time he had reached the end of his street, he decided that he would call Hartmann, apologize, and ask for another meeting. The call from his cellphone was answered by the departmental secretary and he arranged another meeting with Hartmann for the following morning. Ryan then pulled out a small notebook and pen and began making point-form notes on the meeting just completed. After filling five pages, he pocketed notebook and pen, and strode off toward his flat.

Rick was waiting for him outside, a backpack at his feet.

"Come on in", Ryan said roughly, brushing past Rick. "I hope you brought your antidote."

"Right here." Rick opened the top of his backpack to reveal a small barrel of Bitburger.

"I might have guessed", Ryan said. "All right. Let's get stuck into it."

They poured two large glasses and sank half of each. It tasted good, even though, at barely eleven o'clock, they were at least six hours from yardarm time.

Ryan laid out the whole story for Rick.

"Definitely sounds fishy", Rick said. "Was Hartmann nervous?"

"Not at all. At least not initially. Later, I would say he looked uncomfortable."

"Like a man who feels he's come to a meeting holding all the cards?"

"Probably, yes."

"Have you found out anything more from Angelika?"

The sudden switch caught Ryan off guard.

"A bit. She said the woman who contacted her spoke good English but wasn't a native English speaker. Apart from that, she knows nothing."

"Not a native English speaker? What kind of speaker then?"

"Angelika thought Austrian, but might have been Bavarian", Ryan replied.

Rick poured them each a second glass of beer.

"I have some news about the guys who duffed you up", he said, looking at Ryan over the top of his beer glass.

"And?"

"They were paid to do it."

"Paid?"

"Yes. By a woman. Someone from Bavaria."

Ryan looked up sharply.

"I guess it's too much to suppose that the same woman was involved in both these events."

"Well, it's an assumption at this point, not a proven fact", Rick said. He looked at Ryan for a long moment. "But I know who she is. Well, let me correct that. I have a name."

Ryan set down his glass carefully.

"How did you find out all this?"

"I have friends. Believe it or not. And one of them owed me a favour. He and a couple of colleagues visited the man who lost his bus pass and might have been one of your muggers – Sieghard Lehmann – and Mr. Lehmann was very co-operative. 'Sang like a bird' is how the expression goes, I think."

"Shit! What are you dragging me into?"

"Not at all, Ryan. You're welcome."

"Er, yes. Sorry. I do appreciate you doing things for me. But how can you get information about me being attacked without alerting the attackers that it's my case you're looking into and that I know who at least one of them is? Where does that leave me now?"

"Do you have any idea", Rick began, "how many assaults, street attacks, muggings – call them what you want – occur in Karlsruhe in an average month?"

"Probably not many. Five?"

"Try twenty. There's about the same percentage of assholes, misfits, head cases in Germany as in any other country. We don't have the bullshit American reverence for the rugged individual, and we don't walk around armed to the teeth, but we're not all saints either."

"So?"

"So, the case presented by my friend went something like this. Herr Lehmann, you and your friends stand accused of being involved in quite a few street beatings here in Karlsruhe over the past few months. One of your victims was my good friend Ralf Klein. Could you tell me why you decided to pick on Herr Klein?"

"Who's Ralf Klein and when was he beaten up?" Ryan asked in puzzlement.

Rick shrugged. "Fucked if I know. Probably never."

"Then what . . ."

"They kept asking about Klein, and Lehmann kept declaring his innocence, then they got rougher with him. After some generous bruising and threats of worse if he didn't start talking soon, Lehmann was shit-scared and began babbling about everything. Looks as though Lehmann and his friends make some decent pocket money every month by beating up and robbing random strangers, only your case wasn't random. They were paid to do you over."

"So in addition to my ten euros . . ."

"Yes. They got a fee."

"But what's to stop them trying to get even?" Ryan asked.

"Well, first, they don't know who Ralf Klein is, but they think they know that your name isn't Klein, so they have no reason to suspect that the visit to Lehmann was instigated by you. Second, my friends told Lehmann that Herr Klein is a dear acquaintance, and that they would be deeply disturbed if they got wind of anything unpleasant happening to him. So they warned Lehmann to stay well clear of Klein or they'd be back, and that any subsequent discussion would make today's chat look like a walk in the park. My friends can be very scary. So I know that Lehmann and his crowd are likely to have twitchy sphincters for some time."

"The woman who paid them", Ryan began, "do you know who she is?"

"One of my friends asked Lehmann if they could borrow his cellphone. By then he was practically a gibbering idiot. He gave them the phone. From the dates in the call log, there were incoming calls from only three numbers around the time of your beating. With a little more specialist help, I was able to identify the important number."

"How does this help us?" Ryan asked.

"How does this help us? You know, Ryan, you really can be a thick bugger when you put your mind to it. We have a name, man! We can find out things about that name. It's hard to be anonymous today if even only part of your life is in the real digital world. We need that sort of information so that we can start making connections and figure out just what's going on here and how far it extends."

"Who is it? What's the name?"

"Brigitta Fleischner. But that's almost certainly a false name. I looked. Couldn't find anyone called that."

Ryan went quiet at that point. Wondering why all this was happening to him. Wondering whether it might be best just to sidestep the whole thing. But then the potential stigma – quitter – flashed through his mind, and he realized that the only way through it was forward. He had come this far. He had got a long way through the project his father had made it possible for him to undertake. More important, he had gained a solid foothold in Germany, something he hadn't even dreamed of a few months ago, and the personal horizons this had opened for him were tremendous. His project had begun to change his life in a positive way. He had made good friends, and one of them was sitting opposite him now.

Thirteen

Rick had another glass of the Bitburger, left the remainder of the small barrel with Ryan, and said he had to go off to study. Rick walking away from a decent amount of good beer because he had to study made Ryan suspect that he might be unwell. But they agreed to meet back at Ryan's place at six that evening.

Ryan went out and bought a new cellphone and account, thought about calling his father, but then decided to wait. Maybe a bit of time to think over the situation would bring new information or new possibilities to light about what had been happening and how this might affect the future of his project. The rest of the day he spent fretting over his meeting with Hartmann that morning, cursing himself that he hadn't tried to squeeze out more information on what had caused Hartmann's change of view, and scribbling many pages of notes in an attempt to guess at what could be behind all this.

The day crawled by. Ryan's confusion, dismay, and anger at the interview with Hartmann settled into mild depression by two thirty but had begun turning to some sort of resolve by late afternoon. At five thirty, his door buzzer sounded, and he pressed the door release without asking who it was, assuming it was Rick. So he was surprised when Angelika walked into his flat.

Her stride was confident and she was smiling as she came straight over to him and gave him a friendly peck on the cheek. "Rick told me about your meeting with Hartmann. An unpleasant surprise."

Ryan gave a single nod. He was aware but unconcerned about how he must have looked, up to his elbows in paper, his hair a mess, and two empty glasses on the table in front of him, smelling of stale beer.

"Didn't do a lot for your day, I expect", Angelika said.

Ryan shook his head.

After a long pause, Angelika said, "We could always go to bed. From recent experience, I can vouch for it as a mood changer."

Ryan looked up and felt some of his downer mood evaporate when he saw Angelika's impish smile. She sat down opposite him.

"What do you want to do tonight, Ryan?"

"What do you mean?"

"Ah! I meant, what did you want the three of us to discuss?"

"Three of us?"

"Rick visited me in my flat this morning. He said that you and he were getting together here tonight, and that I should be there too. I know he doesn't trust me. I expect he suggested I come here tonight so that he could grill me, see whether I need to be unmasked."

"You're judging him harshly. I think you'll find that he considers us all to be on the same side."

"After what I've done?"

"He doesn't have the full picture on that. And I think he considers that the real problem lies elsewhere."

"Elsewhere. Sounds as though you and he have got a lot of it worked out already."

"Not at all. I really have no idea what's going on."

"So what do you want to do? What do you want to talk about?"

"I don't know. It was Rick who suggested getting together."

"Yes. But you must have some idea of what you want to do to get past this . . . this problem."

"That's probably the first thing we should talk about – just what is the problem", Ryan said in a deflated tone. "I don't mind admitting that I could use your help just now."

"Have you eaten today?" Angelika asked.

"No."

"That's likely part of the difficulty right there. Do you have enough in your fridge to make a meal?"

"Not for three people."

"So. A good strategy would be to have a short discussion when Rick arrives, then go out somewhere for a decent meal."

Ryan was about to utter a kind of "yeah, but" response, when the door buzzer sounded again. A few moments later Rick entered the flat. He and Angelika said their hesitant hellos then fell into a carefully neutral discussion in German. Since it was evident from Angelika's expression that she was relaxing noticeably, Ryan let them carry on for a bit, then interrupted, also in German.

"As the object of the exercise, I think I should have some say here."

"Certainly", Rick agreed. "But by the end of this evening, you need to have a plan for getting past the problems that have surfaced today."

"Yeah, well, they are *my* problems . . ."

"But you're my friend, and I'm not prepared to watch you wallow in a sewer and complain about the smell."

This could easily have been the beginning of a whiny argument. But when Ryan looked at the two young people standing next to him, he smiled wanly.

"Okay. Let's talk."

Angelika and Rick both began speaking simultaneously.

"Okay", Rick said to Angelika. "You first."

"What I wanted to say is simple", she began. "You have to finish your project."

Seeing the doubtful look on Ryan's face, she continued. "Just look at the situation. Your father has set up a once-in-a-lifetime opportunity, and you've taken it. You have your project here, but that's only half the picture. You've moved here to Germany, worked your way into the language and culture, and you've done all that on your own and in just a few months. You just can't throw all that away. As far as I'm concerned, making the decision to push ahead in your project should be your first priority. And I suspect that you feel the same way and that's why your interview today with Hartmann, and the possibility that he could derail all this, is bothering you so much."

"That's all true, but it's not so easy . . ."

"Shit, Ryan!" Rick interjected. "Of course it's not easy! If it was easy, you would have brushed the whole thing off hours ago and we wouldn't be here now!"

There was silence for a few seconds.

"So", Rick said, placing a hand on Ryan's shoulder, "let's agree at the very least that this should be the basic direction, then we go out and get some nosh."

Ryan nodded half-heartedly.

"We could go to Ludwigsplatz", Rick said, hoping that the promise of people and friendly social chatter would appeal to Ryan.

"No", Angelika said. "It's a nice atmosphere, but it will be too noisy. We need somewhere to talk. I know just the place." And she rose without waiting for a response. "Come on guys", she said, allowing a hint of impatience to show when they remained seated wearing obtuse expressions. "The evening's not getting any younger."

Angelika led them off without saying where they were going. When they arrived, Ryan didn't recognize the place at all. He knew he had walked past it several times and had paid no attention to the small sign – Enrico – just to the left of the door. Inside, they were faced by a stairwell, and Angelika began walking down. At the next level she pushed open a windowless wooden door, and they entered a large high-ceilinged room. Soft music was playing. Almost all the twenty or so tables were occupied. People were eating and talking quietly, not having to make themselves heard above excessive background noise.

A waiter approached them, gave Angelika a smile of recognition, and wished them all good evening.

"Is the alcove available?" Angelika asked.

The waiter nodded and led them to a recessed area in the rear wall of the room, large enough to seat six people comfortably. He lit the two candles on the table, placed three menus in front of them, and moved away. By means of some signal that Ryan missed, or perhaps it was just common practice for Angelika as a known customer, a litre of white wine and three glasses appeared on the table. The menu was straightforward and unpretentious and included quite a few classic dishes from German and Italian cuisine. Reading through them, Ryan realized that he was famished and decided on the fettucine Bolognese, hoping that it would be done in the proper Bolognese style.

Angelika poured out wine for them. The waiter returned and took their orders, placed a basket of bread on the table, and moved away.

"I agree with Angelika", Rick said suddenly, and Ryan didn't realize immediately that he was continuing on from Angelika's comment back at Ryan's place. "Your father has given you this fantastic opportunity, and by the way you've handled yourself over the past few months here, I would say that his judgment was spot on."

"You don't know anything about my life back in Toronto, so I'm not sure how you can say that."

Rick was shaking his head. "I don't need to know anything about your former life. For anyone to be given the chance at a spurt of intellectual growth like you have here really is a gift, no matter what came before. I'm guessing that your father wanted you to be able to work in a completely different context, and I'm guessing that you saw the advantage in that. Otherwise you wouldn't be here now. So, the hows and whys don't matter, and if I was handed an opportunity like yours, I know what I would do."

Rick's blue eyes gave added significance to his words, animated as they were by a clear and active intelligence.

"This all sounds good if you say it quickly", Ryan replied. "But it hasn't been downhill coasting by any means. There have been times when I was inclined just to say fuck it and back out."

"But you didn't. And that's the point. Now you've hit another bump in the road. No reason to back out now either."

"I know you're on my side", Ryan said, "but locker-room pep talks aren't what I need. It's the mechanics of carrying on that's the problem now."

The conversation around them was a comforting buzz. The dark oak wall panelling offered its own quiet welcome, and Ryan continued. "Tomorrow, I have another appointment with Hartmann. I'll do a bit of grovelling and try to get out of him what has changed since our previous meeting. He took such a firm stand today that I doubt very much he'll backtrack at all. The best I'm hoping for is to get some kind of insight on why there's been this shift in his position and what direction he wants my project to take from here. Maybe I was too hasty this morning. Maybe what he'll propose is not so unreasonable. But I just have this deep concern because of the way he broached the thing today . . . that he'll try to push me down a track that leads to a hugely unspectacular result for my work or even leads to failure."

Ryan lapsed into silence. The sound of cutlery at work filled the room. The unmistakeable aromas of Germanic dishes drifted past them, singly and in combination. And Ryan was aware of Angelika's bare arms, her face now just a little flushed from the wine and the heat in the room, and the sound of her speech, the clear vowels, the surprising softness of the *r* and *ch* sounds, having a feminine quality that he had not expected from high German when spoken by women, and which still intrigued him.

"You really think that?" Angelika asked.

"It's not a question of thinking. It's little more a feeling, but it's supported by all the facts of the case, or perhaps more importantly, it's contradicted by none of those facts. And if there's one thing I've learned from my father, it's that we ignore subliminal or visceral signals at our peril."

"You could always part ways from Hartmann and just carry on independently. Rick and I could give you access to whatever you need from the university library."

But Ryan was already shaking his head.

"My father wants my project to be a demonstration. So it needs to follow some rules. It has to be done within a university. No good taking it outside. Could be seen just as a privileged kid being bankrolled in Europe by his old man. No. It's got to have the stamp of the university. Otherwise it's worth nothing."

"Can't your father intervene with the university?" Angelika asked.

"Of course he could. And I think he wouldn't hesitate to do so. But the more I think about this, the more I have to conclude that he's given me this opportunity so that *I* can solve the problem, so that *I* can do all the stick-handling. The only way out of this would be if it becomes reasonably clear that Hartmann has caved to some sort of external pressure. Then I wouldn't hesitate to talk to my father. But just me having an unfounded suspicion of that isn't enough."

"What kind of proof would you need?" Angelika asked.

"I think that there won't be any proof, in the usual sense of the word. Of course, if Hartmann just came out and said that he was told to force my project to change direction, that would be as close as one could come, but that's not going to happen. The next best thing would be for Hartmann to fail to give a convincing reason for why he's changed his mind so abruptly and why he thinks my research direction is wrong."

"So, a lot depends on what happens in your meeting tomorrow morning."

"Yes."

"Then I guess we just wait and see", Rick said.

"I guess so", Ryan said.

Their food arrived, and all being hungry students they set to immediately.

All three of them surfaced, set down their forks, and reached for their wine glasses at the same time. Angelika being suckered into the role of unwilling spy was something Ryan wanted to discuss, but he was concerned that it was still a sore spot. But the three of them would need to air it at some point. Soon.

Angelika looked at Ryan. "I'd like to know a bit more about your project, Ryan. I know it's important, but it's not much more than a black box for me."

It was that request which ultimately took the three of them onto a different plane. Ryan looked into the space beyond them and then tried to summarise weeks of work for them.

"I wanted to look in depth at something in the nineteenth century. A few things of significance were beginning to happen in the US and Canada, but the real world beaters were here in Europe. What I really wanted was something that epitomized the emergence of the modern world, something that hadn't already been studied to death. And I found it. It was something that happened in Karlsruhe."

Ryan went through the background, then focussed on the individual who had attracted his interest.

"The 1860 conference here was the first ever international scientific meeting. And the meeting was a success partly because of one guy. A young Italian chemist called Cannizzaro. The more I looked at him, the more interesting he seemed. He was an Italian patriot associated with Garibaldi, and that opened out for me all the history of the time. When I combined that with what was going on in physics and chemistry, well, here I am."

"It does sound interesting", Rick said.

"More than that", Ryan said. "It's overwhelming."

"Well," Angelika said. "I can see the attraction. I want to learn more."

"But", Ryan added, "it's not going anywhere unless I can get past my Hartmann problem."

They looked at one another, caught, or so it seemed, on some logical merry-go-round.

"Okay, look," Rick said. "Tomorrow is tomorrow. It might work out. Let's just hope that it does. If that happens, some of the problem, the trouble we seem to be having, could just fade. Although, for the life of me, I just can't see how this sort of historical research could possibly trigger any kind of intrigue today. How could it possibly be threatening to anyone?"

"I'm afraid I have absolutely no idea", Ryan said with feeling. "I'm just focussing on tomorrow."

"And after the meeting tomorrow? What's next?" Rick asked.

"One step at a time", Ryan said. "I need to see what Hartmann says, not go into a meeting having my head full of conspiracy theories. I have no proof that his odd behaviour is linked to my street beating. Frankly, it would be very odd if that were the case. But, being realistic, there is a chance that tomorrow's meeting could be the swan song for my project."

The looks around the table were signs of internal personal denial, an unwillingness to think that such an outcome would arise.

All at once, Rick's expression cleared, and he gave Ryan a direct, penetrating look. "On a more important question . . ."

Ryan looked back at him in puzzlement. "What? More important?"

"Yes. Much more important. The wine's all gone, and what do we do about that?"

There was a general laugh, the tension drained away from their table, and they became just three students once more.

Fourteen

They finished their meal and sat over the last of another half litre of wine, talking about everything and nothing. A few serious questions came up, but in general frivolity reigned. There were laughs, drowning any concerns about drawing more heavily than usual from budgets that were otherwise carefully watched. A nominal protest was raised when Ryan said he would cover the cost of the wine but faded when it became obvious it would take a lot of arguing to change his mind. Ryan posed a desultory question to Rick on how his work was going and was given a desultory reply, full of confidence on the content and progress but comfortably devoid of facts. By ten o'clock, they were back out in the street, radiating a collective glow of satiety into the chilly but pleasant evening.

They walked together for fifteen minutes, but then Rick went his own way, his lodging being well removed from either Angelika's or Ryan's. As Angelika and Ryan approached the point where they had to part company, she took his hand, did a walking cuddle for a few steps, and smiled at him. At the far side of the intersection where Angelika would have to turn right to continue on to her flat, Ryan turned to say goodnight. But when he looked at her, he knew that wasn't the way the rest of the evening was going to unfold.

***

It seemed that Ryan's alarm sounded insanely early the next morning, and he awoke in a pleasant tangle of arms and legs. They both had to get moving early, Angelika to collect the things she needed for an early class and Ryan to prepare and to psych himself up for the meeting with Hartmann, which he began doing while Angelika had a quick shower. There was time for a stand-up cup of coffee and a lump of cheese, then Angelika gave Ryan a hug and a smile, and vanished. Looking through the meeting notes he had prepared the previous day, along with four pages of thoughts that had occurred to him before Angelika and Rick had appeared yesterday, Ryan felt about as ready as he was ever going to be, had a shower and a shave, dressed, and left for his meeting.

He arrived at Hartmann's office a good twenty minutes early. Hartmann hadn't made an appearance yet, so Ryan spent time going over his notes.

"Professor Hartmann hasn't arrived yet." Ryan looked up to see the departmental secretary at the door. He was suddenly aware that his meeting should have begun twenty-five minutes earlier.

He smiled at the secretary. "That's okay. I can wait."

"No. Um . . . I mean, I've tried to contact Professor Hartmann. Several places where he might be. I can't find him."

"Maybe something came up. I can wait."

The secretary smiled uncertainly, then left.

Ryan turned back to his notes but reflected that it was very unusual for Hartmann to be late for anything and that, in his schedule, he was as predictable as Immanuel Kant. But Ryan had welcomed the delay. In fact, he now felt better about the coming meeting mainly because he had spent so much time preparing.

At eleven fifteen, the departmental secretary reappeared, this time clearly anxious.

"I'm afraid that Professor Hartmann isn't going to make it."

"Not a problem", Ryan said, trying to radiate confidence and unconcern. "Perhaps I can make an appointment for this afternoon or tomorrow morning."

The secretary's hesitation gave Ryan the first clue that something might be amiss.

"Professor Hartmann is not answering his home telephone or either of his cellphones. Someone has just gone round to his house. He isn't there . . . and his car is gone."

Nobody could raise Hartmann during the rest of the day. Or the following two days. Or the day after that, which was a Friday.

As Ryan learned later, Hartmann's absence had been reported to the police on Saturday morning by the university rather than by family, since he had been a resolute bachelor from the age of twenty-nine, following an early, disastrous, and short-lived marriage. It didn't take long for the mills of the gods to begin grinding.

There was little else that Ryan could do except continue working on his project. That's what he was doing when his door buzzer sounded on Sunday afternoon, a rare occurrence.

"Who is it?"

"Polizei! Police!"

Ryan buzzed them in, and moments later, two young but large police officers were seated in his flat. They introduced themselves and said they wanted to ask a few questions about Professor Hartmann. Neither of them had good English and rather than let them struggle, Ryan jumped in, making it clear that to continue in German was a perfectly good option.

"Wir können Deutsch reden, wenn das leichter ist", Ryan said calmly.

A combination of relief, mild embarrassment, and surprise swept across their faces, but they quickly accepted the offer to carry out the interview in German.

"How well do you know Professor Hartmann?"

"Personally, not at all", Ryan began. "He's my project adviser. I've met him six times."

"How long did your meetings last?"

"Never more than an hour."

"When was the last time you saw him?"

"Monday morning. We had a meeting from nine o'clock to just after nine thirty."

"And this was to discuss your project?"

"Yes."

"And you met in his office?"

"Yes."

"How did he seem? Did he act normally?"

"Initially, he acted no differently than he had done the other times I met him."

"Initially? Did something change later?"

"He did seem to be concerned about something."

"Concerned? Did that have something to do with the meeting? Was it an important meeting?"

"No. It was just a regular review meeting."

"Was there anything different about the meeting?"

"Yes. In all my other meetings with him, he was very pleased at how my project was going and he gave me suggestions on things I might check. At Monday's meeting, he said that my project was moving in the wrong direction, that I needed to make changes to it."

"It sounds like this was a surprise to you. Yes?"

"Yes."

"Did you ask for his reasons? How did he respond?"

"He wouldn't tell me what was wrong, why a change was needed."

"Do you have any idea what he was concerned about?"

"No."

"And what happened then?"

"I was upset. I felt he was keeping something from me. I got up and left."

"What was it that he might have been keeping from you?"

"I don't know."

There was a pause here while the two policemen looked at each other and flipped through the notes that one of them had made.

"We understand that you were in his office again the next morning. Why?"

"After Monday's meeting, I realized that perhaps I should have asked him about the changes he wanted to see, given him more chance to explain. I requested another meeting with him the next morning. I hoped that he would say what changes he wanted to see."

"When was your meeting to start on Tuesday?"

"At nine thirty."

"And?"

"I waited until eleven fifteen, then the secretary told me that they couldn't contact the professor, so I left."

The note taker checked through his notes once more, looked up, smiled, said that they didn't have any more questions, and they rose to leave.

"You speak very good German", the note taker said, in halting English.

"Thank you."

"Where did you learn it?"

"Here. In Karlsruhe."

The officers smiled again, then left.

It was then that he phoned his father, and things began to get exciting.

Fifteen

Ryan's conversation with his father was uncomfortable. He was aware that he had deliberately withheld all information about his mugging from his parents. He felt that to have done otherwise would just introduce an enormous complication, and given them unnecessary worry. It was all in the past now. There had been no recurrence, and he was quite sure that Rick's friends had thrown the Fear of the Lord into his attackers, that there was no concern that they might try something again. But Ryan's discussion with his father was also a surprise in some ways. It was civilized, matter-of-fact, and consisted of a lot of questions asked by his father once Ryan had explained about the meeting with Hartmann. But he had expected all that. What he hadn't expected was the suddenly clear and immediate image of his father's face, of his own living quarters in the house, and of the house itself. Familiar smells and sounds came back to him. He didn't feel homesick, but he did have a sense of disconnection, that the life he was living now was distantly related to the place he had always known as home.

"What do you plan to do now?" his father asked.

It took Ryan a couple of seconds to drag himself back to the conversation. "Oh I'm carrying on, as usual, working to complete my report."

"How much do you have left to do?"

"I would guess about another four months. There are a lot of loose ends I need to deal with. My draft now is a little over a hundred and forty pages."

There was a short silence from the other end of the line.

"I'll contact the university, see about finding another professor to take over where Hartmann left off. We can't let this drag on. It's now well into November."

"Should I wait to see if Hartmann turns up?"

"I don't think so. It looks as though he might have abandoned his post, and the abrupt change in his advice to you seems very odd. No, I think we have to forget Hartmann. Can you give me access to the notes from your meetings with him?"

Ryan promised to send his father the location and access information for the backup server in Toronto.

"How do you feel about the project? Is it what you expected?"

"I'm not sure what I expected, but it's been a pleasant surprise in almost every way. I think it's one of the best choices I've ever made."

"I'm very pleased to hear that, Ryan. Very pleased. When you've finished, I'll want to talk to you in some detail about the mechanics of the whole thing, what went right and what went wrong in setting it up."

"I've been keeping a diary, and I've noted down a few things like that."

There was some further desultory discussion of family matters, Ryan's father said that his mother sent her love, and then they said goodbye. Afterwards, Ryan sat for a long time thinking about the telephone call and his now confused feelings. He had been delighted to hear his father's voice. He was still surprised at the clear images of his family home that came to him as he and his father talked, but he had no sudden wish to go back there. The word *home* kept intruding into his thoughts, and he realized with a start that his flat in Karlsruhe now had just as strong a connection for him to the notion of *home* as did his family home in Toronto. In the end, he faced a phalanx of impressions that had arisen from his new situation in Germany. And as he considered that situation, it suddenly became clear to him that "sense of direction" was one of the descriptors at the centre of it all. Another descriptor was "abruptness", and a French word that was at one time a favourite suddenly came back to him: *déraciné*. Almost immediately, a related German word flashed across his mind: *umgepflanzt*. Yes! It was the abrupt transplantation to another culture, but a change that he had chosen, not one that had been imposed upon him. But more than just a transplant. The root had struck in this new soil. Yes! That was it!

The implications of this hit him like a flash flood. Just as he was experiencing this shock of transplant, so the changes in the nineteenth century that he had been studying must have delivered similar shocks to the people who had experienced them. Ryan had spent more than four months in intense study in areas he had never ventured into before.

The notion that stood before him now was that our world, in any century, was a world of ideas.

This bit of his own experience now stood out in his mind as a valuable lens. He had to look at the Karlsruhe conference through this lens, at the people who attended the conference, and at the things happening around them that they couldn't help but be aware of. He took a few minutes to note down his thoughts.

And then he decided to go for a walk. He had to gain control of the superheated buzz in his head. On the off-chance, he tried to call Rick, but Rick's phone went straight to voicemail. *Good idea*, Ryan thought. And he turned off his own cell, wanting his storm of ideas to be brought under control, not interrupted.

He walked the streets of Karlsruhe, past the bronze statue of Karl Friedrich and out into the Schlosspark. His mind was a maelstrom of questions and ideas. A plan! His project needed to be re-envisioned, not redirected as Hartmann had insisted so opaquely. He had to work out how to do that. But for the moment, he just wanted to walk about the city and enjoy the avalanche of thoughts that were reconfiguring his outlook.

There were benches all around the Schlosspark – some facing the open park area in the full sun, others set further back among trees and shrubbery, offering shade and seclusion. Ryan chose a sunny but secluded spot, since Karlsruhe was by now into the chill of late autumn and early winter, and then settled into a long mental ramble through the reams of material he had researched thus far. Initially it seemed to be little more than a hail of people, concepts, and events, but slowly a different format began to appear. There was a timeline and a string of faces, French and German and English chemists. Then ideas, historical events, cultural shifts, scientific discoveries, engineering advances began to appear. Almost without realizing it, Ryan had pulled out a pen and notebook, and soon had filled several pages.

The pale sun swung across a milky sky, and Ryan had to move twice to stay in the sun and its warmth. The names of five chemists began emerging from the throng on his timeline: Gay-Lussac, Ampère, Berthollet, Dumas, and Cannizzaro.

He put a star beside Cannizzaro's name. Here, he felt, lay the key to the whole thing. He had to dig deep into Cannizzaro's science.

People had crunched past him on the gravel at intervals for several hours, or however long he had been sitting here. There was more crunching now, someone walking faster. Ryan paid it no attention.

"Shit! There you are! I've been looking all over for you!"

"Oh, hi, Rick. I was just–"

"Come on! Get up! We've got to move it. They found Hartmann. Or what's left of him."

Sixteen

Rick accompanied Ryan to a nondescript office in central Karlsruhe. A plainclothes policeman led Ryan to a small room where he was interviewed. It took very little time.

"We had some trouble finding you today", the policeman began. "Can you tell me where you were?"

Ryan said he had gone to the Schlosspark.

"You had a meeting with Professor Hartmann last Monday. Is that correct?"

"Yes."

"And you didn't hear from Professor Hartmann again after that meeting?"

"No. That was the last time I spoke to him."

"But you went back the next day to his office."

"I did. But he wasn't there, so I left without seeing him. I told all this to the police who visited me at my flat."

"Yes. I'm aware of that. But now a death is involved, so I need to go through it with you again."

The next fifteen minutes were spent examining all Ryan's relevant recent exchanges with Hartmann. The man made what appeared to be some elaborate notes, then looked up and said thanks and that Ryan could go now. Ryan remained seated for a moment.

"I would like to ask you a few questions", he said at length.

The policeman looked up in some surprise and fixed a gaze on Ryan for a few seconds.

"Fine", he said. "But there might be nothing I can tell you."

"Hartmann's behaviour on Monday was so out of character that I strongly suspect he was acting under some sort of duress." Ryan stopped there, waiting to see what the policeman would make of his foray.

"You said you had some questions."

"Yes", Ryan responded. "Do you have any information on what might have caused Hartmann to behave in that abnormal way?"

"I can't comment on the investigation, but the simple answer to your question is no. Why do you ask?"

"Hartmann was my academic adviser. I want to know whether these events might have any implications for me in the future."

"Hartmann was adviser to many students, and–"

"Yes, he was. Did he show the same abrupt change in behaviour toward any of them?"

"Once again, sir, I can't comment on the investigation. I can't offer you any advice. But just speaking as one person to another, you shouldn't be making decisions or actions based on assumptions that might wrong."

"I understand that", Ryan replied. "But what I need is information. If I can't get that information from the police, where should I be getting it?"

"I'm afraid I can't help you there, sir."

"Can you tell me a bit about what happened to Professor Hartmann? Where was he found?"

"It was a single vehicle accident, sir. I'm afraid I can't say more than that."

Ryan returned to the public area of the building and told Rick what had happened. Rick just shrugged as if to say *What did you expect?* and they agreed that they needed more information.

They found out the next day that Hartmann's car had left the road and ended up wrapped around a large beech tree. Hartmann had been badly mangled, his body was in more than one piece, and his days as a professor and a human being had come to a quick end. Significantly, the police were looking at foul play as a possibility.

Two days later, their plan to get reliable short-term information bore even more fruit. The scheme involved Angelika, and it provided some further interesting details. Using the story that she had been considering asking Hartmann to advise her on an upcoming project, she approached the six other students who had been under his guidance. Now that Hartmann was ... no longer available, she would have to consider one of his academic colleagues.

But just for background, what was Hartmann's faculty like? And how had Hartmann been as an adviser? The six students said that Hartmann had been a kindly man who was thorough and offered good consistent advice. No surprises.

So Ryan was very definitely the odd one out. It was evident that Hartmann had been acting apparently out of character toward Ryan for some reason, and it was difficult to avoid the sense that there was something dark behind all this.

Back alone in his flat, Ryan tried to bring everything together in his mind. Why had Ryan been the odd one out? Had Hartmann behaved that way because he was under duress? And there was no doubt about it now. Before much more time passed, he had to talk to his father.

But a new and increasingly insistent tributary of information to his project was claiming Ryan's attention. Opening his laptop, he pulled up the notes he had begun making in an area that seemed initially far from the main theme of his work.

He had been driven to follow this lead just out of curiosity. It involved that interesting pair of men, Cannizzaro and Piria. They both came from the south of Italy. They were both republicans. In fact, Cannizzaro had gone into exile in Paris after the 1848 revolution in Sicily had failed – an uprising in which he had taken an active and enthusiastic part. Less than two years later, Cannizzaro was back in Italy to begin his long academic climb, during which he attended the Karlsruhe conference. It hadn't occurred to him previously that ordinary history, as opposed strictly to the history of chemistry, would play any role. It looked like he might need to change his mind on that.

And once Ryan had started down this road, it took little time to identify one man who was at the centre of things. That man was Giuseppe Garibaldi, who ended up being one of the most popular and best-known figures in the entire western world. When he visited London in 1864, a half million people turned out to see him. A hundred years later, English historian A.J.P. Taylor described Garibaldi as "the only wholly admirable figure in all of modern history".

Did all this affect Cannizzaro's behaviour at the Karlsruhe conference? Almost certainly not, at least not in any direct way. Was it something that could have affected his outlook? It's hard to see how that could not have been the case.

As Ryan had done many times during his research and during his writing, he sat back now and pondered. *How is this advancing my project? And what is actually happening here?* What was happening seemed fairly clear to him. He was being drawn in by the magic, the excitement of the Risorgimento, the story of Italian unification. And he could see nothing wrong with that. It was part of the spirit of that time in Italy.

Tantalizing as all this was, Ryan needed to have a clean line forward. That meant finding some way to come to terms with the things that looked set to derail his work.

A clean path forward would appear soon, but it wouldn't be something Ryan could anticipate.

Seventeen

That afternoon, Ryan crossed part of the Schlosspark and found a bench at an ideal spot in the Botanical Garden, in the open and having unobstructed sightlines in every direction so that nobody could approach him unobserved. It was cool and crisp, nearing the end of the calendar year.

Using his new cellphone, he talked to his father for just over an hour. He knew that his father was fully engaged because the conversation was really a tight and closely argued cross-examination. No aspect of Ryan's term at Karlsruhe was left untouched. Ryan came away with tasks his father had asked him to undertake.

First, Ryan would speak to the chairman of Hartmann's department and ask for access to any notes on his project. Second, he would introduce himself to Dr. Alan Mitchell, who has just begun a sabbatical at Karlsruhe from Simon Fraser University. Third, at some point in the near future, he would schedule a trip away from Karlsruhe, to a place of his choice but for at least one week.

This had come as a complete surprise to Ryan.

"Why?" he asked his father bluntly.

"Several reasons. Hartmann's death represents a discontinuity in how Karlsruhe is guiding your project. I know that you've been working hard. And these, let's call them disruptions, at Karlsruhe aren't good. You should carry on for now. But eventually I think you should take a break. You choose the time. But in the last phase of your work I think a change of scene would be good. I'll be speaking to people at Karlsruhe. I want to make sure that things go smoothly for everyone."

"What about Professor Mitchell? He could take over."

"At the moment, he's just an academic on sabbatical. I'm hoping that eventually he'll fill Hartmann's role as your adviser, but that's

Karlsruhe's decision. In the meantime, I'm going to suggest that Karlsruhe assign someone on an interim basis to advise you."

"I could just as easily take a break here."

"You could", Ryan's father said. "But I think it will be the change in setting that will be good."

This made Ryan wonder just how much of his situation in Karlsruhe his father was aware of. James Chandler was not a man to be underestimated. In the end Ryan agreed to take the break his father had requested at some time to be specified in the future.

There was also a fourth task. James Chandler asked his son to do something that hashaving academic credibility that would give Ryan visibility at Karlsruhe. Ryan knew instantly what he would do. Calls to Angelika and Rick resulted in them getting together for a scratch lunch, where Ryan brought them up to date on his discussion with his father and let them know about his upcoming absence from Karlsruhe.

"When?" Rick asked.

"No date chosen, but not imminently."

"For how long?"

"Maybe two weeks."

"Two weeks!" Angelika exclaimed, in a reaction Ryan hadn't expected. He said nothing at the time, but her response to the news and her facial expression stayed with him.

"It won't happen for some time yet. It's starting to feel like the project that never ends. Every item of research I deal with seems to identify two more. I'll keep you up to date." He told them about his upcoming meeting with Alan Mitchell and how he hoped Mitchell would become his new project adviser.

"For your time off, where will you go?" Angelika asked.

"Not sure yet. Perhaps Strasbourg."

They chatted for another five minutes, then Angelika and Rick had to be off to lectures.

Ryan walked back to his flat and set to work on his fourth task, which would be an article for one of the non-technical publications produced by KIT. By midnight he had a rough draft of an article provisionally entitled "A Worldview Lesson from the Nineteenth

Century", which he was quite confident would be accepted in the university's magazine *looKIT*. This name of the magazine signalled both the level of formality and the linkage to Karlsruhe Institute of Technology. When he met Mitchell, he would discuss this article and ask Mitchell to propose a reviewer. Ryan was hoping that Mitchell would have some formal role in his project.

Despite the late night, Ryan was up and wide awake the next morning at six thirty. He spent an hour going over the draft article, tidied and tightened it in several areas, and revised the first and last sections. He then contacted Alan Mitchell and asked to meet. An e-mail returned to him almost immediately giving an address and suggesting a meeting at nine thirty that morning.

Ryan had no trouble finding the building and the room where Mitchell was holed up. The door was ajar, and Ryan tapped lightly on it. He was surprised to hear an immediate and unselfconscious "Hinein!" and he pushed the door open.

Mitchell was about fifteen years older than Ryan and had a slight but athletic build and wavy sandy hair. He rose, extended his hand, and smiled. Getting past the good-to-meet-you and how's-it-going informalities, Mitchell waved Ryan to a round table on one side of his small office and gazed at him in frank openness for a few seconds.

"Tell me a bit about your project."

Ryan gave him a summary of what he was trying to do, how far he had got, and then related a short timeline of his experience with Hartmann. He described an extended abstract on his project and the article destined for *looKIT*, waved a thumb drive containing them both, and said he was hoping to pass it over to him. Mitchell nodded agreement and they spent a few minutes discussing the rationale for the *looKIT* article.

"I don't know yet what my formal status will be within KIT with respect to your project. I've suggested that I could take over from Hartmann but haven't heard back yet. In any event, I have no problem acting informally as a reviewer and adviser, either in the interim or over the longer term."

"Let me know when and how you'd like to organize that", Ryan said with relief.

"I'm still figuring out how things work here, but it seems pretty straightforward. I'll call you when we can make some firm arrangements. In the meantime, let me have a look at your draft article. That seems to be the only urgent item at the moment."

The thumb drive was handed to Mitchell, the file was downloaded, and since that seemed to be the business contracted, Ryan began making time-to-leave noises.

"Before you go", Mitchell said casually, "it doesn't need to be all work and no play. How about lunch or dinner one day soon?"

Slightly surprised, but pleased, Ryan agreed to dinner the following evening.

"Excellent", Mitchell said. "I can pass on any comments on your article then." They shook hands and Ryan left.

Dinner the next evening was a very enjoyable affair. It was clear to Ryan that he and Alan Mitchell were going to get along well.

"I understand you'll be leaving Karlsruhe for a couple of weeks."

"My father's suggestion. He seems to think I've been spending too much time in the same place hammering away at the same thing." It was close enough to the truth.

Even though it was still some way off, Ryan began thinking about his trip, how long he would be away, what he needed to do before leaving, and how he wanted to use his time. Before retiring he checked his bank account. Unsurprisingly, the money his father insisted on sending him was already there. He had tried to convince his father that no more money was needed, but his father had just said, "My idea, my quarter." Two weeks after Hartmann's death, Mitchell was appointed interim adviser for Ryan's project.

But now that he thought about time away from Karlsruhe, he felt oddly uncertain, hesitant about the whole business, as if he would be squandering time or risk losing momentum. As he climbed into bed, he brushed those thoughts aside, restating his personal commitment to get on and break the back of his problem.

Eighteen

It was a short run by train from Karlsruhe to Strasbourg, and finding himself outside Strasbourg station when it was not yet ten o'clock the next morning left Ryan feeling a little disoriented. He was also tired. There had been no fixed date for the Strasbourg break but there always seemed to be something that delayed it. The end of the year came and went uncelebrated. Then the days of January drifted by. Then February. Ryan worked like a slave, following up what seemed to be innumerable loose ends, making revisions to those sections of his report where he knew changes were needed, and struggling through other sections that were evidently either vague or incomplete or that contradicted text that appeared elsewhere. He kept coming up with more dangling threads that needed to be tied off. It was infuriatingly slow work, and time seemed to flow even faster, making it uncomfortably clear that he had been nowhere near as advanced as he thought and that his planned departure from Karlsruhe would turn out to be a pipe dream. Finally, the day before he was to leave, he'd packed, printed his train ticket, and put calls in to Rick and Angelika to arrange dates for weekend visits by each of them to Strasbourg, and to Mitchell to discuss the state of his draft report.

Now, standing outside the Strasbourg station in chilly air but under a clear bright late February sky, he soon got his bearings and, after a little wandering, found a good spot to stay for two weeks. It wasn't cheap, given that it was just a stone's throw from Petite France.

But, what the hell, Ryan thought. *I'm here. I might as well do it right.*

The hotel was small, tucked in a side street not far from the Église St. Thomas. The river was less than a hundred metres away, and it was a pleasant walk to the Place Kleber through a maze of small streets and lanes. Ryan filled out the registration form under the watchful eye of the no-nonsense Madame Chatelaine, half of the older couple who ran the hotel. Seeing Ryan's Canadian passport, the woman tried to engage him in somewhat painful English until he found a way to divert into French. The smile split her face, and Ryan was delighted to see her inner young person as she chattered about Strasbourg and displayed her somewhat raucous sense of humour. When she discovered that Ryan was studying in Karlsruhe, she made a tentative foray into German, then smiled broadly and picked up speed when she found he was having no problem keeping up to her. Her husband seemed to be an omnipresent entity. Ryan could hear him moving crates of something and humming what sounded very much like a revolutionary song. After Ryan had been in the hotel two days, he saw the man in beret and pencil moustache – the wiry Frenchman in every regard – except that he was singing something in German. In short, a pair of lovely eccentrics.

After settling his things in his room and taking a quick stroll along the River Ill, he was still in time to be seated at eleven thirty for an early lunch of a quarter litre of wine and a nice tarte flambée.

Make the most of it, Chandler, his Inner Voice said sternly. *In three days Angelika will arrive, and by then I want to see some solid progress.*

Being in a French environment after his lengthy Teutonic immersion was surprisingly welcome, ignoring the fact that for the first while whenever he opened his mouth to say something in French, German came out. But here at lunch he just let the ambience swirl around him as he sipped the wine and slowly consumed the food. At quarter to one, he paid and made his way back to his accommodation. It was small but light and airy, and he opened most of the windows before taking out his laptop and spreading files on the desk and guest chair. Although a continuous chatter of voices rose from below and entered through his open windows, there was no vehicular noise, no blaring horns, no blatting motor bikes, and that struck Ryan as being just about as civilized as it gets.

But now it was time to work.

It had been only a few weeks earlier that he had come upon the idea that had breathed fresh life and new direction into his project, a much more refined idea of worldview, focussed on what one could call the chemical spirit of the times in 1860, and how this manifested itself in the minds of the participants. Ryan immediately pulled out his notes and went through the thoughts that those notes had captured, thoughts that still were not completely fleshed out. He had done quite a bit of research on the notion of worldview, and had turned up a huge amount of fluffy, breathless, and almost useless material. One exception was the well-written book by Richard DeWitt, which he had read carefully and had brought with him. He had also gone over some of the literature that Thomas Kuhn's classic on scientific revolutions had prompted. Apart from Kuhn's book, he had dug out about twenty solid articles from a vast sea of dross and redundant clutter.

A primary task before him was to view the time during and just after the Karlsruhe conference, to look over carefully the communications among some of the conferees, and try to assess all that in the light of Kuhn's insights. His immediate aim during this Strasbourg sojourn was to produce something that articulated a spirit that he was pretty sure lurked there. But it had to be credible and it had to have solid academic legs. His extended abstract, now with Mitchell, contained marginal notes and questions on just these things, and he hoped that Mitchell would be able to steer him away from any cliff edges.

But, basically it's up to you, Chandler, he said to himself.

He set to work. The afternoon flew past. Ryan filled more than twenty pages in notes. But it was at about seven o'clock that evening when a lamp switched on in his head. A faint glow, to be sure, but . . .

By eleven o'clock, he was light-headed. It wasn't from tiredness, although that was there. After going through five drafts, he now had four pages of closely argued description interpreting what had happened during and after the Karlsruhe conference in terms of a worldview event. At one in the morning, he called it quits, opened the bottle of Alsatian wine that came with the hotel room, and had a 750 ml nightcap.

At seven thirty the next morning, a crustless Alsatian breakfast tarte, a croissant stuffed to overflowing with smoked salmon, and a cup of strong coffee all looked up impatiently from his breakfast table at a slightly bleary Ryan Chandler.

He shook himself back to reality from a mild state of shock brought on by the hallucination that his breakfast had been speaking to him.

Nous sommes ici pour toi! Vas-y! (Why aren't you eating? Get on with it!)

A fresh, coolish morning breeze and sunshine beaming down from an early springtime sky of scattered cloud got rid of the last of the night's cobwebs, and he began firing on all cylinders. In twenty minutes, he felt completely re-energized. A brisk one-hour walk, during which he slowed considerably around the storied Cathedral of Our Lady, ended back at his hotel and he was ready to don harness for another day's work.

Pulling up the four main sections of his report on his laptop, he reviewed them closely. Keeping the finish line in sight, he bent his back again to the work. By late afternoon, his stomach was barking impatiently that not even an Alsatian breakfast could fuel this sort of effort indefinitely. He found a good place for dinner, had one of those superb Alsatian French-German meals, said hello and goodbye to a half litre of very good white wine, and by eleven thirty was tucked nicely in bed.

Nineteen

Sunlight and fresh air had Ryan up early. He decided on a very quick breakfast. The high of the previous day's progress was still with him, and he wanted to get back at it right away.

Checking his e-mail, he found a response from Alan Mitchell offering a few suggestions and outlining a path that would lead to formal review of his report within KIT. Ryan smiled at this confirmation that he was in the home stretch.

By six o'clock in the evening, he had come within sight of the finish line for a first very rough draft.

Good start, the Inner Voice pronounced tartly. *Another five serious passes and it might be just about ready for eyes other than yours.*

All the major revisions he had foreseen in his plan for this draft had now been made, at least on a first-cut basis. Two fairly late nights and continued close application had worn down his cerebral horsepower, so he decided that he would throw in the towel for the day. A leisurely dinner and an early night seemed entirely in order. Ryan spent a final half hour preparing a detailed list of the nine separate spots in his report where he had seen the need for some further elaboration.

Ryan allowed himself a few minutes to bask in the glow of something hovering on the horizon: a full first draft ready for a thorough review by Mitchell.

Just then his cellphone buzzed.

"Ryan Chandler."

"Hello, Ryan. It's good to hear your voice again."

"Hi, Dad. I wasn't expecting a call from you. Is everything okay?"

"Yes. Fine, fine. I'm in Berlin. Some business came up, and I decided to fly over and handle it."

"Berlin!" Ryan said. "How long will you be there?"

"Not sure. At least four days."

They talked briefly about Ryan's work.

"I was in touch with Alan Mitchell this morning", his father began. "I'm very pleased that he's now the adviser for your project."

Ryan's father said there was no chance of them getting together while he was engaged in Berlin, but that he planned to stay on in Europe and then go on to Rome for more business meetings.

"I'll be meeting your mother there. As soon as I let her know that things are wrapping up here in Berlin, she'll fly to Rome. If you're able to, we'd love to have you join us. I'll let you know the details when I have them."

Ryan then outlined for his father the spin-off interest from his project, the "Cannizzaro connection", something that would lead him to a number of places in Italy. His father reacted positively, and they talked for ten minutes about what Ryan had in mind.

"I look forward to reading your report myself, once it's been published", he said, preparing to end the call. "I can't be seen to have any involvement until then. Look after yourself, son. See you soon in Rome."

When Ryan put down his phone, he had an immediate sense of disconnection that went well beyond just telephonic. His project soon would be coming to an end. And apart from following the threads that had emerged from that project as areas of personal interest, his stay in Europe would soon be coming to an end as well.

That meant, presumably, going back to Toronto. And that meant finding something else to do. But how could he find anything that could come close to what he had been doing here, what he had found, what he had experienced? And then there were the other connections . . .

Get yourself to the point where the report is publishable. Shove all the rest of it aside.

Good short-term advice, Ryan had to admit, and although there were longer-term items in his life that couldn't just be left to chance or to some foggy Micawberish hope, now wasn't the time to become embroiled in planning on that time scale. There were practical things to prepare for: time to be spent with Angelika and then with his parents.

Ryan tapped a pencil on his desk, his thinking stuck in a closed loop.

You have a shitload of psychic work to do, Chandler, said the often helpful, frequently sadistic, and always irritating Inner Voice.

He sat there for some time, captive of a river current that sent him off on wild eddies but at the same time seemed to be carrying him somewhere, on a slow background flow.

Angelika.

How would they spend the weekend? There was plenty to do and see in and around Strasbourg, and there was enough German spoken in the area that she wouldn't have to fall back on what might be limited French.

Okay, Chandler. Din-dins, said the irritating Voice, *then another early night. Solid progress tomorrow by three o'clock.* Angelika's train was due to arrive at just past four.

Ryan decided that din-dins would be an excellent schnitzel, and that he would be between the sheets by ten o'clock. A good night's sleep was in order. This would allow him to awaken full of optimism, or so he hoped.

But the conversation with his father had done something. References to *final report* and *end of project* rattled around in his head. There was something unsettling in the background.

That something was the realization that this theme of things coming to an end had stripped him of a sense of complacency. He had become used to seeing his comfortable European path extending indefinitely into the future. But now the end of that path was in sight.

Twenty

Friday saw Strasbourg greeted by sharp fresh air and brilliant spring sunshine under a canopy of azure. But this was just backdrop to another day of work. And by two forty-five, Ryan had a good rough first draft report completed. He shipped it off to Mitchell for a first review.

Time to do some practical preparation for Angelika's visit.

Looking around his room, Ryan felt it was just large enough for two people, but he wasn't going to make an assumption that could set them off on the wrong foot. Other rooms were available in the hotel, and that possibility would be offered to Angelika immediately. The main thing would be just two people enjoying themselves, whatever that might mean.

For a longer time scale, but beginning sometime soon, he would need to think about what would happen over the remaining few months, looking at not only the end of his project but also the end of his stay in Karlsruhe, in Europe. Ties form. Tendrils take a grip. They all had to be cut. He wasn't really prepared to admit that these were just hollow words, somehow expecting that a new reality would be just an uncompromised extension of the old one. But the Inner Voice could see through Ryan's self-deceptive smokescreen, and wasn't at all happy.

You know that you're just creating potential problems and unhappiness, don't you, Chandler.

Ryan knew that the Voice was right, but insisted to himself that these matters weren't susceptible to detailed prediction. Sometimes a large piece of life's puzzle had to be dealt with just by winging it.

At three forty-five, he set out for Strasbourg station to meet Angelika. There were any number of equally attractive routes leading from Ryan's hotel to the station, but he chose to walk along Grand'Rue and cross the river at Rue du Maire Kuss, which leads directly to the main station entrance. On the way back, he and Angelika could follow a different route, or if she was a bit tired, they could take a tram through Place Kleber and walk five minutes to the hotel from the nearest stop.

Ryan wasn't keen on doing the tourist bit – he and Angelika could attend to that later if that appealed to her – so he just looked around in general interest, consulting his map regularly to make sure he kept on the right track. The lovely old buildings smiled down on him from every side. Conversations in French filled the air. He was acutely aware of being in a city that called itself the capital of Europe.

He crossed the forecourt in front of the station and entered. Inside the station, the indicator board for train arrivals showed that Angelika's train was due to arrive at 4:20 p.m., so it was running about ten minutes late. That meant a total wait for Ryan of about twenty minutes, time to do some book browsing. After what seemed like a short browse, a glance at his watch indicated that time had flown and the train had arrived five minutes ago. Rushing out into the station, he found the track he needed. The train was there and people were streaming from it.

Ryan moved back into the station and scanned the concourse in case Angelika had already alighted and was waiting somewhere for him. He couldn't see her anywhere.

And suddenly, there she was, walking down the platform, carrying a small pink case and wearing a huge smile. Something funny was going on in Ryan's chest.

I warned you Chandler, the Voice intoned sternly.

Ryan told it to crawl back into its hole.

He took Angelika's case and they embraced in a way that seemed slightly puritanical, then set off toward Ryan's hotel.

"There's quite a lot to see here, and I have a list of some of the things you might be interested in", he said.

"I have my own list", she countered and then immediately began asking him questions about what he'd been doing.

They settled into a comfortable chatter, and Ryan pointed out a few things along the way.

"What's the hotel like?" Angelika asked.

"It's a middle-of-the-road place, small, clean, not luxurious, and close to Petite France. We can see about accommodation for you when we get there."

For a fleeting moment Angelika looked puzzled. "Is your room not big enough for both of us?"

"It is. But I wanted to offer you the choice."

They looked at each other, laughed, and it was clear that the matter was closed.

"This is nice!" Angelika said as Ryan opened the door and stepped back to let her enter first. "Lots of light. Lots of fresh air. Let me just use the toilet, then we can go out and do a bit of walking before dinner."

And walk they did. For an hour and a half. Being European, Angelika was not surprised at how much there was to see, but she was delighted at the mixture of French and German, in conversations, in shop windows, in names. It took about half an hour to decide where they would eat. Ryan made a reservation, they walked around a bit more, and by seven o'clock, they were back at the chosen restaurant, seated at a table for two looking out over the river. Angelika tried her French but then decided that German was much less effort. They both settled on using German and that suited Ryan. *Stay well away from English*, he thought, and his unavoidable North American accent. Don't risk the virulent looks that might be directed at him as an assumed representative from Trumpland.

Dinner was a languid affair. Their main courses, *Flammkuchen*, matched the outstanding Alsatian wine, and both Angelika and Ryan shared a sense that it was over too soon. Pleasantly sated by the meal, shadows having fallen across Strasbourg, the last of their wine now drained, they made their way out of the restaurant and through the city to the hotel.

Once in the room, Ryan kicked off his shoes in perhaps too much familiarity and was about to flop into the large armchair. But then he hesitated.

"Or, maybe the bed would be more comfortable", he said, as he turned to face Angelika. She was standing there smiling in mock innocence, as the skirt she was holding negligently by one finger dropped to the floor. "Just what I was thinking", she said.

Twenty-One

They awoke early, looked at each other, and smiled like naughty children.

"Hungry?" Ryan asked.

"Yes. But let's just lie here for a while."

From outside came the sounds of birds and urban activities. A street sweeper went past. Several "Bonjour!" greetings could be heard, and a bicycle bell sounded.

"My project will be ending soon", Ryan said, not being quite sure how to get into his topic. "There are things we should talk about."

"Has this got to do with the future?" Angelika asked in a tone that sounded confident, not the least bit hesitant or uncertain.

"Yes. My future. But also your future. And maybe our future."

"For the next little while, I suppose things will continue as they are", Angelika began. "But then your project will end. Soon? I'm not sure when. And then what?"

Ryan stumbled around mentally for fifteen seconds then explained where things stood at present, what he expected to happen and when, and gave a rough timeline up to the point when he expected his connection with Karlsruhe to be ended.

"And then what?" Angelika asked.

Ryan's reply came after a short delay and emerged from a clouded expression and slightly knitted brows.

"That's the problem", he explained. "I really don't know."

"But you'll be going back to Canada, won't you?"

Her hair was attractively tousled. Ryan was aware of their feet touching, the warmth of her body.

"That's one possibility."

"What do you mean? Are you thinking of staying on in Europe?"

Ryan gazed at the ceiling for a long time.

"I don't know, Angelika. In less than a year, I've had some of the most significant experiences of my life. Now I'm confused. Looking back on my past life in Toronto, I see just a shallow adolescent dream. But that was my home. That's where my mother and father live. And they're still two of the most important people in my life."

Ryan was aware that Angelika was observing him closely.

"But I do feel that I've become now something close to a bona fide resident of Germany. I know that it's been only a short time, less than a year. But I feel that I have some understanding of the place. It's different from anything that I've known . . . the old Ryan now feels like a child."

Ryan gazed at the ceiling for another minute, then turned his head to look directly into Angelika's eyes. She shifted slightly under the sheet.

"And then there's you."

She made to say something, but Ryan carried on. "I know. We're friends. Perhaps something more than friends. How much more than friends . . . well, that's what I think we need to talk about."

They looked at each other for another minute. Angelika's hand sought out his.

"But first", Ryan said, in a more pragmatic tone, "we need a shower and some breakfast. Then we need to explore Strasbourg and not spend all day mooning. But I think we should talk about all this before you return to Karlsruhe. So, shower? You know that if we have one shower it will save water." And Ryan poked Angelika at the bottom of her rib cage where she was so exquisitely ticklish.

"Stop! Stop!" she shrieked, leaping out of bed and heading off to the shower.

The shower was a vigorous four-handed soaping exercise that suddenly gave the bed renewed allure. But they resisted this hormonal tug, towelled each other amid outbursts of giggles, dressed, then headed off into the morning.

Sunshine laughed down onto every corner of Strasbourg from a crystalline blue sky. The day was unforgettable – a stream of food and wine, taken as the mood struck, a close study of buildings, statues, and all the delightful ornamentation that Strasbourg offers. Ryan didn't allow himself to drift off into the emotional weeds, but more than once he cast a glance at Angelika, saw a carefree and relaxed young woman, and was sure of a sense of rejoicing in both of them, at a feeling of life, of things on the cusp of discovery, of a large and inviting world urging them both to explore.

They walked for many kilometres. By six o'clock, despite youth and energy, they were tired, and they stopped for a glass of wine at a small restaurant tucked into a byway. It looked like a good place to have dinner, so they lingered over a second glass of wine and glided naturally into their evening meal.

At eight thirty, they stood on legs that were now decidedly weak and wobbly, and tottered toward the hotel. They walked quietly, hand in hand. Light had already drained from the sky. Shadows carved by streetlights clothed the city in its evening garments.

Back in the room, Ryan excused himself a bit sheepishly.

"My dad's in Berlin. I just want to check on whether he's sent me an e-mail. Sorry. Won't be a second." Ryan fired up his computer. There was no message from his father, but there was an e-mail from Alan Mitchell. He opened it and read, standing in what evidently seemed to Angelika to be an immobile pose.

"Is something wrong?" she asked.

"No. Not at all", Ryan answered. "It's a message from my project adviser at Karlsruhe, requesting a meeting on Monday." He turned to Angelika. "What time is your train back to Karlsruhe?" Ryan asked.

"Seven", Angelika replied. "Will you come back with me?"

"Yes. I think I should. Mitchell wouldn't ask if it wasn't important."

Ryan spent three minutes replying to Mitchell. The distant cloud bank had returned, at least in Ryan's mind. The end of his project. The end of his stay in Karlsruhe. The end of – what else?

It was clear that Angelika sensed his change in mood.

"Well", she said in a matter of fact tone, "there are things to do between now and train time."

"Things? You mean pack?" Ryan was still feeling somewhat derailed, thrown off a trail they had been following all day.

"Well, yes. But there's other stuff too", she said, as she slid both hands under Ryan's light jersey.

Once again, Ryan was astonished at the response speed of the human male to anything even remotely resembling a sexual stimulus. Angelika smiled at him, telegraphing a mixture of satisfaction at the fine and instant control she had over him and her own sense of anticipation, something that had apparently been simmering for some time.

The bed enfolded them eagerly once more.

***

The following day was overcast, and after a slow breakfast, they decided to spend time looking at Strasbourg Cathedral and then indulging in a three-hour guided tour of the city. It turned out to be exactly the right sort of agenda and the rest of the day flew past. A good deal of laughing and joking, another excellent meal, and the day ended with tourist fatigue and an early night.

Monday broke like the first morning.

There was a brisk walk to the station, where they grabbed breakfast rolls and boarded the train. As Ryan had experienced before, once the train began moving, a different mental framework fell into place.

He made a vague attempt to restart their pillow discussion from the previous morning, but Angelika picked up the thread decisively.

"After I finish my course, I'm going to have a career. I plan on making sure that nothing gets in the way of that. There will be other priorities, I know. But I'll find a way to make them fit into that framework."

It was evident that they were wrestling with the same thoughts.

"Can I suggest that we work out a plan?" Ryan asked.

"A plan?"

"I don't want to throw anything away. But I don't want to decide anything too quickly either. Can we continue on the way we are and just see where things go?"

"You make it sound as though some decision has been half made already." She looked down at her hands, brows slightly knitted.

The indicator over the door to the carriage told them their speed was 280 kilometres per hour. The subdued sounds of wheels on rails was a background murmur. Outside, the supports for the overhead wires flashed past in metronomic regularity. Ryan turned to look at Angelika.

"I like you. I like you a great deal. But there are some important things I need to work out. What I want to do, what I want my professional life to be. And where it is that I'll be doing what I want to do. I can't divorce any of that from you. Not easily. Not with anything as simple as a snap of the fingers. So can we just hold steady for a while, see where each of us might be going?"

"How long?" she asked, looking at him.

"Well, you have two more years in your course. I have what looks like it might be another three months, tops, in my project. I have a lot of things to sort out. Are you happy just to wait? Think about things? See where it all might be going?"

"Yes", Angelika said at length, still hesitating a bit. "But no real commitment beyond that. Is that okay?"

As a path forward, it was more than a little hazy, but Ryan felt that it was good enough for now, that it didn't feel like any sort of dodge or cop-out, and that it was something they could make work, no matter which way things headed for them in the end.

They lapsed into a companionable silence for the rest of the trip, and Ryan reflected that, for the first time in his life, he was considering what it might mean to lock in place large blocks of the future.

Twenty-Two

Ryan unlocked the door to his hotel room and experienced an immediate visceral hit. Some essence of Angelika still perfumed the air, but it was something subtle that he felt or sensed rather than *smelled* in the blunt and crass way implied by that verb. Images from the past two days welled up powerfully. But then Ryan moved to open windows, retrieve his laptop, pull out notes and books, and get down to work, pausing only to send a text to Angelika: *Meeting with Mitchell was excellent. Back in Strasbourg now. Path forward on project clear. Wonderful weekend Angelika. Thinking of you.*

The meeting with Mitchell had fired Ryan's enthusiasm once more. They had reviewed Mitchell's comments on Ryan's draft report, and the entire effort now felt a large step closer to being finished. Ryan now had more papers to read, and an armful of books each containing multiple tags on chapters Mitchell suggested Ryan read.

The journey back to Strasbourg had been a working trip. Ryan scribbled twelve pages of notes based on his discussion with Mitchell, then plunged into a close reading of the papers he had been given.

Settling at his desk, Ryan worked through the day.

And through Tuesday and Wednesday.

Thursday morning. He could see the metaphorical finish line, could almost taste the victor's cup of wine. At two o'clock, he leaned back in his chair, and let out a mild whoop of victory. He now had a revised report ready for review within KIT.

Twenty minutes later, Mitchell acknowledged receipt of it. After a much needed shower and shave Ryan headed out for a late lunch.

Lunch was a tall glass of blond beer and a lovely onion-and-bacon tarte flambée. Life was good. Mitchell indicated that he would look through Ryan's revised report but he expected not to have any further substantive comments. Detailed comments could be handled at any time. The formal KIT review likely would not begin for another week at least.

It was time for Ryan to turn again to his areas of personal interest, including specifically digging out more detailed background on Cannizzaro, his period of exile in Paris after the abortive Sicilian rebellion, his intriguing and touching and permanent link to Harriet Withers, and, something Ryan had begun to appreciate only lately, Cannizzaro's link to Garibaldi, the Risorgimento, and his rise to the status of scientific elder statesman.

And then there were those papers that he had found buried in a dusty book deep in the KIT library. Notes. Letters. Folded and slipped in next to the back cover of that book. The notes were a mixed bag, associated with times that were years apart. How they came together, and by whose hand, was a mystery. Why they were squirrelled away in that particular book was unknown. But there they were, found entirely by chance while Ryan was digging in a quiet and unfrequented corner of the KIT library. Ryan had copied those papers, then replaced the originals in the book, which he eventually returned to its gloomy library shelf without informing anyone.

Having a good stretch of time now at his disposal, Ryan could slow down from the frenetic pace he had set over the past weeks, before and after his arrival in Strasbourg. He strolled back to his hotel, intending to spend the rest of the afternoon planning a trip to visit his parents in Rome for a few days.

By five thirty that afternoon, Ryan had an itinerary and a plan. His father called just before six o'clock that evening. His parents would be in Rome the following afternoon.

He found that he was looking forward very much to seeing his parents again, especially now that his project was nearing its endgame.

But it would turn out to be more than that. Much more.

And much worse.

Twenty-Three

On Thursday evening, just before turning in, Ryan took stock.

Dealing with the tail end of his report and his project were things now on the back burner. Foremost in his mind was the business of changing mental gears. He would be burrowing into a different chapter of the nineteenth century. Cannizzaro would still be there. But now he would be linked not to chemistry and chemists but to a different set of people and events. Garibaldi, Mazzini, and Cavour would be there. Garibaldi's Thousand would be there, as would their voyage from Genoa to Marsala – Garibaldi's conquest of Sicily and his advance up the Italian peninsula. And then there was that particular *Garibaldino*, the almost mythical figure of Ippolito Nievo. Nievo was someone new to Ryan. As he dug further, the story of Ippolito Nievo came out. It took little time for him to come across the book *Il Caso Nievo*, and little more time to recognize that this book was probably the last word. The significance of Nievo and of the notes from the book in the KIT library had really placed an increasingly tight grip on Ryan over the past while. But this all had to be set aside. Visiting his parents took precedence.

It was an insanely early high-speed train that Ryan caught the next morning, one that would put him in Rome just before four in the afternoon. To have finished his work and be heading off across Europe by train was more than enough to power a contented smile. Having his mind in neutral and watching the changing countryside through the window was a luxury. Thoughts of Angelika came and went. But mostly he just gave himself over to a long series of thoughts and images, each triggered somehow by its predecessor, like a long ramble through a photo album on a rainy Sunday.

The train sped through Switzerland on its way to Milano Centrale, Bologna, Florence, and on to Rome. Glimpses caught through the carriage window confirmed a reality that Ryan had just let slip past him. The deep freeze that would just be releasing its grip on Toronto did not exist here. There were definite signs of spring everywhere. And thinking back, he now recalled that snow in Karlsruhe remained on the ground typically for just hours, that the winter air was cool and clammy rather than frigid, and that there were warmish days even in December. Now as he sped south, March had overtaken February, and in Rome and points south, the days would be mild.

Rome.

There were so many places Ryan wanted to see. It would be essential to visit the location on via Panisperna that had been Cannizzaro's final residence. But first he would meet Professor Nino di Biasi, emeritus at the University of Rome. Mitchell had suggested that Di Biasi was someone who could help ensure that Ryan maximized the value of his visits. To anyone outside looking in, his whistle-stop route across Italy would have appeared as the most self-indulgent boondoggle. All the people and events that had caught his interest had been studied to death. He wasn't going to turn up any astonishing original information. But then, he wasn't expecting to do that, just to immerse himself in the locations and settings that would be reminders of the link connecting Cannizzaro the chemist, one of the fathers of Italian chemistry, to Cannizzaro the republican, a link that had been brought out by the material in his draft project report.

Then there was the whole Nievo business, a mystery shrouded at the centre of so many things . . . Ryan expected nothing, literally nothing, from any focus on Nievo. It was all just a romantic fling, romantic in the historical sense, a nominal chase after something tantalizing that had sung its siren call to so many individuals before him.

The train was still quite a few hours from Rome. Ryan pulled out his cell and a notebook, made the call to the number for Di Biasi that Mitchell had provided, then stumbled through a few lines of Italian after Di Biasi's "Pronto!"

"Buona sera, professore."

"Buona sera. Signor Chandler?"

"Si, si. Ryan Chandler."

"I'm very pleased to hear from you", Di Biasi replied in almost perfect English. "Alan Mitchell has spoken at length about your work. What can I do for you?"

Ryan explained the situation.

"Yes, most certainly. I would welcome a visit. Take a taxi from Termini." Di Biasi gave Ryan his address. "Ten minutes at most. I look forward to seeing you at about four thirty."

Well, that went well. And he could feel the wheels of his Italian "adventure" begin to turn.

Time passed. Ryan dozed briefly, read in short spells, but mostly he just gazed out the train window.

The stunningly beautiful and remarkably varied Italian countryside drifted past. Towns and villages flashed by the window. Olive groves, vineyards, orchards, and winding lines of signature Lombardy poplars decorated the landscape in an exquisite display of random order. Having spent quite a few months now coming to terms with life in Germany and acquiring something approaching functional fluency in German, Ryan was astonished by an urge to do the same thing now in Italy. As a serious intellectual consideration, the notion could be dismissed out of hand, but he relished the visceral sense of how challenging, how exciting, how satisfying it would be to launch himself into just such an activity. For about half an hour, he allowed the passing countryside to raise self-indulgent images in his mind, but then he took a grip, pulled out a file folder, and began thinking seriously about the discussion he would be having with Di Biasi in less than two hours.

Ryan had taken a crash course in Italian in Karlsruhe. How much he had learned was evident to him as he listened to and understood portions of the conversations taking place around him in the carriage. He had been surprised just now, although also a bit mortified, at his sputtering telephone conversation with Di Biasi. Whether this nascent grasp of another language would take hold or just fade away was yet to be seen.

More dozing. Another half hour of languidly reviewing the passing landscape, and then another spell of light reading.

The announcement that the train would be arriving in Rome in ten minutes had him glancing at his watch. As he put away his papers and the book he had been reading, Ryan felt some excitement at the upcoming meeting. Here was a man who Mitchell described as having spent a professional lifetime studying the development of Italian science. Ryan could hardly have hoped for a better contact.

The sounds, sights, and smells of Roma Termini were like those of Frankfurt, Brussels, Strasbourg, or any other large European railway station, but at the same time were utterly different. The odd blend of controlled chaos that has resulted in all the extraordinary things Italy is known for was all around him in an intensely sensual presence.

Outside the station, Ryan found a taxi easily enough and gave the driver Di Biasi's address in via Agrigento. Close to the university, according to Mitchell. Quiet, at least by Rome standards. Not large, but then Di Biasi and his wife also had a place at Porto Santo Stefano, where they spent most of the time from April to November. Ryan paid the taxi, went to the door of a well-kept but not ostentatious building, and pressed the button labelled *AdB*.

When the door was opened, Ryan was surprised to be met by someone who was a dead ringer for Vittorio de Sica – not too tall, very distinctive features, knock-'em-dead, thick silver hair, laughter lines from the corner of each eye, and a smile that seemed to illuminate his entire face and everything around him.

"Ryan Chandler, I presume. How delighted I am to meet you. Please. Do come in. My apologies for not coming to the door sooner. I was just speaking to my wife at our summer place. Come in! Come in!"

"Thank you, professore", Ryan said, allowing himself to be led to a comfortable living and dining room, where Di Biasi had papers spread over a desk to one side. Against the far wall was a table that could accommodate four cosily. On it was a platter containing an attractive display of cheeses and cold meats and an invitingly chilled bottle of Frascati.

"I thought that a nibble and a sip might be just the ticket."

Di Biasi made pleasant and relaxing small talk but broke into a spell of essential multi-tasking by pouring out two glasses of wine, after first inclining his head toward Ryan and receiving a "si, grazie" response.

They clinked glasses, sipped, and then Di Biasi led the way by selecting meat, cheese, and bread and loading it onto a small plate.

"Alan Mitchell warned me that you might be getting in touch, but he didn't give me any idea what you might want to talk about. He did tell me about your project however. I'm intrigued. Someone having your background . . . Alan tells me that you now have a draft report."

"Yes", Ryan said. "He's given it a first review."

"Alan gave me only the barest outline of what you've been doing. When I say that I'm intrigued . . . well, it's the Italian connection and Cannizzaro. Can you give me a quick summary?"

"Certainly. Alan probably told you that the central idea in my report is that there was a clash of chemical worldviews at the 1860 conference, and that it was Cannizzaro's particular approach, the details of his worldview that ultimately helped carry the day. It's this notion of worldview rather than just some listing of physical and chemical arguments that I've been focussing on."

"Indeed. Very interesting. Alan did tell me that you would want to have a discussion, but I'm not sure how I can . . ."

Ryan nodded acknowledgment. "I really should have given you more warning", but Di Biasi waved that off. "What I'm looking for", Ryan continued, "is more background. I don't expect to be modifying my report, but I do want to get a much clearer picture of what was in Cannizzaro's mind. He came from Sicily. Did that influence his outlook in any fundamental way? What was the effect on him of working with Piria? How was he affected by his period of exile in Paris?"

"These were all influences", Di Biasi said. "But if you don't plan to modify your report, I'm not sure what will be the use of any further information."

Ryan set his glass down. "Once I got the idea of worldview as a central concern for the 1860 conference, I realized that Cannizzaro and others were products of their time. Political views among Italian scientists appear to have been spread across an unusually wide spectrum, and I want to get a better feeling for the dynamic that must have been at least partly responsible for the development of Cannizzaro's views. Second, if there is something here of real interest, I would prepare a short paper for publication. I fully intend to produce a paper summarizing my report. The possibility of a second more focussed paper might make a nice contrast."

"Most interesting. Of course, I will help any way I can."

Even as Di Biasi was speaking, Ryan was pulling a sheet of paper from his case, with names and addresses of people or places he wanted to visit. He spent a few minutes explaining to Di Biasi how his project had led to a strong interest in the events of the Risorgimento that were taking place at about the same time as the Karlsruhe Conference.

"I want to visit the places that might give me a better feel for things. But I don't have a lot to guide me on where to go. What to look for. Which places I can skip."

Di Biasi sat nodding and munching his bread and cheese.

Ryan hesitated a moment before moving in a different direction.

"I'm also interested in Ippolito Nievo."

Di Biasi looked suddenly confused.

"Nievo?"

"Yes. His name keeps coming up and I have a feeling that there's background there I should be aware of."

Di Biasi still looked somewhat dubious. "You know the story, I assume", he prompted.

"Yes. Well, at least in outline."

"I just want to sound a warning", Di Biasi began. "The Nievo story has become something of an industry in Italy. It's become a huge conspiracy, an unsolved mystery that invites everyone to pose their own theories, a story of international intrigue, a national cause celebre, and just about anything else one can dream up. There are still people who don't agree that Lucio Zinna had the last word when he wrote *Il Caso Nievo*. In fact, we still haven't recovered from the aftershocks that Umberto Eco generated. Interesting book, *Prague Cemetery*, but, my goodness! Did he really need to drag Nievo into it? What am I saying though? I know very well that this *nuvola di Nievo*, this Nievo cloud, isn't going to go away. I know about a dozen people who are obsessed by the whole thing, who think they will be able to get to the bottom of it, resolve all the remaining elements of mystery, make their name. So, Mr. Chandler, I would advise caution. Go ahead and inform yourself on the details. But I strongly suggest that you don't let anybody know what you're doing. Say the wrong words in the wrong ears and you might be branded a nut."

"Don't worry, professore. It's just an area of personal interest."

"Hmmm!" Di Biasi grunted, looking unconvinced and perplexed. "What was it that caught your interest?"

"Once I started exploring the consequences of Cannizzaro being a republican, his involvement in the 1848 Sicilian rebellion came to light, his obvious interest in what Garibaldi was doing, the story of Garibaldi's advance up the peninsula, and then inevitably, it seemed, the Nievo story. I started looking for any commentary on how those events affected Cannizzaro and other republicans."

There was a period of silence during which they both just allowed this topic to drift quietly into the background. Di Biasi selected more meat and cheese, poured them both more wine, and moved briskly onto a different topic.

"I am intrigued, very much intrigued, that you have taken such an interest in Italian science."

"Well, I was really just led to it", Ryan replied. "A lot of it seems to be linked through Cannizzaro. At least", he added quickly, "if restricted to the nineteenth century and by my own very sketchy knowledge on science of any sort, place, or time."

Di Biasi smiled indulgently, confirming that ignorance is a blanket curse under which all humans labour, experts and ignoramuses alike, and nodded some more.

"Yes. I just hope you won't be too disappointed in what you find. Or don't find."

"I'm not sure I follow you, professore."

"Many of my colleagues would disagree with me, but I've always been disappointed at the shamefully superficial efforts that have been made to preserve and promote the history of Italian science. There are some bright spots. The people at the University of

Palermo have done tremendous work on Cannizzaro's legacy. But the fact that none of Cannizzaro's lab at Genoa has survived is just one indication. So, when I come across your work, as Mitchell has described it, work done by a non-Italian, non-chemist, non-scientist that rivals a large fraction of what has been done here in Italy, well, I'm impressed and depressed at the same time."

More wine was poured, and Di Biasi gestured to Ryan, urging him to help himself to more meat and cheese.

"We should talk more about these papers you want to write, but there's time for that. I think I have a good idea what you have in mind."

Di Biasi paused here and looked at Ryan.

"I would be very pleased, Mr. Chandler, if you were to undertake work on these papers under my auspices here at la Sapienza."

"Here? With you? But, professore, I am nobody!"

"Without wishing to offend, I think I'm in a better position to judge that", Di Biasi said, as a twinkle flickered across his face. "No need for an immediate answer, Mr. Chandler. But please think about it. I can make some funding available. And the library at la Sapienza as well as my own collection probably represents the most complete set of documentation on these areas anywhere in Italy."

"I-I really don't know what to say. A very generous offer, and one that is completely unexpected, I can assure you! Thank you!"

"Not at all. Now, let's take a close look at the visits you propose."

It took Di Biasi only a few minutes to consider the items on Ryan's sheet, and he then began making annotations. Within fifteen minutes, red ink covered most of the blank space, Ryan's list of six visits had been expanded to nine, and Di Biasi had promised to send Ryan a list of questions to consider and other sources to consult before he began his visits.

Ryan checked his watch, and after another round of pleased-to-have-met-you remarks were exchanged, he found himself back on the street with instructions on where he would be most likely to find a taxi.

"Hi, Dad", Ryan said twenty minutes later. "I'm in the lobby."

Twenty-Four

It was a family reunion like none Ryan could remember. James and Michaela Chandler were evidently relaxed and greatly enjoying each other's uninterrupted company. But an aura of expectation seemed to fill the room when Ryan entered and met his parents face to face for the first time in more than six months. Ryan walked straight to his mother and enfolded her in a huge grown-up son hug. He was sure she had damp eyes as she pulled away, and Ryan turned to exchange a strong handshake and bear hug with his father. There was a bottle of prosecco and three glasses on the table, and Ryan's father ushered them all across the room and poured.

"You look absolutely stunning", his mother said. Ryan's father just stood looking at him, beaming and nodding through a smile that was a mixture of barely contained pride and lump-throated astonishment.

"Here's to us", James said, raising his glass, and they all drank.

"Come and tell us what you've been doing", his mother urged, one hand on Ryan's forearm, gently leading him toward a large sofa.

Ryan gave them a very quick summary of his project, told them about Rick and Angelika, and soon found that he was extolling the whole experience of living well outside his accustomed box and fending for himself. He became self-conscious when he realized that he had been delivering a monologue for almost five minutes. His parents couldn't stop smiling.

They explained their plans, their intention of staying in Rome for another six days before flying back to Toronto.

"It's been a long time, far too long, since we spent relaxing time like this together", James said, glancing at Ryan's mother as he spoke. Ryan realized just then how little real investment he had made in the three of them as a family, how much he had taken for granted, and the depth of the commitment his parents had made to him over many years.

"But you must be hungry", James said. "I know I am. There's a superb little patio restaurant just around the corner. It might be a bit cool to sit outside, but let's not prejudge. So. Andiamo."

Dinner was relaxed and relaxing. In response to questions, Ryan filled in his parents on what he planned to do next, the timing he expected for the review of his project, the unexpected spin-off interests the project had thrown up, and how he wanted to pursue them over the next few weeks. He drew out his parents on their lives back in Toronto, and this delivered one surprise. Ryan's father related, in a way that seemed somewhat distant, almost relieved, how his business was changing, how he was beginning to hand off more and more work to his principals, and how the bottled excitement over Ryan's project had made the steering group noticeably eager and impatient at their two most recent meetings.

"It seems to me", his father said, looking into the distance, "that they want this whole effort put onto a more structured basis. But they'll need to wait for the formal process on your project to be finished. And they'll be looking to me to take a lead role in the management of the effort. I would welcome that. It would be a pleasant change."

James turned to look directly at Ryan. "So, I guess you and I are somewhat in the same boat, dipping our toes into new seas."

Gliding down a relaxing post-prandial grade, and over glasses of sambuca, the three of them put together a plan for the next day. After a few more minutes' conversation, they said goodnight.

Ryan's father had booked him a single room in the same hotel, and Ryan tumbled into bed. The world stopped for about eight hours.

Over strong coffee and bread the next morning, and wearing a common uniform of jeans and light short-sleeved shirts, and light jackets just in case, they discussed what they would be up to. Ryan's parents had decided to take a six-hour bus tour, and knowing his mother, Ryan guessed that she had already studied an armful of guidebooks. It was certain that the tour she had selected would not miss anything important, not mislead them on anything, and not include anything trivial.

"Where will you be going?" Ryan's father asked him.

"To Cannizzaro's last residence in Rome, in via Panisperna. One of Professor di Biasi's students documented Cannizzaro's work in modernizing the chemistry department at la Sapienza and has offered to meet me there and talk about Cannizzaro's time in Rome. Then we'll have a tour of the chemistry department itself."

"Is this part of your follow-up work?" Michaela asked.

"Yes. It's the first stop Di Biasi recommended."

They finished breakfast, arranged a time to meet back at the hotel for lunch, and then went their ways. Ryan watched his parents leave the hotel, hand in hand, and realized how much he was looking forward to the next few days in their company.

Ryan met Di Biasi's student, spent an hour with him, and took many pages of notes. At the edificio Cannizzaro in la Sapienza, Di Biasi met them and gave Ryan a quick half-hour tour of the chemical museum and the department.

"I hope your time here has been useful", Di Biasi said.

"Very much so. Thank you, professore."

They shook hands and Di Biasi handed Ryan an envelope.

"There are a few copies of my business card in there and the names and numbers of the contacts we discussed yesterday. Feel free to call me any time. And none of those contacts will be surprised if you call them, so don't hesitate."

They were still in handshake mode and Di Biasi's grip tightened.

"I hope we will be able to meet again."

"I'll make sure of it", Ryan offered. "And I expect to be in touch with you again very soon."

Ryan had no idea how prescient that statement would turn out to be.

Twenty-Five

Ryan and his parents met back at the hotel, had a leisurely lunch together, and then discussed the next few days. James and Michaela were in full tourist mode and were off to spend an afternoon in specialist museums. By the end of their week, Michaela's research would ensure that they were minor experts on all things Roman.

Ryan told his parents he planned on a cycling visit to part of the Appian Way in the morning, then some research in the afternoon in preparation for all the places he planned to visit.

They talked in a desultory fashion for a few minutes longer, then Ryan's mother collected her shoulder bag, probably containing at least one guide book and some well-organized notes. At eight forty-five, his parents walked out into the day's sunshine. Twenty minutes later, Ryan did the same.

The morning went well for Ryan. Despite the fact that he had done a great deal of reading about various aspects of Rome, he had no doubt that he was cycling past quite a number of important locations but in complete ignorance of what they were or why they were important. There were many stops for photos.

Over the next two days, Ryan felt that the three of them were making up for at least some of the time that he had wasted in his dissipated lifestyle back in Toronto. Odd, and in this case sad, that he had to travel thousands of miles to find what has been right under his nose all along.

In no time at all, it seemed, they were down to Ryan's parents' last two days in Rome. His father gradually became quieter, probably ticking off in his mind all the things that would be awaiting him back at his office in Toronto. Ryan's mother had clearly enjoyed the three of them having so much time together and wasn't looking forward to that experience coming to an end. But they ventured forth as usual on the second-last day, which Ryan planned to spend wandering among the ruins in Ancient Rome.

In that timeless place, time had a funny feeling.

Quite a few dozen pictures later, after several hours drifting at that dreamy pace known as "tourist wander" and multiple stops for close examination of various arresting bits of architecture, Ryan found a bench and began munching the apple he had brought from the hotel's breakfast display. The sun and breeze added just the warmth and caress needed to complete one of those perfect settings, the sort of occasion you know you will remember for a long, long time. As he had found over the past days in Rome, his thoughts had gone back repeatedly to the nineteenth-century Italian at the centre of his project: Stanislao Cannizzaro.

Looking at his watch, and realizing with some surprise that it was already quarter to two, Ryan packed up his reverie and began making his way back to the hotel. There was still plenty to look at, and it occurred to him that he could easily wander for a week and not exhaust all the possible sites that Rome offered. By two fifty, Ryan was back in his room and making more notes on what he would see, and should see, in the cities he planned to visit.

He hoped that a number of threads could be drawn together by the information, or at least the sense of time and place he expected to collect, and he even dared to begin sketching out in his mind some details for the articles that he should be able to produce. He was aware of new anchor points related to people and events, foliage that added depth and contrast to an emerging picture. A faint smile – the outward sign of a successful response to an intellectual challenge but also recognition of his scarcely believable personal luck – played across his features.

The phone vibrating in his pocket caused Ryan to break off from thinking and making notes.

"Pronto", he said, not looking at the display.

"Ryan?" A quavery voice. His mother.

Something was wrong.

"What is it, Mother?"

"Your father has been in an accident. It's serious. We're at the Salvator Mundi Hospital."

Ryan raced to the nearest main thoroughfare and hailed a taxi. During the ride to the hospital, the confident mental architecture that Ryan's visit with his parents had constructed over the past several days came crashing down like buildings after a Richter 10 quake.

An accident. It's serious.

No. He wasn't about to lose his father. It couldn't be.

Panic began rising, but then Ryan barked silent orders to his mental world, ordering them all to SHUT UP! and wait for some real information.

At the hospital, he spoke to a calm gentleman at the information desk, then sprinted through the hallways, ignoring the words of disapproval directed toward him, until he saw his mother in the waiting area next to a group of operating rooms.

She was red-eyed, shaking, barely on the cusp of control.

"He's in the operating room", Michaela said when she had brought herself almost under control. "I don't know what kind of injuries he has."

They exchanged a long hug. Dabbing a handkerchief at her eyes, she told him they had been crossing a street when a car came out of nowhere.

"Your father pushed me across the street and I fell. When I turned, I saw the front of the car catch one of his legs and he was thrown against a tree. The car just screeched out of sight."

As she related events, it was evident that things became confused for her. A man on the path about fifty metres away had got onto his cellphone immediately, and Ryan's mother learned later that he had called the police and an ambulance. He had rushed over to Ryan's mother, but his little English, her little Italian, and the stress of the moment meant that they just stayed with each other until the emergency services arrived.

The police turned up first, followed by the ambulance less than a minute later. There was a very brief discussion between the police and the Italian witness. Ryan's father was moved to a stretcher and then placed in the ambulance, which rushed off to the hospital. One of the policemen had reasonable English, and he spent about fifteen minutes speaking to Ryan's mother and the witness, took many notes, and said that likely there would be some follow-up questions.

Ryan led his mother to a seat, they sat together, and Ryan held her for a long moment.

At length, Ryan said he was going to try to find someone, get some information, and that he would be right back. He was gone about an hour but kept in contact with his mother by cellphone. When he returned, he also had a plastic bag containing his father's personal things.

"He's going to be okay", Ryan reported. "He'll be in intensive care and likely won't be conscious for at least another twelve hours. They told me he has multiple fractures in his right leg, a cracked pelvis, six broken ribs, a broken left wrist, and some internal injuries. But there's nothing life threatening."

Ryan paused here. "He'll need to stay here for at least ten days."

Michaela nodded, and it was evident that despite the anxiety and the physical and mental shock, she was relieved to know something concrete.

"Can I get you anything?" Ryan asked.

"We have some time", she replied. "Let's go and find someplace where we can get a strong drink."

Over a glass each of Martini Bianco, they held one of those conversations that results in no information being exchanged but generates a feeling of being connected. When Ryan's mother had drained her glass, she made to rise, but Ryan suggested that they have another.

Ryan noticed that the second glass of Bianco caused a perceptible easing of his mother's tension, or maybe it was just mild emotional anaesthesia. Didn't matter. In due course, they made their way back to the waiting area. Ten minutes later, an orderly wheeled Ryan's father through the double swing doors. He was elaborately swaddled and had connections for tubes and drips protruding from several parts of his body. A doctor emerged from the operating room.

"This is my father", Ryan managed in Italian. "Do you know when he will be conscious? Do you know his condition?"

"He is in serious condition, but he's out of danger." The doctor spoke accented but grammatical English. "He will spend the night in ICU, and if all goes well, he will be moved to a private room sometime tomorrow morning. You should be able to see him tomorrow afternoon, but only for a very short period. And now, excuse me."

The bed, the doctor, and the orderly moved off down the hallway and vanished around a corner.

Ryan's mother had begun to weep again.

"Let's go back to the hotel", Ryan said. "I'll give our cell numbers to the information desk. There's no point in staying here."

His mother hesitated, but then allowed herself to be led away to the elevator lobby. Outside the hospital, Ryan found a taxi and they headed back to the hotel.

Twenty-Six

Ryan and his mother went directly to her room once they reached the hotel. She sat stiffly on the sofa and looked around as though lost.

Most of the day had passed. It was now late afternoon. Ryan asked about dinner, but Michaela just shook her head.

"Something light from room service?" he urged. "We should eat something."

His mother looked completely distracted and it became clear to Ryan that a unilateral decision on dinner was needed. Flipping through the brochure on the desk, he called room service and ordered a small salad, some focaccia, and an antipasto platter. When the food arrived, Michaela ignored it initially, then picked at the salad, and finally managed to eat a decent amount. When they had finished, Ryan cleared the trays away to one side.

"I'll go to my room and get my pyjamas. I'll come back and stay here in your room tonight, on the couch."

"You don't need to do that . . ."

"I think I do. Neither of us should be alone tonight. I'll be right back."

Ryan slipped out and returned five minutes later carrying his small suitcase, toilet bag, a folded blanket, and a pillow. His mother remained in the same stiff sitting position on the couch, still looking off into the distance in what appeared to be a combination of expectation and uncertainty.

Ryan went over and sat next to his mother. They spoke about practical things. Flights needed to be changed and the airline had to be consulted about special arrangements to get James home as soon as he was able to leave the hospital. They had to see about extending the hotel reservations. Ryan offered to contact his father's office and let them know what had happened. But all that could wait. Ryan's mother nodded vaguely to this list of tasks. She was beat, emotionally exhausted, and needed rest.

"Go to bed, Mother. Things will look a bit better in the morning." Ryan accompanied his mother to the bedroom door, kissed her goodnight, and wished her a sound sleep.

Back on the sofa, he didn't feel like going to bed, didn't feel like sitting up, was just unsettled. He made the bed, which was really nothing more than spreading the blanket over the cushions, then sat down heavily as if waiting for something to happen, magically.

It wasn't magic, but the question that popped into his mind suddenly had his attention.

Why would someone try to run down one or both of my parents?

The question neatly sidestepped the assumption that it had been an accident. From Michaela's description, it was no accident. It had been a deliberate hit-and-run.

Ryan's mother knew nobody in Rome, of that Ryan was quite certain. She was here just to accompany his father. And after pondering the matter for a few minutes, Ryan could find no rationale for anyone wanting to kill his mother.

What about his father?

James' father had business connections in Rome. He had been here several times over the past five years. But as far as Ryan was aware, there was nothing that could prompt anyone to find advantage in his death. His dealings in Rome had always been international legal consultations. There were no investments involved. His father owned no shares or interests in Italian companies, as far as Ryan was aware. It was conceivable that there were situations he was unaware of, which might alter that conclusion, but he couldn't think of any example that was even remotely credible. Ryan sat undecided, thinking in circles.

A further question began forming itself. But it seemed absurd, impossible . . .

Could this possibly be related to the bizarre events that had been occurring over the past months in Karlsruhe?

Ryan's immediate impulse was to reject the possibility out of hand, but he hesitated. There was the beating he had suffered in the street, the "snooping" incident involving Angelika, and the very odd about-face that Professor Hartmann had made on the direction Ryan's project should take. And as far as Ryan was aware, the Karlsruhe police had got nowhere in determining any of the details surrounding Hartmann's death, particularly who might have been involved.

How could this Roman hit-and-run be connected to any of that?

Ryan knew from idle internet searches that Rome is the most dangerous capital city in Europe in terms of traffic accidents and pedestrian deaths. Could this have been just another random event, someone driving too fast and carelessly causing an accident, panicking, and then fleeing the scene? His mother said that the car had accelerated, so he was inclined to believe that it wasn't just an accident, however irrational the alternative might seem.

Ryan walked over to the desk, picked up the pen and small notepad that sat by the telephone, and began making a list of the items he had just ticked off in his head. He scanned through his list, looking for things that could be missed in a mental list but are often suggested by a physical one.

But then another question arose almost immediately. Suppose his father's "accident" was indeed linked to the Karlsruhe events. Could it have involved the same person or some group of confederates? How would they have known that Ryan's parents were in Rome? Would it not be more likely that this deliberate hit-and-run had been orchestrated from Toronto? But by whom? And why?

This was spinning out of control.

Okay. Practical stuff. Contact the senior partner in his father's business. Let him know the situation. His father's cellphone. Contacts.

Ryan busied himself with this for a few minutes. It made him feel as though he was actually doing something, at last.

And then, suddenly, Ryan was dead tired. He moved silently to the bedroom door and checked that his mother was sleeping. Returning to the sitting area couch, he undressed, pulled on his pyjamas, wrapped himself in the blanket, and could remember nothing until the following morning, when very early dawn turned everything in the room to a dream of mixed pastels.

Ryan folded the blanket, had a quick sponge bath in the guest bathroom, shaved, dressed, and then returned to the notes he had made the previous evening. Something had changed during the night. The razor-edged shock of the previous day's events was now blunted, and he wanted to explore the postulate that he was at the centre of whatever had led to the hit-and-run. He had spent months in Europe, he was the one around whom the odd and violent events in Karlsruhe had occurred, and it now made eminent sense, in the growing light of a new day, to assume that a common cause was behind all this and behind yesterday's events as well.

What could anyone in Rome possibly want from Ryan?

Indeed, who knew that he was in Rome?

Di Biasi knew. But did he know about Ryan's parents or where Ryan might be staying? Ryan had not said anything to him about that, so the answer was very likely no.

Could it be . . . No. He didn't want to believe it, wouldn't believe it. Angelika?

He had told Alan Mitchell about Rome, but in even more brief terms, so Mitchell knew even less than Di Biasi. Besides, it was quite ridiculous to think that either Di Biasi or Mitchell was involved in any of this. Mitchell had not come on the scene, had not even been in the picture, until all the serious aggro at Karlsruhe was finished. And it had been Mitchell who contacted Di Biasi.

So how could–

Cellphone tracking. Somebody could have tracked Ryan through his cellphone or could have tracked his father. Ryan then remembered that he had replaced his cell after he received the call from his school friend Ted. Did that mean that none of the people who must have been behind the violence in Karlsruhe, the people he thought of as "the watchers", had his new phone details? Did that mean they couldn't track him? Well, if they did have his details, he could certainly put a stop to any further snooping. And taking the back cover off his cell, he made sure that that became impossible. This meant that he couldn't use his phone now, but that was no hardship. He would get a cheap replacement.

Where did that leave things?

Suppose somebody had been able to track him. They might know that he was staying at the Hotel Quarto, almost certainly were aware that his parents were staying there. But they wouldn't be able to tell which room he was in.

On the other hand . . .

No, the Voice said. *You need to stop going in circles.*

If they had the appropriate information, the simple approach would be just to follow Ryan, if they could, if it was him they were after. Or follow his parents.

Ryan took a long moment to ponder all this, then began making notes to capture his thinking over the past twenty minutes. Two pages later, he stopped abruptly and looked up.

Sources.

And timing.

It surely could be nothing in his project report. All of that rested on information that was already out there. Looking through his notes, it did seem that he was at a dead end. But he couldn't stop now. The more time he took to find out what was going on, the more anyone watching them, if indeed anyone was, would be able to make up for lost time. No. He had to keep hammering away at this until he could see some path.

He puzzled over it for another twenty minutes and almost missed the key piece of information.

Twenty-Seven

Is there anything in my project that would raise interest?

The short answer was *no*.

What else then?

There were those sheets he had found. A request from Cannizzaro to have copies of his *Sketch of a Course of Chemical Philosophy*, his *sunto*, distributed to the delegates of the conference. This led nowhere..

His beating that night in Karlsruhe? Why was it . . .

Shit!

Had someone hoped to raise concern with his parents?

No. It was all ridiculous. An absurd conspiracy worry.

You're going soft in the head, Chandler, and for once he had to agree with the Inner Voice.

Hartmann? His U-turn on Ryan's project?

Did someone have some dirt on Hartmann?

Hartmann's death? Tying off a big lose end?

Then, much later, the hit-and-run attack in Rome?

He looked again at his notes. Something needed closer checking. Rummaging in his accountant's case, he drew out the copies of the sheets he had found in the book in the KIT library. He had already gone through these once closely. Had he overlooked something? Thank heavens he had stuck the Italian dictionary in the case before leaving Karlsruhe.

It took about an hour of detailed checking, but just as he heard the toilet flush in his mother's en suite bathroom, he had picked his way through the sheets again thoroughly.

They were in two sections, as he recalled.

It appeared that the first pages were addressed to Professor Piria. Piria died in 1865. So these words had been penned more than a hundred and fifty years ago. Two names appeared at the bottom of the first sheet: Sergio Cesare and Giovanni Pozzuoli. Ryan pulled out his computer, switched it on, and did a quick search under each of these names.

Nothing.

Maybe they had been students of Piria. If so, it looked as though they had not gone on to become well-known.

Ryan looked through the text again. The request, which could have come only from Cannizzaro, was clear from the scribble, partly smudged, at the bottom of the first page: *Sunto. Copie per i delegati.* Give copies of the sunto to the delegates.

It took a moment to sink in.

They were there! Those two guys, Cesare and Pozzuoli, they were there! In Karlsruhe! Not at the conference, certainly, but in the city. The notes likely were written by Cesare and Pozzuoli after a discussion they had with Cannizzaro.

In which case . . . probably nothing.

The other two pages were something different. They were written by someone else, had flowed from a different hand. Then he stopped.

At two words. Two words whose significance he had missed before. Words that set him off on a new course.

Bice carissima.

Immediately Ryan knew what was before him. *Bice* was Beatrice Melzi, before she was married and became Beatrice Gobio. She was a close friend of Nievo, and the two pages he had been struggling through appeared to be part of a letter. There were what appeared to be personal comments, in a sort of shorthand that Bice evidently would understand. There was a comment about how abominable life was in Palermo. And then there were the words *grazie al cielo per i documenti mandati in precedenza.* (Thank heaven for the documents sent in advance.) How did these two very different fragments of document come to be put together? Did these last words really mean–

"Good morning, Ryan."

Ryan's mother looked a hundred percent better, dressed in relaxed summer clothes and even wearing a faint smile.

"Good morning, Mother. You slept well I hope?"

A nod.

"Shall we go down to the restaurant and have some breakfast?" Ryan asked, scooping papers together and having his watch surprise him by relaying the information that it was almost nine o'clock.

They set off almost immediately. They didn't linger over breakfast. Soon they had hailed a cab. Many things needed to be done, and priorities jostled in Ryan's head.

Twenty-Eight

During the taxi ride, Ryan's mother had been quiet but calm, apparently wrapped in her own thoughts.

"Mother", Ryan began, "a few weeks after I went to Karlsruhe, we spoke on the telephone and you asked me whether everything was okay. Do you remember that?"

"Yes. I remember how good it was to hear your voice. Even though it was only a few weeks, it seemed like you had been gone for months."

"I remember assuring you that everything was fine, but you seemed worried."

"No. I wasn't worried. I guess I just missed you."

Ryan's mother had never been good at massaging things or hiding her feelings, at least not when it involved Ryan or his father. And now Ryan just held her gaze without saying anything further.

"Oh, well", his mother said at length. "Yes, I was worried. But in hindsight it really was nothing. I had read an account of street violence in Europe. It upset me. I began worrying about you. Your father said that this sort of thing wasn't really news. He knew that I was worrying about you. He suggested that I just call you. So I did."

Ryan nodded.

"And this account of street violence. Did you just happen to see it? In the newspaper?"

"I don't remember now. No, I think there was some more specific reason why I came across it. It was months ago now. After our telephone discussion, I forgot all about it." And his mother gave Ryan a wan smile of reassurance.

Ryan smiled back. But he knew there was more to it than that. He suspected that his parents had a discussion, his father would have assured his mother that Ryan would have called them if there was any problem, and that their subsequent telephone conversation had put the whole matter to rest for Ryan's mother. At least nominally.

But he also suspected that his mother didn't just happen upon the account of street violence by chance. He expected that it had to do with that dreadful woman Sarah Brimley.

Ryan knew the story. His mother and Sarah Brimley had been fast undergraduate friends and friendly competitors through graduate school, but then had fallen out seriously when Michaela had snapped up the lecturer's spot they had both been angling for. Brimley soon found another staff position at the university, and the rivalry reignited, worse than before. In the end, Michaela sailed on ahead in her career, leaving Brimley fuming in the dust. Things were made worse when Michaela resigned her position after Ryan's birth, a position that then was not available to Brimley. There was a final terrible scene, after which they hadn't spoken again.

That was one thing clarified for Ryan. Most likely, Brimley was trying, once again, to take some sort of revenge, to sow fear and worry in his mother's mind. They rode the rest of the way to the hospital in silence.

By ten thirty, they were with Ryan's father once more. James had been moved from the ICU to a private room. Ryan made sure that his mother was settled there, outlined his proposed schedule for the morning, then set off for la Sapienza. In the hospital lobby, he made a quick telephone call.

"Professore di Biasi?"

"Good morning, Mr. Chandler. I hope this is to tell me that you will do your research here in Rome."

"I have indeed thought about your offer, professore, but there's something else I want to discuss. Does your library have a copy of Nievo's complete letters?"

"Nievo? Mr. Chandler, I sincerely hope that you have not been, how does one say in English, bitten by that particular bug."

"No, professore. But I would much rather talk about this face to face."

They agreed on a meeting time at the edificio Cannizzaro, and it was clear that Di Biasi was intrigued. But Ryan knew that there were three important items to discuss. First, he wanted to get Di Biasi's view, the view of a fully galvanized Nievo conspiracy sceptic. Second, if the fragment Ryan had was part of a letter, did the text in those two pages from Karlsruhe correspond to any of Nievo's complete letters? And third, he would ask Di Biasi to get into contact with KIT immediately.

At la Sapienza, Ryan was met by a down-to-business Di Biasi, who whisked him upstairs to his office and had a book of the complete letters of Nievo open even before Ryan was in his seat. It took very little time for the two of them to confirm that no letter in the book reflected what was on Ryan's sheets.

"But that's not proof of anything", Di Biasi said. "These sheets could be fakes."

"That's true", Ryan agreed. "But there are plenty of people who will believe what they want to believe. As long as anyone thinks that there might be a missing Nievo letter out there, there will be a clear possibility for trouble."

Di Biasi nodded. "Especially a letter that seems to promise what this one does."

It was immediately clear to Ryan that he had missed something and equally clear to Di Biasi that that was the case, prompting a brief explanation from Di Biasi.

"Nievo sailed on the *Ercole* from Palermo to Naples, but the ship never arrived. It is presumed that the ship and everyone on it was lost somewhere in the Tyrrhenian Sea. But Nievo was also transporting with him the account books for Garibaldi's campaign. They were presumably lost as well. These sheets that you found imply that Nievo had a second copy of the books and that he sent them on ahead, to somewhere, in advance of his voyage. If that's true, and if another copy of the accounts exists, that really would be dynamite."

"Do you think that's likely?"

"Remember that you're talking to a Nievo conspiracy sceptic. No, I think it unlikely that there was a second set of account books." Di Biasi was lost in thought for a moment.

"Can I leave these copies with you, professore?"

"Most certainly. I will lock them away right now."

Ryan waited while Di Biasi secured his sheets.

"There's something I think we need to do, or at least that you need to do, professore. Right away."

Di Biasi jumped in surprise, as though he had sat on a tack. "What?"

"The originals I copied these pages from are back in the book where I found them in the KIT library. They need to be made secure. Not only to have them available to check the authenticity of the notes in them but also to prevent the whole lot disappearing permanently and untraceably into some private collection. Here is the shelving reference for the book. Could you contact KIT and make sure that's done?"

"Very good thinking. Yes! Right away."

"There's something else", Ryan began. "I've told you of the events that have occurred during the time I've been on this project, including my father's very recent hit-and-run horror. Suppose these sheets here really are a lost letter from Nievo. What would they be worth?"

"To some people, a great deal indeed", Di Biasi replied. "But based on what you've told me, how would anyone know that you have these sheets?"

"I don't know, professore. I'm grasping at straws really, just trying to find some explanation for what's been happening. I was an obvious anomaly at Karlsruhe, a non-German studying the significance of an international conference and being particularly interested in the role played by an Italian chemist. I had also begun asking around about Cannizzaro's connection to Garibaldi, and my own developing interest in Nievo. People would know about my interest. A story like that could spread. I really don't know, professore. None of this comes together as a completely coherent story. But my father was nearly killed. And to be quite honest I'm worried about my parents. Whatever the reason was behind that hit-and-run, maybe these sheets, maybe something else, I'm very concerned that they're still in danger."

Ryan stopped here and looked at Di Biasi.

"I have nobody else to turn to, professore. My parents need someplace to hide, putting it bluntly, and I'm hoping that you might be able to suggest something."

"Indeed I can", Di Biasi replied without missing a beat. "At our summer place in Porto Santo Stefano, we have plenty of room. They could both stay there."

"Oh! That's very generous, professore, but I'm not sure my father would be able to accept that." Ryan was not entirely certain that he could convince his father about the need for any such plan, although he was prepared to try anything, including bullying an invalid, to do this. But even supposing that his father was convinced, Ryan was sure that he would not want to be beholden to Di Biasi to that extent.

"In that case", Di Biasi continued, "there are guesthouses very near our place in Porto Santo Stefano. They are run by friends. I doubt there would be any difficulty arranging for your parents to rent rooms for as long as needed. This could be arranged at short notice."

To Ryan, this had the ring of a workable plan. A private ambulance to spirit his parents off to Porto Santo Stefano, and the trail in Rome would suddenly go cold. Apart from Ryan himself.

Ryan felt his cellphone vibrate. It was from his mother, saying that Ryan's father was awake.

"Sorry", he said to Di Biasi, slipping his phone back in his pocket. "My father is awake now. I'm going back to the hospital. Is tomorrow too soon to have my father taken to Porto Santo Stefano?"

Di Biasi waved off the apology. "Tomorrow is fine. Get back to me as soon as you can. And if you need any assistance on anything", Di Biasi added, holding up his cellphone and waggling it at Ryan, "I'm this close."

It was then a straight run for Ryan from la Sapienza to the hospital. His father was indeed awake, looking somewhat disoriented, but able to offer a smile to Ryan when he entered the room.

Even through a pain-killer fog, Ryan's father wielded a mind that would have struck apprehension into the hearts of most people. Ryan was more forthright with his father than he had ever been, and it was clear that this came as something of a surprise to both his parents. In his own mind, he was convinced that in some real sense he had to take control, to tell his parents what was going to happen, and that there would be little room for negotiation.

"I don't know why you were targeted in that hit-and-run, Dad. And yes", he added, seeing the objection his father was about to raise, "I think the only safe assumption is that it was indeed a hit-and-run, and that whoever was behind it might try again. So let's not argue about the 'why' of it. You need to be safe. Both of you. And you're not safe where you are now." In the end, it was the need to guarantee the safety and security of his mother that won the day. Ryan's father did not like it at all, but logic won out over pride. There was a condition, however.

"You must promise me", Ryan's father intoned, "without hesitation, to keep in touch with us daily, and to call me immediately if any problem develops. Promise me that now."

Ryan promised.

"And I want to have a discussion with Professore di Biasi before we leave Rome."

Ryan passed his father's cellphone over to him. "I called your office and explained the situation. And I've rescheduled your Toronto flights."

Ryan's father just nodded, a hint of surprise and respect in his face. Ryan then said he would make arrangements through the hospital for a private ambulance for tomorrow morning and ask about any nursing assistance that might be needed in Porto Santo Stefano. "Once I've done that", he added, "I'll call Di Biasi and ask him to contact you. Okay?"

Ryan's father chuckled, then winced in pain. "Yes, son. Very much okay. Thank you."

Ryan looked at his father and sensed that their roles had been reversed, for the first time ever. A new sort of bond was forming.

"What about you?" his father asked.

"I'll be striking out right away on my tour through Italy. I'll be leaving Rome the morning after you do. Don't worry about me, Dad."

It took some time to arrange the private ambulance since Ryan had to be absolutely sure that it would be an unmarked vehicle and that the departure would be unobserved. He then telephoned Di Biasi, told him what had been organized, confirmed that guesthouse accommodation had been booked, gave him his father's cellphone number, and promised to be in touch again soon.

Ryan headed back to the hotel, wanting to make more notes on the things he had discussed with Di Biasi about the presumed Nievo letter. But he also wanted to consider the deception he had just pulled off. He had no intention of leaving Rome immediately.

Back at the hotel, he tidied up the notes he had scribbled that morning, added another five pages of points, stuck them in his accountant's case, and sat back to think.

His cellphone buzzed.

He recognized Rick's number from the display.

"Rick, you old fiend! How are you doing?"

There was a delay here, a premonitory delay that wiped the smile from Ryan's face and sent a shiver through him.

"Bad news, Ryan. Very bad news."

Another delay.

"It's Angelika. I'm afraid that she's dead, Ryan."

Twenty-Nine

There was the image of an impish smile.

There were three students enjoying dinner and discussion, a wine glass held in conversational suspense in mid-air, and he could tell from the eyes that an active intelligence was preparing a comment for delivery, a comment sharp with meaning but softened by humour.

He could see a colourful patterned skirt, sliding off a negligently extended index finger, and dropping in slow motion to the floor.

He could feel her smooth skin through soapy hands.

I'm afraid that she's dead, Ryan.

How could Angelika be dead?

It's not . . . It was only . . . They were just . . .

The account was clear in Ryan's mind later, but he couldn't remember any other of Rick's words.

Someone had found her that morning. On the concrete pad below one of the windows of her fourth floor flat. Lying on her back. One leg beneath her, bent at the knee, her body cold. Evidently she had been lying there for hours. Nobody had heard anything. Indicating that she hadn't screamed, hadn't cried out? Indicating . . .?

"Ryan? Ryan? Are you there?"

"Yes. I-I'm here. Do I need to come to . . ."

Long pause.

"I don't . . . no, I don't think you need to come here. Although the police might want to talk to you at some point."

"Could you speak to them? Tell them . . . tell them where I am. I'll come . . . I can come back to Karlsruhe. Tomorrow afternoon . . ."

"Yes. Yes, I'll do that."

There was an uncomfortable pause here at both ends of the line.

"I really am terribly sorry, Ryan. I'll meet you when you come in to Karlsruhe. By train?"

"Train? No. Fly . . . I think. I'll let you know. Right now, I can't . . . I just . . . Oh, damn it all to hell!"

And Ryan hung up. And went into a long weeping jag. And then must have dozed off.

It was sometime in the afternoon when he awoke. He sat up on the bed then groaned as he remembered Rick's words, and an ugly pock face of defeat rose up before him.

Rome. Father. Time. Four forty-five. His emotional world was full of jagged pain. But there were important things to do. Ryan summoned an enormous effort. He had to get back to the hospital. Pack his parents off to Porto Santo Stefano. There was no way he would tell them about Angelika – completely out of the question.

Fifteen minutes later, Ryan entered James' private room. Michaela was there keeping company with a patient who looked improved already. Michaela sported a faint smile, and the anxiety furrows on her brow had been smoothed. Ambulance arrangements had been confirmed for the following morning. Accommodation at a guesthouse in Porto Santo Stefano had been organized. Ryan and his mother eventually rose and waved goodbye to Ryan's father, lying on his bed amid snaking tubes and wires. He looked increasingly like the restless convalescent.

The taxi ride back to the hotel was mostly quiet.

"Are you okay, Ryan?" his mother asked at one point, an expression of concern, dangerously intuitive, on her face.

"Yes, thanks, Mother. Just a bit tired."

In fact, he was struggling just to keep it all together.

They had a light dinner and then Michaela retired.

Ryan awoke the next morning, feeling drained and listless despite having a sound sleep behind him. He could hear his mother moving about in her room, and by the time he had emerged from the guest bathroom, abluted and shaved, she was sitting on the sofa, bag packed, prepared to go. She was ready to look after her James.

They skipped breakfast and went straight to the hospital. An orderly accompanied them to the basement, James' large hospital bed having been replaced by a lighter gurney, and Ryan's parents were soon in the ambulance. After a last round of goodbyes and promises to be in touch daily, the ambulance pulled out of its basement bay into a bright Roman morning and headed north.

Back at the hotel, Ryan checked out of his single room and had the double room his parents had been occupying changed to his name. There was a text from Rick saying that the Karlsruhe police would be grateful for the chance to interview Ryan today, so he spent some time organizing a flight. He tucked the loose papers he had been scribbling notes on into the accountant's case and was making a mental list of what he might need in terms of documents and clothes for his upcoming sweep down the peninsula. His enthusiasm for this venture had evaporated. But there was nothing for him to do in Karlsruhe except mope. A jagged loose end gnawed at him, the fact that he was swanning off while Angelika's body lay somewhere . . . but what could he do? What should he . . . how could he . . .

Focus, Chandler. There's nothing you can do. Get back to Karlsruhe. Pick up what you need. Talk to the police. Get on with it.

Looking back much later, Ryan remembered little about the trip to Karlsruhe that day. Rick was waiting when Ryan stepped into the airport terminal. They exchanged a hug and then spoke of odds and ends on the way into town. The first stop was Ryan's flat to drop cases, then a walk to the police station.

Before they had gone very far, Ryan stopped and turned to face Rick.

"Do you know anything more about what happened to Angelika?" Ryan asked.

Rick hesitated for quite a long time. Ryan gave him a look that was grief-stricken, but also demanding. He had to know.

"Not much", Rick began. "I spoke to the maintenance man who found her . . . found her body. Had to tell him I was her fiancé to get him to say anything. He said that she had a large bruise and broken skin on the side of her head, the side facing up."

Tears were streaming down Ryan's face.

"I'm so, so sorry, Ryan", Rick said, and embraced his friend unselfconsciously.

Ryan pulled away, wiping his cheeks.

"What does . . . is there . . . some explanation?"

Rick hesitated again, and continued only when Ryan looked at him once more.

"I'm only guessing. I don't ... I think she might have been struck ... before she fell. Or was pushed."

Ryan shook his head. The depth of his grief was evident.

"So, what– ?"

More hesitation by Rick.

"That would be consistent with nobody ... having heard screams", Rick said. "It's hard, in fact, pretty much impossible, just to ... fall from one of those windows. Being pushed out ... while she was unconscious ... well, it fits the facts."

It was ghastly. Ryan didn't want to think about it, couldn't handle the images this information raised. But he knew he had to understand and his look invited Rick to continue.

"This whole business makes me just white-hot angry." Rick practically spat out the words. "Maybe it just happened that nobody heard Angelika. But a lot of people live around there. It's a quiet neighbourhood. And nobody who's conscious falls from a fourth-floor window without making a lot of noise, whether they're pushed or not."

They walked on in silence for a while.

"Does the building have a surveillance camera at the entrance?" Ryan asked.

"Don't know."

"Maybe the police will tell me."

"You'll be lucky."

"Do you know just when the ... when she ..."

"No. Not exactly. But from what I've heard, I suppose that her body was lying there quite some time. Possibly a whole night."

Ryan said nothing. He was a mass of turmoil, trying to erase or ignore the images that kept returning to fill his consciousness. But that exercise was shelved as they approached the police station. Inside, Ryan was conducted through a security door and asked to wait in an interview room. Ten minutes later, two men, not in uniform, entered. They introduced themselves, thanked Ryan for taking the trouble to come to Karlsruhe, sat down, and the questions began.

"Tell us a bit, please, about how you come to be in Karlsruhe."

Ryan did.

"And how did you know the . . . young woman?"

Ryan gave as short an explanation as he thought would satisfy them.

"So, there was no real link between you, apart from being students?"

"We were friends", Ryan answered neutrally.

"And where were you when the event occurred?"

"That's hard for me to answer, since I don't know when the event occurred. When did it occur?"

They evidently wanted to give away as little as possible. "We believe that the young woman fell sometime around ten o'clock, two evenings ago."

"In that case, I was in Rome. Spending time with my parents."

"Is there a way we can confirm that?"

"You can check at the hotel where we were staying. The costs were logged to my parents' credit card and I expect the staff would remember us." A pad was pushed before Ryan, but instead of writing down the information they wanted, he handed over the hotel and restaurant business cards.

"You have a student flat here in Karlsruhe?"

Ryan gave them the address. The note taker looked through the several pages of scribbles in his notebook, then the two looked at each other and nodded.

"I think that's all, Mr. Chandler. Thank you once again for making time for us." And they made to rise.

"I wonder", Ryan began, "if there's a possibility of learning a bit more about her . . . death."

The two sank back into their seats.

"The investigation isn't finished, Mr. Chandler. I doubt there's anything we can tell you."

"I understand. But let me try asking a few questions anyway."

They nodded uncertainly.

"What was the injury that killed her?"

"She fell from the fourth floor."

"Are you saying then that she died as a result of the fall?"

"We can't comment."

"Has an autopsy been performed?"

"Yes."

Ryan nodded and looked at each of the policemen. "May I leave now?" he asked.

"You have asked quite a few questions . . ."

"She was a friend. I just want to know what happened to her and why."

A silence indicated that the two policemen had said all they were going to say. One of the officers accompanied him to the security door, thanked him again for his time, and then Ryan and Rick walked out into the street.

"Learn anything new?" Rick asked.

Ryan walked Rick through the questions and answers as they started back toward his flat. He had four hours to collect the things he needed and get back to the airport.

"How about a quick glass of beer, Rick? I expect that I won't be back in Karlsruhe for some time."

Rick seemed to have a built-in beer GPS, and instead of continuing on toward Ryan's flat, he immediately turned right, leading them to a small beer garden. Fifteen minutes later, beer having been consumed and comradeship reaffirmed, they made their way to Ryan's flat. Ryan retrieved what would be needed, and then offered his hand to Rick.

"What's this?" Rick asked.

"Just thanks. I'm going back to the airport now."

"Yes, I know. I'm coming with you."

"You don't need to."

"Need doesn't enter into it. Let's go."

At the airport, Rick gave Ryan an unexpectedly warm hug.

"Look after yourself, man. And keep in touch. I've become interested in what you've been doing here. I want to know how things turn out. I just wish I had the application to do what you're doing. And if I learn anything new about Angelika, I'll let you know right away."

There were things Ryan wanted to say, but the words wouldn't surface.

"Thanks. Thanks for everything."

"Not at all. Now go on. Get out of here."

On the way back to Rome, random thoughts kept vying for attention in Ryan's head. But there was one that kept coming back again and again.

He had, in fact, learned something from the interview with the police. And he was now convinced that that information would give him a foothold in determining who was doing what and why.

Thirty

It seemed thin and watery, the gruel of information Ryan had obtained from the police interview in Karlsruhe. At least it looked like that when Ryan took a second close squint at it. The police had said that an autopsy had been performed, but they weren't prepared to say that she had died as a result of the fall itself. This might confirm Rick's suspicion, that it had involved something more than just a "fall". If Angelika had been murdered, and Ryan had now managed to admit that this was likely, then it was something of a stretch to believe that same person had been involved in both her death and his father's hit-and-run in Rome.

Not impossible. But unlikely.

Although given a flight time between Karlsruhe and Rome of about an hour . . . But then why would someone rush – and that's what they would have needed to do – to stage these two events so close together? There seemed to be no rationale for that. The alternative explanations were that either two people were operating as a tag-team, or the two events were independent.

This didn't get him much further ahead. Things were not in much better shape on other fronts. Ryan had to keep reminding himself that some large assumptions underlay any deductions he might make, the main one being that those old sheets of paper he had found in the KIT library book really were at the centre of it all. But other questions swirled around, for example, how anybody else could have known about those sheets. But he had to remind himself that he had made no particular effort to be discreet, and people in Karlsruhe might have become aware that he was digging into the story of Cannizzaro, Garibaldi . . .

You're going in circles again, the Voice said.

So, Ryan thought, *what am I going to do?*

Internally, he was a mass of turmoil, something he tried unsuccessfully to sidestep. But how could he? Apart from wishing he could turn back the clock, what did he want? Well, he wanted to ... but that was ... He had to get on with his peninsular travels (as a means of taking his mind off ...), but without having to watch his back all the time. By now, he felt fairly sure that whoever had been after him would know which hotel in Rome his parents had been staying in. But if they didn't know that Ryan was there? Could the objective of the hit-and-run been not to kill Ryan's father or even to injure him seriously but to bring Ryan running to help? If the watchers had been watching all along, they would have realized that Ryan had disappeared suddenly from Karlsruhe, that they had lost track of him, and this might well have alarmed them. *This makes no sense. If they had been watching my parents, surely they would have seen me as well.* He shook his head. There were still way too many unknowns.

But why just at this time? What could have sparked this surge in interest?

Rick had suggested one possibility. For someone having the skills, it wouldn't be difficult to set up a few computer sites having catchy names and content that would appear meaningful but was really dummy in nature to lure in and identify individuals looking for sources of information in a particular narrow subject range – for example, anything to do with "letters by Nievo". The right sort of cookie could identify where any such inquiry had originated and could keep an eye on the location, perhaps even try to peek into material stored on the computer that was doing the inquiring.

But that could end up being a lot of work. A source at Karlsruhe made just as much sense. There was also the significant point that Ryan's departure for Strasbourg had occurred very soon after he had found those sheets. And his appearance in Rome, his making contact with Di Biasi – well-known as a critic and sceptic in Nievo circles – had taken place almost immediately, as had his father's appearance in Rome. All this might have become known to someone well prepared. These were coincidences that a suspicious mind would want explained or could see as harbouring some deeper meaning.

So, Chandler, the Voice asked again, more insistently, *what are you going to do?*

Good question, Ryan thought sarcastically.

But, surprisingly, some answers came right away.

Ryan pondered, then picked up the telephone in the hotel room.

"Hier Rheingold." Rick once again in Wagnerian mode.

"Hello, Rick. It's Ryan."

"Ah! You made it back to Rome all right."

"Yes. I want to ask a favour."

"Okay. Shoot!"

Ryan could still feel the oppressive weight of recent events upon him, but even this first proactive step, reaching out to Rick, made a small flame, a feeble ember, light up somewhere inside.

"Could you check at KIT to see when an academic from the University of Toronto spent time in Karlsruhe? Her name is Sarah Brimley. If possible, try to get a head and shoulders picture."

"Okay. Shouldn't be insurmountable. Anything else?"

"No. That's it for now."

"Are you okay?"

"Yes. Thanks. I'll be in touch again soon."

Rick had not asked any why or how questions concerning Ryan's request. He could likely work out the why for himself, and he would never ask how. Rick loved a problem, and he would find some deviously elegant way to get his hands on what he wanted.

One down.

Ryan thought for a long time about the second prong of an offensive. He ticked off in his head a list of the people he knew or had met in Rome. Very few. His parents were out of reach to anyone but him. Di Biasi himself would be in Porto Santo Stefano by now. The student who had shown him Cannizzaro's last Roman residence would have no reason to contact Ryan again. None of those people would try to get in touch with him at the hotel. He found some hotel notepaper and an envelope and wrote out a two sentence missive. Sealing it in the envelope, he wrote on the front *To Be Given To Anyone Asking For Signor Chandler* and then took it down to reception.

"Could you place this in your hotel safe please?"

"Certainly, sir. Let me give you a receipt for it. Are there any specific instructions?"

"Yes. As directed on the envelope. Someone might ask for me. If that happens, please give this to them and let me know."

"Very good, sir." And he entered something into the reception computer before carrying the envelope through a door marked *Privato*.

Back in his room, Ryan murmured "two down" and sat before his laptop. During the following three hours, he sent nine e-mail messages and saved various Trenitalia timetables and hotel website links. *Catch me if you can*, he thought.

Ryan then settled in the big armchair to think about bait. Two hours later, he had fanned a prematurely born spark into a roaring bonfire. Returning to his computer, he began assembling information on Palermo. At ten thirty, he began a wrap-up step, walking around a single question: *In what ways could any of this go wrong?* The number of screw-up possibilities was depressing, but he dredged up as many as he could think of and made notes.

An e-mail message from Rick arrived at eleven o'clock.

Brimley had been in Karlsruhe for the past month working on a joint project of some sort. She had also been there for a month in November of the previous year. Picture attached.

Ryan checked his diary. Brimley's previous visit had coincided with Hartmann's abrupt about-face on Ryan's project and also Hartmann's fatal accident.

Not proof of anything, but . . . you see smoke, you look for fire . . .

Ryan sat back, drained.

It had been a day of continuing effort just to do what he needed to do, and not keep asking himself *why* – a question to which there was no answer.

That night, he wept himself to sleep.

Thirty-One

Ryan's first thoughts on awakening were of Angelika. His conscious mind still would not accept the reality, but parts of that great visceral system that gives people their resilience were already adjusting to the change. That much Ryan could feel, without any real doubt. There was unfinished business here, mental cuts and bruises that challenged him. But how could he wrap this up?

He set out at seven thirty. It took a total of fifty minutes to make his way to Roma Termini, deposit his bag and accountant's case in a locker, and return to the hotel. He had no choice but to re-enter the hotel through reception and hope that at that early hour no watchers would be about. None were, as far as he could tell. Back in his room, he ordered a light breakfast from room service and made some attempt to plan the day. His breakfast arrived and he ate it mechanically. Having finished all that, he settled back on the sofa to work on plans for his sweep through Italy. But almost immediately images of Angelika and a multitude of questions flooded his mind once more.

How can I say goodbye to Angelika?

He asked himself what responsibility he had toward her parents, two people who must be in the worst state of anguish – of not knowing *why*. Did they know about him? Were they aware that Angelika and Ryan considered their situation an amorous flower on the point of opening? Ryan realized that he didn't know much about Angelika's family, just that she was an only child and her father was a professor of something at the University of Stuttgart. Ryan felt responsibility, felt that he had some answers, information that might salve wounds, but it seemed to him that any attempt he might make to provide an explanation to Angelika's parents would just open other equally difficult questions. He needed to get Rick's advice here. But at the moment, he had to set these matters aside.

The envelope he had delivered to hotel reception the previous evening was an attempt to get ahead of the game. But he was very much aware that he would be in the crosshairs once someone read his note. He had spent some time working out its exact wording: *The documents you want are locked in the hotel safe. You no longer have any access to them.*

Opening his computer, he noticed that replies had been returned to four of the nine e-mails he had sent out the previous day. This meant that he could begin putting together some travel specifics, and he would spend the next half hour doing that. The telephone rang. He hesitated before picking up.

"Good morning, Mr. Chandler. This is reception."

"Good morning."

"You asked to be informed if your envelope was passed to anyone."

"You have given it to somebody?"

"Yes, sir. Just ten minutes ago."

"Can you describe the person please?"

A description of a man was given.

"Has the gentleman left the hotel?"

"No, sir. He is sitting here in the lobby reading a newspaper. Would you like to speak to him?"

"No, thank you", Ryan concluded and hung up.

Ryan now undertook what he thought would be the riskiest part of the day. Leaving the room, he made his way down the stairwell and moved along the corridor toward reception. In the lobby, there were people coming and going, two small clutches of people stood chatting, a pile of suitcases was being brought in from a tour bus. Peering around the corner, Ryan scanned the room quickly then ducked back out of sight. The staff at reception were busy. There was hubbub throughout the lobby. Lots of diversion. Peering again, he focussed on a well-dressed man reading a newspaper. *A possibility.* As he watched, the man turned a page, looked around the room, glanced at his watch, turned another page, looked at the desk, and then stepped up to reception during a lull and said something to the woman working there. *He's not reading that paper at all.* Ryan looked him over more carefully. Fortyish, dark medium-length hair, strong features, high forehead, aquiline nose, light-brown slacks, very good-quality brown leather shoes, tasteful lime-green short-sleeved shirt. It took less than three seconds to take several pictures using his cellphone. "Gotcha", Ryan said and returned to his room.

Ryan checked his watch. Ten minutes to ten. It didn't take long for the next scene in this little tableau to play out.

The phone rang.

That would be *them*. No answer is probably what the caller expected, and after eleven rings, that's what he got. In any event, if it *was* them calling, no answer would keep them guessing.

Ryan had already decided on electronic checkout and he used his cellphone now to do that. Okay. Lights, action, and roll 'em.

He went back down and took a quick look at the reception area. Aquiline Nose was no longer there. Returning to the hallway, Ryan opened the exit-only door a crack and scanned the side street. Nobody lurking. In the side pocket of his computer carrying case was a detailed street map of Rome, folded to show an area that included his hotel and Roma Termini.

Thinking of the several possibilities a watcher had to consider – taxi from in front of the hotel direct to Leonardo da Vinci airport, taxi to Roma Termini, one of two metro lines, rental car from a number of locations, train – Ryan chose what they might consider least likely. He set out on foot. He took a dog-legged route through backstreets, emerging on a more major avenue where taxis waited near three hotels. He bundled into one of these taxis and gave directions for Roma Termini.

The railway station was heaving. He stuck to crowds, avoiding open areas, keeping an eye out for Aquiline Nose, but he reminded himself that Aquiline Nose might be only one of several. Too late to worry about that, and no remedy in any event. Ryan headed for the bank of lockers where he had deposited his bag and accountant's case earlier. From within another crowd of people, he scanned the area.

Still no Aquiline Nose.

Making his way quickly to the bank of lockers, he found number 1063 and looked around to see whether any trap might be closing.

Nothing.

Ryan had chosen Genoa as his destination and the e-ticket was now in his cellphone. Wanting to get his stuff and head for his platform, Ryan began moving quickly. Maybe, just maybe, he had outsmarted them.

"Ryan! Imagine running into you here!"

The voice had come from behind him, and he turned to see who it was.

Aquiline Nose.

He was about fifteen feet away and not making any determined attempt to close that distance.

"Look!" Ryan said in a loud voice, almost shouting. "I've told you many times that we're not making a deal! This is approaching harassment! We'll see what the police have to say about this!"

People looked up. Heads turned. It sounded like a fight was about to break out. Ryan moved as quickly as he could. Metro entrance. Hoped that Aquiline Nose would not pursue him, not raise even more suspicion, not bring attention to himself.

At the Metro entrance, Ryan broke into a run. Raced down the stairs. Pushed through crowds. *Shit!* He had no metro ticket. *Not true*, the Voice said. *Check your pockets.* Yes. He had tickets from earlier. From the trip to la Sapienza. He used one now to enter through one of the barriers.

It was hot. The platform was crowded. *Your advantage*, the Voice said as Ryan squeezed his way along the platform. A train was entering the station. He had two choices.

As the train slid past him, he stopped and pressed himself into a recess. Roman bodies surged toward the opening train doors. He used this human screen and skipped further down the platform, but his sightlines were obscured. Couldn't see Aquiline Nose. Meaning that Aquiline Nose couldn't see him.

The crowd was thinning now. Ryan looked around feverishly. *See where the people are going*, the Voice said. To the left, along the platform. There was another exit from the station. He pressed his way toward it. Took the stairs two at a time. Now outside the metro again.

Ryan looked around. Saw that he was in a different spot within Termini. There was an exit to the street right in front of him. Racing out into the city again, he found a decent-sized restaurant. Pushed through the doorway. Located the signs to the washrooms. Took refuge in a cubicle.

"Shit!" he said, something both appropriate and inappropriate at the same time.

Now what? *You have a little time,* the Voice said. *But it's no time to relax. Think!*

Okay. He was fairly sure that Aquiline Nose had not seen what he had done in the Metro. And he presumed that his pursuer would simply return to the lockers and wait.

But the big question rose up, as if emblazoned on a Jumbotron: *How did Aquiline Nose know that I would go to the lockers?*

No answer was forthcoming. Rather than fret over this just now, Ryan had to determine what to do next. He could see only one way forward.

He had been in the cubicle a little more than ten minutes, but it seemed like an eternity. If Aquiline Nose hadn't seen his manoeuvre in the Metro–

Forget Aquiline Nose! the Voice screamed at him. *You know what you need to do. Get on with it!*

And he knew that there was only one path to follow now. It took Ryan some time to build up the nerve to move out of the cubicle, through the restaurant, and into the street. He looked around.

Nothing.

As quickly as he could, he found a taxi. It took a while for him to explain to the cabbie what he wanted – a bargain basement emporium that sold almost everything – clothes, suitcases, toiletries – and eventually the hackie understood. Within five minutes, they pulled up in front of a disreputable place called Eduardo's. Ryan paid the cabby and ducked inside.

One look at the interior told him that this was exactly what he needed. The place was chaos, but he soon found socks, underwear, shirts, jeans, a light jacket, toiletries, and a cheap hold-all – everything he would need to replace the essentials sitting in the

Termini locker. He paid for the heap of stuff, jammed everything into the hold-all, and then checked his map. He found the next thing he wanted: a park that was largish but not famous for anything. Making his way there, he picked a secluded bench and settled down to wait.

Sitting in his quiet park, pondering the ashes of the plan he had been so confident about, there arose in his mind again the question of how the watcher had known to go to the bank of lockers and, specifically, to exactly the right bank of lockers. Panic overwhelmed him when he realized what must have happened. He tore open his computer bag, pulled everything out of it, gave it all the most careful search, and uttered a huge sigh of relief when he didn't find what he most feared: a tracking device.

It was almost one o'clock now. He had missed his train to Genoa. Using his cellphone, he began looking again through train timetables. Ryan guessed that if he waited in the park until about four o'clock, the watchers would be forced to draw some conclusions (that he had given them the slip, he hoped), and he could then make his way back to Roma Termini in time to jump on the train he had just selected. At all costs, he had to avoid any conspicuous waiting, especially out in the open in a place like Termini.

He bought another ticket – a destination that was way down Di Biasi's priority list of cities, but Ryan hoped that it had the fewest and the most obscure links to anything in his report or the documents he presumed his watchers were after.

At ten past five that afternoon, Ryan planned to be on the way to Scilla.

Thirty-Two

On this occasion, Ryan chose first class, shouldering financial caution under the bus. But money had been the least of his concerns over the previous fifteen minutes.

He sneaked back into Termini, keeping a close eye out for Aquiline Nose. If he was spotted now, his plan would be in tatters once again. He found his platform as quickly as possible. Still no Aquiline Nose in sight. He slipped onto his train.

Keeping his face from view through the window of the first-class carriage, Ryan felt a sense of relief flow through him as the express Frecciargento train began moving out of Roma Termini and quickly gathered speed. He was also aware of that now familiar frisson of excitement that he associated with the beginning of any European trip by train. Within twenty minutes, they were sailing through Rome's suburbs. The travel time to Scilla was to be about five hours, meaning that he should be in the station there by ten thirty that evening. Not too late, he hoped, to find a hotel for the night.

On his way to Termini from the Rome park where he had waited, he had found a place to buy what he needed in order to mail the locker key to Di Biasi's residence, thanking his lucky stars that Di Biasi had included his full address in one of his e-mail messages. He sent Di Biasi a long text describing what he was doing, asking whether someone could retrieve his bags from the locker at Termini, and asking that Di Biasi not relate any of this to James and Michaela.

Gorgeous Italian landscape drifted past the window: rugged spurs of Apennines; patches of rich plain tended as fields, orchards, vineyards; and from the other side of the carriage, the occasional view of the Tyrrhenian. Shadows swung and lengthened across the landscape as the afternoon matured. Soon, lights began blinking on, dusk drifted down, and the greens of the fields and rusts of the mountains faded to browns and purples before ultimately being swallowed completely by night.

Ryan was in a state of suspended thought, adrift mentally, but also disconnected from what he should be bending his mind to. He had a vague plan on what he would do in Scilla, but that would last little more than a day. Then what? The watchers were somewhere behind him. Where they were and what they might be doing, he had no idea. Even time had become hazy.

But the heat was off for the moment. A good thing, but also . . .

Having nothing else to occupy his thoughts, images of Angelika appeared before him again. The pain and the loss all flooded back.

What are you going to do, Chandler? the Voice demanded accusingly, unsympathetically. *You have no plan. You're just in denial.*

Ryan couldn't dispute that. What he had really wanted was to get away from his pursuers, spend a bit of time chasing down the suggestions that had simply rolled out of the folds of his project, and try to keep busy enough that his pain over Angelika was dulled, at least a little. But chasing down those suggestions meant digging into a number of things, and the physical markers connected to those things were almost all located in Palermo. That was the world of Cannizzaro. Part of the great world of Garibaldi.

But it was also the world of Nievo – Nievo the *Garibaldino*, that is. If the mess he found himself in was tied to Nievo, then Palermo would be one place in the watchers' sights. They would be waiting there. So turning up in Palermo offered every chance of him being dragged back into the state of being hunted.

But he was convinced that Palermo was where important information lay. And failing to go there out of faint-heartedness would not cause the watchers to give up. It wasn't exactly that he had no choice. It wasn't just a single problem, it was a nexus of problems having no easy entry point. And he guessed that whatever entry point he chose, he would soon discover that there was no easy exit. Ryan decided that he would shelve the whole thing once more and tackle it again in Scilla. It was there he would need to decide what his next move would be.

He drew a small notebook from his computer case and began making a list of loose ends, things he didn't want to trip over. That was at least a start.

Satisfied? he muttered in challenge to the Voice.

A dismissive three word reply came back.

You're pathetic, Chandler.

The train raced south toward Scilla, and in fits and starts, despite his decision to shelve the matter, Ryan continued circling his complex situation, making no discernible progress, seeing just a fuzzy wall of uncertainty.

He had done some research on Scilla. It had attractive features, but his chief interest was in visiting via Raffaele Piria, the street where Piria was born in 1813 (or perhaps 1814), and seeing the marble plaque that had been erected on the wall of his house of birth in 1895. But some rubbernecking was also in order, walking along the sea front, seeing the castle, and in general just enjoying being in the area that had inspired the story of Scylla and Charybdis. If only he didn't have to do this alone . . .

It was clear enough that Scilla was only a way station, that he was going to continue on to Palermo. In Palermo, there were many things on his list, almost all of them having to do with Cannizzaro, but a few linked to Garibaldi. And apart from a visit to the chemical museum at the University of Palermo, it was all just general background – trying to get a feeling for where Cannizzaro came from, what influences might have formed his early ideas – and a chance to acquire some sense of the long history, mix of civilizations, and the almost timeless nature of Palermo itself, a sentiment that several people had expressed to him.

In due course, he arrived in Scilla and found a good hotel. As he flopped into bed, images of Angelika flooded his consciousness again. Tears seeped from the corners of his eyes. There was nowhere to turn, no escape. His mixed anguish and sadness over Angelika, the stress of the day, the lingering shock over his father's hit-and-run – these had all acted to turn his world upside down. "Tomorrow", he muttered, trying to ignore the echoes and fragments of thought that tumbled through his mind.

The next morning was clear and bright. Ryan awoke late and was relieved to feel that his energy levels were back. Breakfast al fresco was just what he needed, and thus began a day having no agenda and no deadlines. The train journey from Scilla to Palermo would take about six hours, so Ryan decided to spend two nights in Scilla and catch a reasonably early train the following morning in what he hoped would be a more rested and relaxed state. The hours slid by, and Ryan wandered from spot to spot, taking in different views of Scilla, the sea, and people going about their business. He felt physically relaxed, if emotionally numbed. He was not worried by the threat of watchers, and his mind ultimately drifted back to the Nievo question.

Back to those sheets, to what he had called the *Nievo letter*.

And back to that phrase in Italian that ultimately had caught his attention: *grazie al cielo per i documenti mandati in precedenza.*

Mandati.

Sent.

Sent where? Nievo couldn't just wander down to the post office and mail things to other places in Italy, or rather to places in the various regions that would soon become Italy. And, it was a time of revolution. The French and the moribund apparatus that was trying to hold together the Kingdom of the Two Sicilies was under attack. Sending anything any distance would be iffy at best. Expecting it to arrive was most likely a pipe dream. It was equally hard to imagine any place in Palermo that might have been sensible for Nievo to lodge a package for safe keeping. But there was another possibility.

It had amazed Ryan to learn how well the identities of the Thousand were known. Many of them had been professionals before Garibaldi's call went out – doctors, accountants, lawyers. Could Nievo have befriended a few of these men, perhaps prevailed on one of them to take a separate set of accounts and carry it onward? Garibaldi had been headed north. He had proposed to reach and take Naples and most likely carry on beyond that to the Holy See, even into Piedmont. Garibaldi, the cool-headed but fiery republican, wanted to end all this regal and aristocratic nonsense. But Cavour –

cunning, resourceful, unprincipled – one of that most unlikely three that included Garibaldi and Mazzini, Cavour wouldn't just let things happen. He was always able to find the right type of sand to throw into anyone's gears. Garibaldi would need to take things one step at a time.

Nievo could have given his package to a chosen *Garibaldino*, and possibly had done so. But which one? And all this had happened, if it had happened at all, 160 years ago. Those accounts might well surface in the twenty-first century, but almost certainly not in response to any focussed search. Any recovery of them would be the result of some random event, an accident of history that unearthed a serendipitous clue, a lucky strike by some researcher. But it was far more likely that there would be no such recovery. Just a possible second set of accounts. Extant but location unknown. If that happened, it would only provide more fodder for the Nievo conspiracy mill.

Ryan was at the point of concluding that this musing was going nowhere when he realized that he had been sitting on just the insight he needed. What was it that was keeping him in the centre of this threatening little circle?

Secrecy.

That alone pointed to a path out of the maze.

He dialled Di Biasi.

"Ryan! I received your e-mail. One of my students is watching for the key you sent and will collect your bags from Termini."

Ryan explained his suspicion that someone had planted a tracking device in them. He then related everything that had happened since Rome, where he was at the moment, what he planned to do, and his idea on how to make any further pursuit of him fruitless.

"Interesting", Di Biasi replied, "but I have some doubts." And Di Biasi made half a dozen solid points then laid out a counter proposal. "So, we don't have Nievo's accounts, and we're not likely to get them any time soon, and we don't know the authenticity of the documents you found, and so we're not likely to convince any average hack that there's an exciting story here. But I know people who pursue this stuff seriously and over the long term, and I'm a known sceptic, not at all viewed as some gullible clown who can be duped easily by something like this. We can put out a story quite readily on – how do you say in North America – on the back channels. Leave it with me."

Thirty-Three

The following morning, an aquarelle blue, the colour of Norse eyes, had washed across the heavens. The sea was calm, the air was mild, and breakfast al fresco, once again, was the only way to go.

There were also voice messages on Ryan's cellphone from Di Biasi and from someone called Angelo Faraci, who had also sent a text message. Faraci could meet him at the station in Palermo. This was initially a surprise, not to mention an alarm, but likely was evidence of activity by Di Biasi. At least Ryan very much hoped this would be the explanation. But all that could wait until breakfast was finished, here in a part of the day and a part of the world that asked to be savoured. If only Angelika . . .

Coffee, some fruit, and some bread can go a long way when you are gazing at a placid sea, have no imminent deadline, and can drift. Ryan suddenly remembered a discussion in one of his classes at the University of Toronto, a century ago now it seemed, when the professor spoke about Homer's repeated use in *The Odyssey* of "the wine dark sea", as in "sailing over the wine dark sea to men of strange speech". Looking out over the sea now, it appeared in no way wine dark, but back then and even now, at times, perhaps it did. And how would either he or his professor interpret those lines now, in this place? Ryan's father had spoken to him about these things on several occasions.

"Not everyone sees what is before them", James Chandler was fond of repeating. But then not everyone knows that what they see before them might not be what it seems. Poets don't always see everything, but they do tend to see things differently. And they encourage us to *Look again. Look more closely.* They also tell us that we need to see the whole picture, and the art of doing all this, indeed our ability to do it, in our vaunted twenty-first century, is a mere shadow of what it once was. Ryan's father had once told him that just reading Homer, immersing oneself in it to the point of oblivion, could reveal a much-enriched version of this *sight* and *insight*.

In other words, the world can be a magical place, if we let it be that.

"But, all things flow", Ryan muttered, glancing at his watch.

And after a last glug of coffee, one more look out over the sea, now trembling in patches of morning ripples, it was time to get a move on. But, as Ryan was finding, the immediate past remained insistent. Images, thoughts, waves of sadness and anger about Angelika would sweep over him suddenly, at random moments. This was one of those moments, and he couldn't help but wonder what it would be like to have her here now.

Ryan's phone buzzed and he glanced down. It was a text message from Di Biasi and sounded promising.

Known Faraci for years. Knows Sicily. Leads tours on Garibaldi. A Nievo conspiracy sceptic (?) but will be interested. Have told him little. Knows about new Nievo letter. Sent him photo of watcher. Knows who it is. Keep me informed.

Time to talk to the man himself.

"Pronto."

"Signor Faraci? Sono Chandler. Il Professore di Biasi vi ha parlato di me." Ryan cringed at his atrocious wording and accent.

"Buongiorno, Signor Chandler." Faraci was speaking very slowly. "Forse più facile in inglese?"

It took a second for Ryan to work out that one, and there would be no question of wounded pride on switching to English. "Yes. My apologies for my terrible Italian."

"Think nothing of it, Mr. Chandler. I always welcome the chance to practise my English." It was clear, however, that Faraci's English needed no practice.

Ryan gave Faraci the details of his train, and Faraci said he would meet the train in Palermo.

Having dealt with minor housekeeping items that had accumulated overnight, Ryan settled down to considering what he wanted to see in Palermo, and beyond that, in other parts of Sicily. But he found that he couldn't concentrate, that he was adrift mentally. An odd sort of drifting, though. He had that strange feeling of not really belonging here or anywhere for that matter. A possible future had been snatched from him. The intellectual anchor, the sense of purpose and direction that had kept him in one place, in Karlsruhe, was now all but finished. It had been so intense, so focussed, that it had blown his past life to matchwood, obliterated it as though it had never existed. And part of him said that that was a damn good thing. But there was now nothing to go back to.

The train cruised along the north Sicilian coast. Occasionally, a place name was visible through the window, and Ryan was aware that he knew essentially nothing about Sicily.

Another name drifted past. Capo d'Orlando. There was a mental connection there, somewhere. Nothing related to his project, just something he had come across, a fragment that stuck in memory. Was it to do with Di Lampedusa? Maybe. And Ryan thought of Di Lampedusa's great book, *The Leopard*.

Up ahead lay Cefalù. Then Palermo. Somewhere off to the left, on Sicily's southern shore, was Taormina, another of Ryan's Cannizzaro stops. And just to the west of Etna was Bronte. It was a dream world . . .

The announcement that the train was about to arrive at Palermo caught Ryan by surprise. Shouldn't have allowed himself to drift into that flabby mental No Man's Land.

Red hat. That was the sign given to Ryan by Faraci, and there he was. Medium height, dark complexion, on the wiry side of an athletic build, an impossibly bright-red cowboy hat and a navy T-shirt bearing the motto *Toronto Molto Meglio*. Perhaps in case of colour blindness?

Ryan walked up to him. "Signor Faraci. Senza dubbio."

"Si, Signor Chandler. Piacere. Vieni." This last request being a sign that they weren't going to rattle formalities at one another. "Let's have a glass of something", Faraci said, having flattered Ryan briefly, but then rescuing him from linguistic embarrassment.

Faraci led Ryan out of the station and across Piazza Sant'Antonino. Within five minutes, they were seated at a small osteria that Ryan would never have found on his own, and a few hand signals had passed between Faraci and someone who appeared to be the owner. Ryan was pleased to have the word *proprietario* pop up instantly in his mind. Twenty seconds later, a carafe of white wine, two glasses, and what looked like a flower vase full of sesame grissini materialized in front of them.

Faraci poured and raised his glass. "Salute!" They both sipped what was a remarkably refreshing wine.

"Alora. Sono molto colpito da tuo italiano. Ma, ciò nonostante . . ."

And just as Ryan sensed he was beyond rescue in linguistic quicksand, Faraci tossed him a lifeline.

"Perhaps it would be easier in English", Faraci said. A huge smile illuminated his features, robbing the previous exchange of anything other than a friendly greeting. "Welcome to Palermo. I hope I will be able to show you some of our fantastic city and its equally fantastic past."

"Thank you. My apologies, first of all, for my poor Italian. I–"

"No apologies needed. Italian isn't a major language, so it is really an enormous compliment to have someone try to speak it. And I must say that given what you seem to know already, if you were to stay here for about, oh, three months, having me as your tutor of course, half the Palermitani you met would be asking you which part of Sicily you are from. We're faced all the time here by people who bark their way in English through a three-day visit, not having armed themselves with a single word of Italian, and whose reaction to any incomprehension by the locals is simply to say it again at double the volume. It doesn't affect me, but I know that Cesare, who runs this osteria, sometimes would like to tell them all just to fuck off."

They both took another sip of wine, Faraci gestured at the grissini, and Ryan took one and began munching as he looked around. They were seated on a large patio, enclosed by a gang of rather stubby fan palm trees, oleander, and blood orange trees. There was colour everywhere. It was one of those moments, and Ryan recalled lines from a favourite poem, "The Buried Life", by Matthew Arnold:

And there arrives a lull in the hot race
Wherein he doth for ever chase
That flying and elusive shadow, rest.
An air of coolness plays upon his face,
And an unwonted calm pervades his breast.
And then he thinks he knows
The hills where his life rose,
And the sea where it goes.

Yet another intrusion from a previous life in Toronto, from Ryan's *studium interruptum*.

"A penny?"

"You'd be over-paying."

They both took another sip.

"I was just reflecting", Ryan said. "Looking around. Things we don't have back in Toronto. They make one think. Why is it that something new pushes some of us to another level of excitement, and yet familiarity can make it all fade away to invisibility?"

"You're too much of a poet for me, Ryan."

Faraci took another sip of wine before continuing.

"So", Faraci said, "we definitely need to talk a bit about history at some point, but later."

They changed course, quickly turning the conversation to Nievo.

"The possibility of a second set of Nievo's accounts is intriguing."

"Do you think there could be real interest in them among collectors?" Ryan asked.

Faraci looked at Ryan in frank interest. "Let's put it this way. I'm basically a pimp. I'll do a lot of things for a euro. Not anything. But a lot of things."

There was a pause here for another sip of wine.

"I'm a tour guide, for example. Every year I lead several hundred people around Palermo and sometimes elsewhere in Sicily. Mostly Americans. But I'm not interested in entry-level tourists – the type who say, *Wow! Syracuse! It's really interesting that there's a place here in Sicily that has the same name as a place in New York. How did that happen?* Among the people I do take around, maybe five percent turn out to have the collector's gene. About five or ten people a year ask about acquiring things for their collections. Almost all those people want to obtain items cheaply and illegally."

"Do you report them?"

"No", Faraci said. "I don't report the people. I report the interest. In Italy we have an agency that looks after our patrimony."

"Must be a big job."

"It's an enormous job, just because the history is so long and so rich, both in events and artefacts."

This comment alone was enough to cause Ryan to look around once more as they both took another sip.

"But I do other things as well", Faraci continued. "I write for various publications. And I have my own interests. One of them happens to be Nievo and all the links that connect him to the Risorgimento and to a lot of other people and events. So, when I learned that you had turned up what might be a missing Nievo letter and that there might be another set of Nievo accounts, well . . ."

"I assume you got this information from Professore di Biasi?"

"Yes. And he has informed me that the documents you found originally are now safely locked away. Even those documents themselves are valuable objects."

"So the people who have been watching me want to know more about these things. In order to try to get to them first?"

Faraci nodded. "Almost certainly. And they see you as the easiest source for the information they want."

"And just what information do they want?"

"Whatever you've got. But it just got more difficult for them."

"And how do I get them off my back? This situation, what I'm in the middle of right now isn't safe."

Faraci was nodding some more. "No. It isn't safe. So let's talk now a bit about a plan I have in mind."

Thirty-Four

Ryan insisted on paying for the wine. Faraci then accompanied him to a hotel nearby, and on the way, they talked about what Ryan wanted to do while he was in Palermo. Faraci nodded at Ryan's list and suggested six other places he should visit.

"Four nights here should be enough. But let's see how things go."

Faraci then suggested a short walking tour that Ryan could make during what remained of the afternoon and offered to meet him later for dinner.

"That's very kind, Angelo, but I don't want you spending a lot of your time on me. After all, I'm here to do a few very specific things."

Faraci was shaking his head in a way that indicated he was going to have things his way. "Your visit here is my chance to get new information, pretty much first-hand, on a topic that most people consider now to be exhausted. Anything new and genuine on Nievo is very much breaking news, and I want to be in on it. I'm the one who's getting most benefit here. So please indulge me."

They arrived at the hotel, and on entering the small lobby, it was evident from the smile and friendly exchange, incomprehensible to Ryan, between the man at the desk and Faraci, that Faraci was indeed a man well-known about town. After Ryan's room arrangements were made, Faraci unfolded a small walking map and outlined what he thought would be a good way to spend three hours of the afternoon in the streets of Palermo. They arranged to meet again at the hotel at eight thirty.

Ryan sat on the bed in his room and thought about things but was suddenly aware that he was tired. A short nap before his walking tour seemed like a very good idea, and the speed at which he drifted off only confirmed this.

At four thirty, Ryan rose, washed his face, pulled a lightweight backpack from his hold-all, slipped his computer and a Palermo guide book into the bag, picked up the walking map, and set off.

Ryan generally followed Faraci's suggestions but spent an hour just walking the streets of the old historic centre of Palermo, then explored several of the grand streets: Villa Giulia, along via Roma, and taking a short side-trip to locate Chiesa di San Domenico where Cannizzaro is buried. He walked along via della Libertà and through the Giardino Inglese. Then there was a long meander back through minor streets and a short stop for another glass of wine, where the waiter took advantage of a quiet time to practise his English. Although he didn't go inside, Ryan spent some time gazing at the impressive sight presented by the Teatro Massimo. By then it was late in the afternoon, and a tour of the theatre itself would have to wait for another day.

Back in his room by six thirty, Ryan decided that another short nap would be a good plan, prior to meeting Faraci at eight thirty, a time that would be, Ryan suspected, ridiculously early for dinner in Palermo. So the evening would likely unfold as a longish meal sandwiched between two longish periods of sipping wine. That would suit Ryan fine. In fact, he planned to try to use the pre-prandial part of the sandwich to find out just what Faraci knew about Nievo and Garibaldi and whether he had any intelligence on links between Cannizzaro and Garibaldi. He expected that Faraci would be well versed on Garibaldi. But Di Biasi had warned him that, although people in the Italian science community were well aware of Cannizzaro, the average Italian knew little or nothing about him.

Ryan emerged from his nap at seven thirty, refreshed, hungry, and ready for the evening. He glanced at his phone. No new e-mail messages. But something else was in his mind. A strange feeling. And it took no time to determine what it was.

Could he trust Faraci?

The question had burst into his awareness suddenly and without warning. And then it vanished as though it had never been. Now he pulled it back forcibly into consciousness.

Faraci had been recommended by Di Biasi who had offered to sponsor Ryan at la Sapienza. Ryan's father would by now have had time to speak to Di Biasi. And Ryan had total confidence in his father's ability to read character. If James Chandler detected even the faintest reason why Di Biasi might represent a problem, Ryan would already know about it. He felt he had been successful in keeping his mugging secret from his parents, but that deception was still causing him concern. Ryan was fairly certain that his father would want to know the full story behind Hartmann's death whenever that came to light. The hit-and-run had been a horrific shock, and the possibility that his wife might really have been the target was the clincher in having James agree to a stay at Porto Santo Stefano. Ryan was certain that his father was concerned for his son's safety. But it was "safety from what", and "protection how" that were the tough nuts to crack. Ryan's father had said several times to him to be careful.

But Di Biasi? As a threat?

No. Through his father's opportunity to get to know Di Biasi, even if only slightly, Ryan felt confident that he was not in any danger from anyone Di Biasi would recommend. This premonition, this false premonition, was just a result of everything that had happened over the past months. Everything now cast a longer and darker shadow, as a result of Angelika's death . . .

Put this all behind you, Chandler. Otherwise, you'll be jumping at every whisper.

Again, he found that he and the irritating Inner Voice were in agreement.

A quick wash in the bathroom, a clean shirt, and he went off to meet Faraci at the small outdoor area in front of the hotel. Three tables nestled among waist-high terracotta pots providing homes to large plants that almost seemed to be whispering "over here, sailor" from somewhere within their extravagant greenery. The modest heat of the mid-March day clung to the air like body warmth to a foam mattress, but puffs of breeze from the sea offered less than subtle Sicilian hints that the day and its residue should by now be on its way.

Ryan barely had time to take a seat before Faraci appeared.

"Ciao canadese!"

Ryan's reply of "Ciao Palermitano!" brought out Faraci's instant smile. He waved Ryan to his feet, and they strode off to what turned out to be just the first of a number of places Faraci had lined up.

The first stop was a flamboyant locale where they sampled a couple of very different white wines, both excellent. The second stop couldn't have offered a stronger contrast. They rounded a corner, entered a small courtyard, and were faced by a modest *ristorante*, windows thrown open, a dozen tables scattered across a cramped patio, many of the tiles underfoot being chipped and discoloured, and a roughly finished outer wall where largish patches of stucco appeared to have sighed and then fallen to their deaths. But there were compensations.

A lively dark-haired server breezed among the tables, flashing smiles that could easily have sunk ships as quickly as Cleopatra launched them. But she couldn't match the smile... The *proprietario* boomed an irresistible welcome and clamped Faraci in a fierce embrace. After a rapid exchange with Faraci, the proprietario led them to a table amid swirls of grace and elegance worthy of royalty. There was another exchange that Ryan assumed to be a wine order, the owner nodded vigorously, but then stopped. He looked intently at Ryan.

"Alora!" he boomed. "Canadese! Benvenuto in Sicilia! Benvenuto in Palermo!" His arm swept through the air, and Ryan looked once more at the foliage, the buildings, the rich Sicilian evening. The proprietario then continued slowly in accented Italian. "Lei è qui da quanto tempo?"

Ryan was amazed at being able to understand the question almost immediately – *How long have you been in Palermo?* – without the usual irritating mental delay and offered a silent vote of thanks to whichever god or goddess in the pantheon looked after language. The deity was clearly at work because a response – *I just arrived today* – was already on his tongue.

"Sono arrivato oggi, e posso dire che Sicilia è molto bella!"

He thought the proprietario would kiss him. Arms pumped the air.

"Parla italiano! Formidabile! Formidabile!"

Faraci managed to reduce the proprietario's agitation enough that the risk to glassware on neighbouring tables was minimized, then he made a couple of rapid hand signals around his own mouth and throat.

"Si! Si! Il vino! Ritorno subito!" And the proprietario regaled a couple of other tables on his way back into his restaurant.

And he did return *subito*. Two bottles and four glasses were rescued from a tray, which seemed to be doing virtuoso biplane stunts. Faraci poured. The first wine was a white – moscatellone. Ryan had never heard of it, but wouldn't have turned down a second bottle. The second was a malvasia.

"Wow!" Ryan said, almost involuntarily. "I've had malvasia before, but never like this."

"Well", Faraci began, his wry smile signalling a plug for Sicilian oenological superiority, "we are blessed here, even if our cretin mainland cousins have trouble with that notion. Did you know that the first wines came from the foothills of Etna? That the grapes producing them came from vines that sprang from the footprints of Dionysus himself? I know that Barolo is a nice tipple, and our wine deity almost certainly did make it up that far. But by then, his palate would have been shot completely, and he would have been as pissed as a newton."

Ryan said nothing, was fairly sure that old Isaac imbibed modestly, if at all, but made a mental note to check. He had to admit, however, that "pissed as a newton" had a certain ring to it.

Dinner was at another place that Ryan never would have found on his own, nestled among trees and large oleander plants. Ryan willingly agreed to Faraci's proposed choice from the menu, and the plate that was soon delivered to him combined culinary elements from Palermo's long history of contacts with civilizations from around the Mediterranean.

Nothing was said while they both concentrated on doing justice to the food.

"That was superb", Ryan said, eyeing an empty plate in some regret and as Faraci refilled their glasses.

"I'm pleased you enjoyed it."

They sipped for a few moments.

Ryan looked directly at Faraci.

"What are *you* hoping to get out of all this, Angelo?"

Faraci twirled his glass for a moment, thinking.

"There's the matter of simple curiosity", he said looking across at Ryan. "The Nievo story is still of great interest to a large number of Italians. It's a delicious mystery, if nothing else. Nievo wrote one of the classic Italian novels of the nineteenth century. In his short life of less than thirty years, he wrote an impressive amount of what I'm assured is good poetry. I would like to know more about his fate, if possible, and about just what he would have discussed in Naples. But I am also aware that being associated with any late documentary find that filled any gap in his story, or extended it, would do no harm to my various lines of business, nor to my reputation."

After a short delay and some more glass twirling, Faraci continued.

"A substantial physical record, like a complete set of Garibaldi's campaign account books, would be a tremendous find. It might contain who knows what sorts of clues to all sorts of threads from those days. It might even shed some light on Nievo's disappearance. If he went to the length to prepare a separate set of accounts and ship them somewhere by a different route, then maybe he had some concerns about his trip to Naples. Perhaps he might even have noted those concerns in the duplicate accounts or in a letter accompanying them."

Another delay and a long appreciative sip of wine.

"And then there is the possibility of dark elements also trying to get their hands on any new Nievo documents. There are plenty of rich Italians. Collectors don't all need to be greedy Americans. Anything that raises the curtain on that world, the time of the Risorgimento, would be chomped on thoroughly by the press and the chattering classes. I count myself as one of them, by the way."

Faraci sipped more wine before continuing.

"You might know that there are strange moods and feelings in Italy today. If you think other countries have fault lines, try comparing northern and southern Italy. And the romantic sheen of the Risorgimento has worn off for many Italians. It would be nice to have another Garibaldi to show us the way, but old Giuseppe is just a shade now. Mazzini was a wild-eyed extremist. Cavour was an exceptionally talented but dangerous fop. These things have all been ground down in modern days by the actions and the misleading platforms of people like Berlusconi. And the same thing is happening in many places around the world. But it's particularly tragic here in Italy, it seems to me, because we have such a rich past that shouldn't just be buried under heaps of modern intellectual sludge. There might be ways past this. Something that tapped into a real person, like Nievo, whose work is still out there, might provide a way to put some of yesterday's ideas into today's clothes. And if anyone's looking for someone to do that, well, I'm their man."

It sounded as though Faraci was trying to cover all the angles.

"And what do *you* want to get out of it?" Faraci asked, catching Ryan somewhat off guard.

"Me? Well, I know some of the story of Nievo, and I also am a bit curious. But I have no real stake in the matter. This all started with my project, some strange things happened, I found interesting spin-off ideas, and that's what brought me here. All I really want to do is a bit of research to clarify those spin-off ideas, see if they lead anywhere interesting. But it's just historical interest for me. I don't welcome any of this intrigue. And there's no way I could keep up with the details of Italian politics, past or present, especially Sicilian politics, which seem very complicated."

"Beyond anything you could imagine", Faraci said with feeling.

"Let me ask you then", Ryan began, "what would the endgame look like? I'm stuck in the middle. I just want the monkey off my back. Those papers that I found at Karlsruhe . . . how could all this be brought to a point where everyone would lose interest?"

"Good question. If a second set of Nievo accounts were found and lodged in the Risorgimento Museum or some other official repository, that would be the end of the line for the treasure hunters. It would be a short-term news sensation, and perhaps a longer-term academic dig."

"But you don't think that's likely to happen."

"No. It's much more likely that no second set of accounts will be found, but also that there will be no evidence indicating that they *don't* exist, and it will be just one of those things that 'might be' in the future. A number of people will keep private watching briefs, hoping some other shred of evidence will turn up. You can publish your story, with my help of course, and that would likely go a long way to having anybody watching you lose interest."

"Do you have any idea who those watchers might be?" Ryan asked.

"I have some names. Probably not all the names."

"Couldn't you just put the word out that apart from the papers found at Karlsruhe, which are now locked away in official safe-keeping, there's no physical evidence of anything concrete being out there?"

Faraci looked at Ryan for a long moment.

"I can imagine your thoughts on your own position. But you need to know just where I stand as well. There are corners of Sicilian, and indeed of Italian society, where it's just not a good idea to go poking one's nose. People do me favours. I do other people favours. But these exchanges will continue only as long as people feel that I'm safe to deal with. So, I don't know most of the people who might be involved in the attention that's being paid to you. I might know of them, but I don't know them, and I'll be keeping it that way."

"So there might be dark elements who know you–"

"Know *of* me", Faraci corrected. "But why are you – Ah! Okay! I get it. You think someone might find it easier to get at you through me."

Ryan just gazed at him.

"Well, let's think about actions and reactions", Faraci began. "The fact that you are here at all says something, but what it says depends on any assumptions that might already be in place. Maybe you're here because you really do know something interesting, something nobody else knows, that you want to confirm something, snatch whatever personal advantage you can."

"But, why would I want to locate Nievo's duplicate accounts?"

"Assumptions, remember? What do people know about you? What do those people want? What are they prepared to do?"

"So, I should just do what I want to do here, finish it as quickly as I can, and leave."

"Possibly", Faraci replied. "But how will they interpret your departure? Did you hit the jackpot? Are you sneaking off with the prize?"

Ryan ran a hand through his hair in frustration. "I need your help, Angelo."

"And you shall have it. We could spend a lot of time running in circles, speculating like this. Let's just stick to the plan you worked out. Make your visits around Palermo. Then go back to your previous existence. I will produce a flurry of articles and interviews, we'll make sure that at least one official body puts out a high-profile statement on this whole business. That should be enough to put out anyone's fire."

Faraci caught the server's attention and asked for the bill.

"There's one more stop to make, then I'll walk back to your hotel with you. One last wine to taste. Mamertino. One of Julius Caesar's favourites."

Ryan seemed hesitant, made sombre by the previous half hour's discussion.

"Come on. Can't miss this one."

Thirty-Five

The next three days were back-to-back visits around Palermo. Ryan took several hundred pictures, spent a full day and a half at the University of Palermo, and communed for two hours near Cannizzaro's grave in the church of San Domenico. In the evenings, he struggled through several accounts, in Italian, of Cannizzaro's time in Palermo as a working chemist. But in all this time he felt flat. Had to force himself to do all that. Tried his best not to think about . . .

He felt that he now had all the local background he needed to begin thinking seriously about the articles he wanted to write, spin-offs from his project. Just thinking about that work reminded him of Di Biasi's offer to do the rest of the work under his auspices at la Sapienza. He could feel agreement to that proposal beginning to take hold in his mind. There was little left to do now in Palermo, although he knew that another week doing more general historical rubbernecking and tourist things would be rewarding. At least, under other circumstances. But he needed to finish in Palermo, visit Marsala and Calatafimi, get on to Taormina, return to Karlsruhe, deal with the review comments on his project report, and then make the big decision on what to do next and where to do it.

This was made even more difficult, now that Angelika was . . .

Ryan spent his last evening meal in Palermo on his own, having dined with Faraci the previous evening and said goodbye. Ristorante Giuseppe, a place suggested by the man at the desk in his hotel, was about five minutes from the hotel on foot, and it was the perfect spot. Small, cosy, quiet, great menu, and a wine selection from local vineyards ranging from Cefalù to Marsala.

The restaurant's own version of *caponata* got him started, Palermo-style baked *anellitti* opened the throttle and moved him into the straight, a generous hunk of *torta setteveli* helped him glide home, and he allowed himself also to be talked into a sliver of Sicilian *cassata*. The evening was mild, a light breeze murmured in the leaves around him, and the quiet chatter from the tables nearby seemed to draw on the richness of Palermo's millennia-long past. It was a reluctant Ryan Chandler who drained his last glass of wine, paid the bill, spent another ten minutes looking around his little oasis, then began making his way back to the hotel.

Thoughts of Palermo drifted off grudgingly, unwillingly, but eventually yielded to next stages – Taormina, Karlsruhe, and the uncertainties beyond that, things that soon would begin demanding decisions.

It was a leisurely walk through the refreshing evening. The Palermo streets were alive, as usual, and the air was redolent of an astonishing range of scents. Ryan halted at a set of traffic lights, and–

Dark.

Not feeling well.

Fading.

Spinning–

Wait.

Lying down.

Weak.

Musty.

Quiet.

Sinking.

My hands are tied.

Sit up!

Tried.

Couldn't.

Something's across my chest.

Confusion.

Falling.

Dizzy.

Panic.

Anger.

"Hey! Is anybody there? Who are you? Untie me! NOW!"

Nothing.

Anger fading.

Think Chandler! said the Inner Voice.

At least, that's something I recognize. What should we do, Voice?

Reconstruct the recent past, the Voice said.

Good idea. Ryan remembered dinner. Food, wine, restaurant – Ristorante Giuseppe. Yes, that was it.

Walking back toward the hotel . . . a traffic light.

Anything broken? Any aches? Ryan let his mind range over his body, tensed muscles starting from the neck and working down. No sharp pains. But there was a debilitating fuzziness in his head.

Shit! Was I drugged?

His conversations with Faraci over the past three days came back to him. He became aware of a sense of letting go, dropping those concerns he'd had about all the unexpected and dangerous things that had occurred to him over a period of months, that whatever had been their causes they were now behind him, gone.

Yeah, right!

So, here we go again, he thought.

Ryan began to heave at his bonds. The restraint across his chest seemed to be the least secure, and as he bucked and strained, it appeared to loosen. If he could just sit up, then what?

Whoever had done this wanted something. By now they might have located his computer, gone looking in it for whatever they were after. If it was the text from the Karlsruhe papers, good luck to them! It was screened behind multiple layers of encryption. The only key to it was in his head. And even if they had some very good tech, it would take them days to get what they were after.

Ryan heaved once more at his chest restraint. It was loose enough now that he could turn over onto his stomach. He flipped over and pushed up using his back. There was a clicking noise, and the restraint loosened considerably. He slid down and felt the restraint pass over his neck. It felt like a broad strip of tough nylon, the sort of thing used to tighten a load on a flatbed truck.

Now he could turn onto his back again and sit up. He brought his hands up to his face. The bonds on his wrists moved across his mouth, nose, felt like polypropylene rope. Very tight knot, but he started working on it anyway.

Ten minutes. No detectable loosening of the bonds. *Don't panic. Don't let anger get in the way. Just keep working at it. It might take–*

Light suddenly flooded the area. He was laid out on some kind of gurney. No. It looked more like a steel carpenter's table. The walls looked to be standard industrial plaster, maybe on top of drywall, painted white. The floor was concrete.

There was the sound of a latch releasing, a grinding of hinges. Someone appeared around the corner in front of him, about five feet away.

Aquiline Nose.

"You!" Ryan spat, surprised at the venom in his own voice. "You bastard!" It was him, the watcher from the storage lockers at Roma Termini. Faraci had put a name to him. *Centrini.* "What's this all about, you piece of shit?"

"Now, now, Mr. Chandler. This doesn't need to be anything more than a simple business deal. No need to make it personal."

Ryan conversed quickly with the Inner Voice, and they agreed that riling this prick while Ryan was in his present state just wasn't a sane plan.

"I need to know what you know about the Nievo documents."

Good luck with that!

"I will get what I want", Centrini said.

"You should believe him, Ryan", another voice said – a familiar voice – and then a second person appeared around the same corner.

Faraci.

Fuck! All this time! I was played like some cheap violin!

"So", Ryan said in as neutral a tone as he could manage. "I guess you're pretty proud of yourselves."

"This really is not a difficult problem for you", Faraci said evenly. "Please believe me. You should just tell this man what he wants to know. Then you can walk away."

"You really expect me to believe that?" Ryan asked, some heat coming back into his voice. "Once he has the information he wants, I'll be just surplus meat."

"No. All he wants is information. That's all there is at this point. And you should believe him when he says he'll get it. Either he tortures it from you or you just tell him what he wants to know."

"You must think I'm as stupid as you are", Ryan shot back.

"No. I know you're not stupid. But you're not thinking clearly. There's the possibility of a big prize out there. That's what he's really after. When he leaves here, you'll have no idea where he will go. You don't know who he is. And you can take it from me that he won't want the trouble of killing somebody, disposing of the body, making sure there's no evidence left behind, cooking up some cover story just in case."

"Oh yeah?" Ryan challenged. "And what if I go to the police?"

"And say what?" Faraci demanded. "That you were nabbed off the street by somebody whose name you don't know, taken to a place whose location is also unknown, and asked to reveal information on some wild story about Ippolito Nievo? A claim about the imminence of the second coming would be more credible. You present no risk to this man."

Ryan had been working ferociously, trying to line up things in his head and separate them from speculation, guesswork . . .

Centrini and Faraci just stood waiting, evidently in no rush. Then Faraci turned to Centrini.

"I'm going to get him a glass of water." He vanished down the long hallway, returned, held a large glass to Ryan's mouth, and Ryan drank. Faraci moved to the other side of the hallway, set down the tumbler, then stood back, next to an open electrical panel.

"I have time", Centrini said, "but I don't have all day. Let me know when you want to tell me what it is that I've come for."

Centrini looked at his watch and began turning, apparently to go back down the hallway, the way he had entered.

He didn't make it.

There was a loud puffing sound. Centrini's body convulsed suddenly, his eyes glazed, and then he just slid quietly to the floor.

Thirty-Six

Ryan cast an alarmed glance at Faraci. The look on his face was stricken. He looked at Ryan, looked down at Ryan's hands, then looked back at Ryan's face.

A third person now appeared from around the corner, a long-nosed pistol in her hand.

Sarah Brimley.

She looked like a Fury.

Ryan had only a photograph to work from. But even given the unreliability of memory, the change in Brimley was undeniable. Her hair had that matted unkempt appearance taken on by the fur of a dying cat. Flesh seemed to have drained from her face, leaving behind skin that hung in uncomplimentary folds and now seemingly hardened to the texture of old parchment.

But it was the eyes. They were no longer human. They were peep holes into a mind now consumed by its own private hell. Utter madness glowed from them. It was terrifying.

"He got in my way once too often", she pronounced harshly, casting one dismissive glance at the body on the floor in front of her. "I have plans."

Ryan recognized immediately the level of danger that faced both him and Faraci, possibly more so for Faraci. Although somewhere in the background he had already consigned Faraci to his own fate, whatever that might be.

What do I do? How does one deal with someone who might well be totally insane?

With great care, the Inner Voice offered.

"What do you want?" Ryan said as neutrally as he could, all the while aware of a very dry mouth and a voice on the verge of quavering.

"What do I want?" she shrieked, turning those terrible Medusa eyes toward Ryan. "What do I want? I want my life, that's what I want! But I can't have my life, can I? That bitch destroyed my life! Destroyed my life!"

Her mouth worked as though trying to utter something further, and her expression hardened even more, as though enraged at not being able to say what she wanted. Unexpectedly, a cold smile began tugging at the corners of her mouth.

"Well, if I can't have my life, then she can't have hers." Her words were cold, expressionless, but at the same time full of dark meaning.

Knowing a little of the background, Ryan could work out what this portended and was chilled to the core. Brimley was talking about Ryan's mother. And he had the powerful presentiment that he would be the means by which his mother's happiness, the value in her life, would be reduced to wreckage.

Ryan cast a glance at Faraci.

"Don't look at him!" the Fury shrieked. "Whoever he is . . . he can't help you now, and in a few minutes he won't even be able to help himself!"

Ryan's state of galloping panic had cooled to just unbridled fear, so the one or two seconds' view of Faraci was enough to register the terror in his eyes. Ryan recognized that Faraci's position was uncertain, probably not the snake-in-the-grass turncoat he had seemed when he and Centrini had been standing together. But the jury was still out.

"What do you want me to do?" Ryan asked, once again offering what he hoped would be viewed as no challenge or resistance.

"You'll do exactly what I tell you to do. In a few minutes, you'll contact your mother. I have some tasks for her . . ." The statement faded away ominously.

"So, you aren't interested in Nievo?"

"What? Who?" The words came out as eldritch screeches.

Ryan's mind was working in overdrive. Here was a clue, possibly, to all the shit that had been happening around him ever since he had come to Karlsruhe. Could it really be that simple? Had Brimley been trying all along to deliver disappointment, injury, psychological wounds to Ryan's mother? Was it all just a consequence of Brimley's slow but inexorable descent into some wild, dark illness of the soul? Holy shit! This was a lot worse than he had ever imagined. And it occurred to him that Brimley and Centrini had been working at cross purposes all along, each of them not really knowing who the other was or what they were up to, but knowing that someone else was there, suspecting that for each of them it was their game to lose. Could it really be that straightforward?

Centrini wanted Ryan's work to succeed, wanted him to unearth as much new information on Nievo as possible before Centrini grasped the reins. He wasn't interested in Ryan. Wasn't the least bit interested in his project, except as a means to deliver information. But Brimley's objectives always had been failure, humiliation, revenge. She had wanted Ryan's project to sputter and die, the result of apparent incompetence, something that would splash failure and shame equally onto James and particularly Michaela Chandler. The fact that Ryan had now essentially completed his project, had avoided all Brimley's traps, mostly by chance, well, that left Brimley nowhere else to go. For Brimley, for Michaela, but most clearly for Ryan, it was the nuclear option.

Ryan cast another glance at Faraci. Faraci hadn't moved an inch, not wanting to offer even the slightest provocation, recognizing that unless something intervened soon, his own remaining life expectancy was probably measurable in minutes. Faraci blinked. There was something . . .

The lights went out without warning. It became pitch black.

Brimley shrieked in rage.

This is it, Ryan thought, his mind suddenly racing. He leapt from his bench, hoping that Brimley had not moved, hoping that the image he had of her was good, hoping . . .

He lunged with all his weight.

He felt his left elbow encounter soft tissue, then grind heavily against parallel ridges.

Brimley's left breast.

There was a quiet crack. Then at almost the same moment, an ear-splitting scream and a *phut* as the silenced pistol discharged again. What felt like streaks of molten wax tracked across Ryan's left calf, but there was no time to worry about that. He had gained a couple of seconds' advantage at the most. He careened down the hallway by which both Centrini and Faraci had entered. Bounced off a wall. Elbows out. Trying to feel his way. Moving as fast as he could. Felt part of a doorway graze his right shoulder. Crashed heavily head first into a wall. Stretched his still-bound hands both ways along the wall. T-junction.

Go right!

Running along the hallway. Hoping not to trip. Equipment left lying? Anything sharp? An irregularity on the floor? Something excavated? A trench? A pit . . .

Just keep running, you asshole! the Inner Voice's screamed.

Crashed into another wall. Saw some light. Off to the left. Began galloping toward it.

Heard moans of agony from behind.

"Chandler!"

An otherworldly shriek. Felt hair lift on the back of his neck.

The shape of a doorway. Straight ahead. Beyond it some steps and a bulky shadow on the ground, ahead, to the right. He was in a construction site.

There was a steady stream of shrieked curses behind him.

Louder now.

Oh shit! Shit! Shit!

The bulky shadow took shape. A metal box. A toolbox. He needed a weapon. Something he could swing, throw. Reached down, felt the shape. Fumbled frantically.

"Chandler!"

Much louder now.

Cut his thumb on something sharp. Narrow. Sturdy. A chisel.

Time running out fast. He grabbed the chisel in both hands. Looked up the stairs. Door before him. Pale fans of light streamed in through gaps between the door and door frame. Looked like light from a street lamp.

Galloped up the stairs.

"Chandler!"

Fuck! She's right behind me!

Reached the door.

Stuck the chisel between his teeth.

Pulled at the door handle.

Nothing.

Shit!

Pushed the handle. Still nothing.

Loud clank of metal on concrete. Down the hall behind him.

"Chandler!" A long, drawn-out demented scream. Half agony, half wild, uncontained anger.

Get that fucking door open! Command shouted by Inner Voice.

Galvanized him. Harnessed his own juddering fear. Bound hands gripped the door knob. Turned. Pushed.

Nothing.

Lights came on behind him.

Fixed the knob in a death grip, then crashed against the door. There was a squeak as the door moved slightly.

"Chandler!"

Crashed again. The door swung wide. Ryan fell through and landed on a patch of gravel. But he was out now, in the Palermo night.

Don't drop the chisel!

A pile of board ends lay to one side. He grabbed a suitable length. Closed the door. Wedged the board under the door knob. Then galloped into the night, heading for trees and a small street off to the right. Rounded the corner. Entered the street, legs pumping. Now charged by adrenaline. Raced madly onwards. Fifty metres along, he turned left into another street.

You need options! Force the fury to make decisions! Move it, you idiot!

The Voice wasn't stupid.

"Chandler!" Further away.

But now she was out in the night as well.

Which is the best way?

Stop dithering, dickhead! Decide!

Left would circle back the way he had come. So. Go left! Maybe Brimley would guess "right". Galloped into the street. *Shit!* At least seventy-five metres to something obscure in the distance. No trees. No cover. What if . . .

Shut up and keep running, you dumb-ass!

Feet pounding on what felt like cobbles.

Don't trip.

Don't drop the chisel.

Faster!

Something dark ahead. Five more long strides.

Shit! Double shit!

It was a wall. He was in a dead end. More panic. Listening for sounds from behind.

Don't worry about her! You're wasting time!

Brick wall to the left. Stone wall to the right. No . . .

Path.

There was a gap, narrow, between the side of a building and the wall that dead-ended the street.

"Chandler!"

Her voice coming from further away now. Or maybe not.

Ryan entered the narrow pathway and was engulfed in darkness. His left elbow struck a protrusion and . . . he dropped the chisel.

It clanged onto stone.

He bent down, vicious curses foaming inside his head, began feeling madly over the surface. Something sticky. Smelly. Garbage residue?

A handle. The chisel. Grabbed it, rose, moved on forward as fast as he could. A streetlamp peered at him over the stone wall to his left. Looked ahead, in the pale reflected light. Not good. The path was dead-ending as well. No option now.

He began working with the chisel. Took only about a minute. Felt like about half an hour. Cut through the polypropylene. Freed his hands, dropped rope and chisel. Kept running and collided with something. Heavy garbage bin. Pulled it toward him. It made a dreadful scraping noise as it moved over the stone surface.

There was a mutter from somewhere on the other side of the wall next to him. A man's voice.

"Che diavolo?"

Ryan pulled himself up onto the bin. More grinding and crunching.

"Chi va là?" Louder this time. There was a sound of inner doors opening. Diffuse light appeared in a small window of frosted glass to his right.

Really out of time now. He reached up, grabbed the top of the wall, hauled himself up, swung his feet over. Lowered himself on the other side, hands still gripping the top of the wall.

His feet swung in the air and he looked down. *Oh fuck!* A platoon of large prickly pear covered the entire ground below him. They were all over Palermo. Looked quaint. Attractive. Until now, that is.

No option.

Keep your legs together! Tight! Cover your eyes!

Good advice, Voice. He didn't want to think about having to pull two-inch cactus spines out of his testicles.

He let go.

The pain was excruciating. The cactus plants collapsed beneath him. Found his footing and stepped back from his landing zone. He pulled ten thorns out of his arms and legs. It wasn't fun.

Looking around, from his spot next to the cactus beds, Ryan found that he was now in a somewhat wider street, not exactly a thoroughfare, but certainly not a side street. Across the street, at his ten o'clock, was what looked like a park. He moved through it at a trot, then located an area where he could sit and be partly screened, with a good vantage and fairly long-range views in all directions.

Ryan sat. The adrenaline was gone. He began to shake. Then he sobbed but eventually pulled himself together and spent five minutes removing the remaining thorns. He then checked his left calf. There were two red streaks across the upper portion, about three inches long, on a rising track. At a third location, there was a puncture mark. A small piece of concrete protruded from it. These were chips broken loose by the shot fired by Brimley when he had gouged her breast. Ryan pulled that out as well.

He then took stock. His watch said eleven fifty, but he couldn't be certain what day it was. He had no idea just where he was. It was somewhere in Palermo. He hoped. He had no map. There would be no place open now where he could get a map. And he certainly wasn't just going to wander about in the hope of finding something he recognized.

Ryan rose from his bench, looked around carefully, then found what he needed. It was a large circular stone wall enclosing a raised garden full of attractive flowers. All around the stone wall were more prickly pear, about four feet high, similar to the ones he had just dropped into. He had determined that the sticky stuff his hand had encountered back by the house was likely cat shit, and he spent a minute rubbing soil over his hands. Hands dirtied by soil were better than hands dirtied by cat shit.

He was able to crawl beneath the cactus, then around between cactus and wall to a spot where the plants were so numerous and dense that he was invisible. This was where he would need to spend the rest of the night. During this exercise he picked up two more thorns and now removed them.

And he listened. He could hear nothing but the sound of night traffic. But she would still be out there, somewhere. For now, the night was his friend.

But it could easily become a dangerous enemy.

Thirty-Seven

Alba.

l'Aube.

Dawn.

Ryan checked his watch. Five thirty. He was cold and stiff. But looking around, he recognized a building, a street. He was still in Palermo. The night had cradled him into a gentle place, perhaps even out onto a wine dark sea. And now the dawn had dropped him gently into a new day.

But his situation was still dire. Except for one thing. They hadn't taken his cellphone. Arrogance? Haste? Carelessness? Didn't matter. A plan was forming already in his head. First of all, no police. In Canada, in his present situation, he wouldn't have hesitated to go to the police. But here, a foreigner, in something involving a death, and the police eager to find someone to link to the body, his story, to be credible, would almost certainly need to make some reference? And if he did go to the police, what would he tell them? Abducted by an unknown someone for an unknown reason? Held hostage in some unknown location? Claiming to be at risk from some woman? No. It was a non-starter from any angle. There were just too many ways it could all slide sideways into the shitter. He had some temporary freedom of movement now, and he needed to use that to get out of Palermo, away from Brimley. But then there was the downside. By following this course, he was putting himself right back into the fray. Brimley was out there. Somewhere. There was now no doubt she was after him. For some reason. She was resourceful. And she was exceptionally dangerous. He lay back to wait, still screened in his prickly pear den, but he felt far from reassured.

Time limped onward. Idle thoughts came and went. The day was gaining strength.

He would wait until the morning was properly underway, say, about eight o'clock. Not so early as to raise concern when he called his mother. Ryan was now fairly sure that Brimley had somehow managed to use the Di Biasi connection to track him down. How that might have come about was unclear, but might just have reflected Brimley's resourcefulness. Ryan had also wondered briefly about Di Biasi and Faraci, whether they were associates in some way. But in the end, he couldn't find any good reason to suspect Di Biasi. It was Mitchell who had given him Di Biasi's name, and that connection alone made the whole matter very doubtful. No. Di Biasi was not under any suspicion.

Ryan checked his watch again. It was seven fifteen. Time flies when you're planning. He decided that he would wait at least another half hour in his lair, then start making his calls.

"Hello, Mother. I hope it's a fine Tuesday morning where you are."

"Ryan! How are you? Where are you? Yes, it is a beautiful day here."

So, he had missed only Monday.

"I'm in Palermo. Are you all right?"

"Yes, of course I'm all right. Why do you ask?" Pause. "Is everything okay, Ryan?" That sensitive intuition at work once more.

Ryan spent a few minutes rhapsodizing over Palermo. He needed to avoid giving his mother any impression that there was a problem.

"How is Dad?"

"He's fine. Taking longish walks now. He's almost recovered his strength."

"So, you will be going back to Toronto soon?"

"We have seats booked on the Thursday flight. What will you be doing, Ryan? How long are you staying in Palermo?"

"Not long. There are a few details I need for my project."

"What do you plan to do next?" Ryan's mother asked.

Ryan said nothing about Marsala, Calatafimi, or Taormina, noted only that he had to return to Karlsruhe to deal with review comments on his report.

"And then?" she asked.

"Well, then it's likely back to Toronto for me too. But that's still some weeks away." Ryan didn't like telling her something that might turn out to be not true, but . . .

They spoke a bit longer. His mother waxed lyrical about the spot where they were staying. Ryan promised to call again soon. They said awkward goodbyes, and hung up.

At Ryan's next call, the phone at the other end rang only twice.

"Pronto."

"So, Mr. Faraci, can you tell me just what the fuck it was that happened over the past thirty hours? Centrini is now dead, as far as I know. It would make things a lot simpler for me if you were dead too, you son of a bitch–"

"Stop, please. This can all be explained. It's not how it looks. It's–"

"We need to get together. This morning. But I'm not meeting you anywhere except in a public place where there are lots of people around." They agreed on a bistro on the Piazza Sant'Antonino, at nine thirty, a bit less than another hour into the morning.

Ryan hung up abruptly, without saying goodbye.

His call to Di Biasi brought ebullient professorial greetings and queries on how things were going, but it soured quickly as Ryan explained what had been happening to him and soon crossed over into outrage at Faraci's perfidy, and Di Biasi's half of the exchange became cold, staccato, business-like.

Ryan had scarcely the chance to get a few words in. Di Biasi outlined what he was going to do. He had calls to make. He was going to set up meetings with people that same morning. He asked Ryan to call him back at noon.

"What are you doing next?" Di Biasi asked.

"I'm meeting Faraci in a little less than half an hour."

"Hrmmph!"

Short pause.

"Have the police become involved yet?"

"Not with me", Ryan replied.

"You haven't contacted them?"

"To tell them what? I don't know what has happened to me or why. I don't know where I was held. Any story I told would be highly suspect. Plus, I would be placing myself, a foreign national, in the middle of what will likely be a murder case."

They talked about this for a few minutes.

"Okay" Di Biasi said finally. "When you meet Faraci, don't tell him your plans."

"He already has some idea of what I intend, based on what I told him a few days ago."

"What was that?"

"That I needed to get back to Karlsruhe to deal with review comments."

"Good!" Di Biasi said. "Stick with that. He's unlikely to follow you back to Germany."

There was a short pause here, before Di Biasi added, "But please call me every day."

Ryan noted that Brimley might have used the connection to Di Biasi as the means to track Ryan's whereabouts.

"You and I discussed it all in some detail", Ryan said in conclusion.

"I'll check", Di Biasi barked. "If there's a leak here, we'll soon damn well plug it."

It was Ryan's hope, and he expected that this was in Di Biasi's mind as well, that if listeners were still hovering around their present discussion, the information they were gleaning would be compromised in a way that would make its use risky.

Ryan thanked Di Biasi, who responded somewhat more mellowly, and they both hung up.

Then he needed to find a map, figure out where he was, go back to his hotel, collect his things, settle his bill, and check out.

There was a risk here. It was possible that Brimley had been able to track Ryan there. Couldn't be helped. If she had done so, that meant the possibility of another large question mark hanging over Faraci. Where the man stood in all this was an unknown. But he likely operated in something of a shadow a good part of the time.

Or had Brimley somehow worked out that Centrini was involved, who he was, what he was up to? Unknown at this stage. In any case, Ryan was pretty sure that Centrini was dead. If Centrini had been working for a third party, what had he told that party? Would someone else just step into Centrini's shoes and pick up the trail? Would Ryan continue to be dogged by watchers?

He needed advice. Probably that meant Di Biasi. But he doubted that he could simply side-step indefinitely what had happened the previous night and his involvement in it. There was now a body. Explanations would be needed.

To his great relief, he found a place that had small tourist maps. He located where he was, got his bearings, and struck out.

For the meet with Faraci, Ryan had hoped to arrive at the bistro first, but Faraci was already there, waiting for him, his features presenting a less cocksure expression than usual. Ryan was fairly sure that Faraci was not a stranger to legal grey areas, that the police probably had a file on him, and that Faraci knew how that would be used in an interview room. Ryan took a seat opposite him.

"Okay. Explain!"

"Ryan, this looks–"

"I know exactly what it looks like! That's why I'm so pissed off! So get on with it! Explain!"

And Faraci did.

It was pathetic, and pretty much what Ryan had expected. Faraci had been trying to play both ends against the middle, maximize his chances of getting a bigger haul out of the situation. A few sharp questions were needed when it sounded like the narrative was drifting off into the vagueness of half-truth. Ryan listened impassively. Faraci's explanation confirmed a few other things as well. It appeared as though Faraci's involvement had nothing to do with Brimley's intelligence on where Ryan was, that his abduction probably would not have been affected either way had Faraci not been in the picture at all. But, again, if Faraci had not been there, not switched off those lights, well, Ryan didn't want to contemplate . . .

Faraci knew the man called Centrini, but was virtually certain that it was a false name. Centrini knew of Faraci, of course, because of his public face, the articles and opinion pieces that appeared under his by-line. But they had never met before last night. Faraci wasn't interested in writing about minor hoods like Centrini. But on this occasion, Faraci knew enough about Ryan to interest Centrini. They had talked. A sort of pact among thieves had been hatched, and so Faraci became involved in the plot to do – what? – after Ryan had been snatched. At least, that's what Faraci might have hoped Ryan would believe. It was all grey, both the story and the background.

"Have you spoken to Di Biasi?" Faraci asked.

"Yes."

"Have you told him what has happened here?"

"Yes."

"Oh."

Faraci tapped his chin.

"We need to speak to Di Biasi, sometime–"

"We? Who is *we*?"

"Well, you and me", Faraci said.

"I've already spoken to him. Whether you speak to him is up to you. I don't know what your relationship is with Di Biasi, but I suspect it just tanked. That's your problem."

Faraci nodded in a resigned way.

"However", Ryan carried on, "I will be speaking to Di Biasi again later today, in a couple of hours, in fact. I know he will be concerned about the body. I can tell him that you will work with him and the police in putting together a reliable sequence of events for last night. If you're not prepared to do that, then I suspect that Di Biasi will accept my account for the time I was awake and find his own means to fill in the gaps. If that should happen to end up looking bad for you, well, tough. What do you say?"

"Maybe we could find some other course–"

"No! What's your answer? There's no time left for pissing around."

Thirty-Eight

The priority now was to get out of Palermo as soon as he could. And to do so while avoiding Brimley.

Brimley.

He stopped in a park, rethinking things for the third time. Avoid Brimley.

Would she be waiting somewhere near his hotel? Possibly. What if she saw him?

There weren't many options. He could just forget about the hotel. Leave his stuff. Not pay his bill.

But then the police would become involved. No. That wouldn't work.

He just needed to minimise the risk.

He found a taxi. Went to his hotel. Rushed inside. Asked at the desk for another taxi to pick him up. Went to his room, packed his things, came downstairs and paid. The taxi was waiting. He jumped in. The whole exercise had taken less than five minutes.

The taxi dropped him at Palermo Centrale, and he hastened inside. Ryan found the most secluded place to park. And watch. Watch for Brimley. There was a train to Marsala in forty minutes. After fifteen minutes, he had been unable to see Brimley anywhere. He bought his ticket, and then at the last minute boarded the train. He was drenched in sweat.

At Marsala, he was first off the train. He sprinted out of the station caught the first taxi he could, and somehow managed to tell the cabbie that he wanted to go to a nice hotel near the sea.

The spot the taxi stopped at was perfect. Not too large. Tucked away. Not on a major street.

In his room, he stretched out on the bed, and was astonished to find himself sobbing, unexpectedly, suddenly, from anxiety and relief. Anxiety because of everything that had happened, to him and to his parents. Relief that he had left Palermo successfully, had at least a temporary reprieve, and seemed to have eluded Brimley. He fell into a deep sleep and awoke nearly five hours later.

A shower, a shave, and half the bottle of white wine that came with the room put things in a better frame. His mood had changed too. His fear and anxiety over Brimley had now hardened into determination. Eventually, when he wandered out into the evening, he could feel that the Sicilian charm was back. Almost next door to the hotel there was a lovely small restaurant that had a nice sea view from a private patio. It wasn't cheap, but Ryan just muttered "Fuck it!" to himself. He sat and gazed westwards into the late afternoon.

Tramonto.

Sunset.

The world was bathed in gold, and not even the stress and horrors of the previous evening, which rushed back into his consciousness at irregular intervals, could change that. But it was all tinged by regret.

Ryan now realized that trying to second-guess Brimley was a dangerous game. She was unhinged, so was likely to do things that could have serious risks attached, things that normal people simply would not do. But once she had chosen a course, he had to expect that she would plan her path in scrupulous detail, and this was what would make her so treacherous. He just needed to try to keep away from her, keep one step ahead. But the deeply worrying thing was that he now knew that she wouldn't give up, that he really wasn't safe anywhere.

The good news was that the information link via Di Biasi likely was shut down now, so her ability to track Ryan easily was gone. Had she been able to overhear Ryan's last discussion with Di Biasi, she might believe that Ryan would be heading back to Karlsruhe and would go there herself. Given the information that Brimley had access to, she would have difficulty guessing at any further destination in Sicily that he might have in mind. So although he wasn't exactly comfortable, he wasn't particularly anxious.

He worried yet again about what to do next. Going back to Karlsruhe right away made no sense. What would he do there? The review comments on his report would not be in for at least a few more days, and he was sure that Mitchell would let him know when they were available. And in Karlsruhe, he was sure he would be conflicted by memories that he couldn't handle. He would see Angelika everywhere there. How would he be able . . .

Then there was Brimley. Brimley might have judged that Ryan would go back to Karlsruhe, as the information trail he had left would suggest. Maybe she would sense that by returning to Karlsruhe she might find some last-ditch opportunity to sabotage Ryan's project. Or hatch some plan to strike at him directly. The concern on Ryan's part was the likelihood that there would be some period of time when she and Ryan could be in Karlsruhe together and he wanted to minimize that time. Give Brimley the least possible opportunity to do something. To attempt another snatch perhaps? To arrange some sort of "accident" for Ryan? It did seem likely that, one way or another, she would move the game on to some sort of final phase. Lifelong agony or grief for Ryan's mother now seemed to be the sole remaining objective.

And if that were the case? Then a primary means for achieving that would be Ryan. Or perhaps Ryan's father. Di Biasi was aware of the hit-and-run in Rome, knew how serious the situation was, and knew that a primary reason for Ryan approaching him about Porto Santo Stefano was to find a very safe refuge, someplace having no link to any of the Chandlers' past travels in Italy. Ryan could only hope that these precautions had put his parents beyond Brimley's reach. If she had been behind the Rome hit-and-run, then her activity here, now, in Sicily could mean that she had been unable to pick up the trail of his parents, and had gone after the next best thing: Ryan.

He decided that he wasn't going to shrink from that possibility. If she didn't find a way to work her evil in Karlsruhe, most likely she would just find some other opportunity, somewhere else. So hiding or running wasn't an option as far as Ryan could see.

The sea and the advancing sunset gradually coaxed Ryan into a less apocalyptic, quieter mood. A quarter of the bottle of wine he had ordered had now been drunk, and Ryan couldn't recall just what it tasted like. This wasn't the way things were supposed to happen. His meal arrived, the waves lapping just beneath him offered a quiet *buon appetito*, and over the following forty minutes, a full evening was woven from light, sound, taste, and texture. At ten thirty, still struggling with the loss and the real and potential conflict that had engulfed him, Ryan fell into his bed and dropped mercifully into an immediate if fitful sleep.

The next three days was a struggle. Too early to return to Karlsruhe. The need to avoid falling into the dreaded slough of despond. Ryan forced himself to seek out traces of Garibaldi and Cannizzaro. There was a short stop at Trapani, a trek to Calatafimi that turned up no physical markers but revealed lots of historical significance, and, in the course of his path back to the mainland, a long visit to Taormina was imbued by an imagined Cannizzaro presence and centuries of eventful Roman ties. Etna oversaw Ryan's visit there: towering, benevolent, and threatening, all at the same time. But at every one of these stops, places he had wanted to visit in a relaxed mode, had become locations where he was always looking over his shoulder, where he sometimes felt very much on the run, and all of them intended to help delay as much as possible a return to Karlsruhe.

And then Ryan left Sicily, and he felt, unexpectedly, a strong sense of separation. This was something to be considered later. For the trip back to Karlsruhe, he chose the train once more, despite the distance and the travel time. On the train, he would have time to think and reflect, and God knew he felt a strong need for both of those just then.

He packed away the trappings of Sicily and unwrapped the elements of his project that had been placed in temporary storage. But these activities were interrupted regularly to look out the window at one lovely scene after another as he made the northward passage through the Italian peninsula.

For the remainder of the trip, Ryan read and slept, by turns.

On arrival in Karlsruhe, the first thing he did was call Rick, very much wanting to hear a friendly voice.

"Hey, Ryan! You're back? Where are you?"

"I'm at the station. Can we get together quickly?"

"No", Rick said. "But we can get together. Come to my place."

The smiles, handshakes, and hugs of a real friend almost brought Ryan to tears, a reminder that he really had been through the wringer. By six o'clock they were at one of their usual watering holes.

"So, tell me all", Rick said, still concerned about his friend but managing to be the nonchalant companion. And then without even thinking about it, or intending to unburden himself, Ryan spelled it all out, everything that had happened. For over an hour and a half. Rick's face registered disbelief, then shock, then sympathy, then anger, and then a deep concern.

"What are you going to do?" Rick asked.

"What can I do? Go and hide someplace? For how long?"

"Well, yes. You can go and hide. You must go and hide. I can arrange a place."

"No, I don't–"

"I'm not going to argue with you, Ryan. Don't be an idiot! I know a place. You're going to stay there. You can't stay at your flat! That's insane!"

They went back and forth for another half hour. Ryan finally gave in, asked Rick to make whatever arrangements were needed. Then they drank far too much beer.

Ryan looked at his watch. "I've got to go. I'm meeting Mitchell tomorrow morning." And he began to rise.

"Where do you think you're going?" Rick demanded. "You're not going home. You're staying at my place tonight."

There was another short argument, but eventually Ryan agreed, exhausted, tipsy, just needing to lie down somewhere.

He was at home, but he didn't feel at home. He had been away from Karlsruhe for what seemed like a very long time. It had been five days since Palermo. His project was now complete. His report had been written and submitted. Did he dare believe that he might be out of the woods? That the threat from Brimley might have eased?

A short rest at Rick's place revived him slightly. Unpacking, laundry, a shower, and change of clothes were the first elements of resumed routine. He then called Mitchell and arranged to meet him the following morning, Thursday, at ten thirty. By then, it was pushing six and Rick said that it was time to have something to eat. Which they did. At eleven that evening, Ryan slid between sheets on Rick's couch.

Thursday morning, ten thirty, Ryan was in Mitchell's office. The review of his project report had gone quickly, and Ryan and Mitchell walked through the comments. Mitchell was pleased. Ryan now had about ten days work ahead of him, the last ten days of his formal project. After the meeting with Mitchell, and as agreed with Rick, Ryan called Rick, met him at an out of the way spot, and Rick led him to some true student accommodation.

"Here's the key. The guy who rents this place will be away for another three weeks. It's your home now. Call me if there's any problem."

And this was where Ryan set to work dealing with the comments on his report. It went quickly. The days he put were long and the work went more quickly that he had expected.

Work on his report was interrupted on Friday afternoon, when he took a call from Di Biasi who had spent time working with the Italian police on the ragged Sicilian situation. All the contentious items relating to Ryan had been dealt with. A notice had gone out to find and apprehend Brimley. Ryan needed to give a statement to the Karlsruhe police. But Di Biasi had tilled the ground well, and all this was now in the realm of formality.

By the following Tuesday, Ryan had made his three-hour deposition to the Karlsruhe police, his first round of responses to the review comments had been returned to Mitchell, and the world was going flat. He had the sense that an ending was coming. That same morning he received an e-mail from his father saying that he and Michaela had arrived back in Toronto, that he would be back at work very soon, was doing some physio, and looked forward to a telephone discussion with Ryan whenever the opportunity for that appeared. Ryan felt fairly certain that his father was also interested in the project report, knowing that things in Karlsruhe were well into the endgame. Resolving to have KIT confirm that a copy of the finalized report would be shipped through official channels to James very soon, Ryan sent an e-mail to bring his father up to date. And then he was definitely in the endgame.

He got back to work.

Wednesday rolled around.

Project clean-up now.

Items were ticked off Ryan's list, but without enthusiasm, because he knew what it all meant: the end of his time in Karlsruhe, a place that had changed the course of his life.

But then there was an item indicating one small gap. Ryan checked through his papers, but what he needed was not in his accountant's case.

His flat. The two files he needed had to be there and he needed them.

He called Rick, explained the situation.

"You can't go back there, Ryan."

"I have to. No choice."

"Wait for me then. You can't go alone."

"Okay. I'll wait for you in the street outside my building."

"All right. But be sure to wait for me!"

Ryan struck out, anxious to get what he needed and finish the project finally. He arrived in front of the building that housed his flat. Nobody around. So he just settled to wait for Rick.

He looked at his watch.

Ten minutes had passed.

Looked again.

Now twenty-five minutes.

Shit.

I'll just go in quickly, get my files, then come right back out and wait for Rick.

His flat was sad and airless. There was the evidence still around of him having left in a hurry. Three empty wine bottles sat by the sink. Glancing through the doorway to his bedroom, he could see that he had left his bed unmade. The door to the large armoire in his living space hung open. On the coffee table was a small plate, a piece of crumpled plastic cheese wrapper, the brown and shrivelled remains of an apple core, and the kitchen knife he had used to cut and eat them just before he had left. How long ago? Seemed like an age.

He spent a few minutes looking through the paper on his desk, and located the two files that he needed. As an afterthought, he collected a pair of clean jeans, several shirts, socks and underwear, stuffed them, along with the files, into an IKEA bag.

That's it then. Nothing more to do. He bent to pick up the IKEA bag, to go back outside and wait for Rick.

"Hello, Ryan."

Sarah Brimley.

She had entered silently. She closed the door without taking her eyes off Ryan.

And, once again, the silenced pistol.

Despite his awareness of the acute danger Brimley presented, anger flooded Ryan and he found it hard to contain. "What do you want?"

"I told you", she said, the same wild glow in her eyes. "I want my life back. But I can't have it back. That bitch, your mother, stole it from me."

There was no point in trying to reason with her. He would just need to talk. The anger slowly subsided. He needed the clearest possible head just now.

"You and my mother were close friends at one time. What happened?"

"What happened? She got ambition. I was in her way. She did everything she could to throw me on the trash heap! That's what happened!"

They looked at each other. Ryan allowed a long interval to draw itself out.

"Well. I am sorry", he said at length.

"*You're* sorry?!" she replied, in a kind of muted bark. "Why would *you* be sorry? And sorry for *who*?"

"I'm sorry because I hate to see people dumped by the wayside. The world should be large enough to accommodate everyone. But it's not always a fair place."

"So. The rich kid philosopher", she said, her words dripping sarcasm. "If it had been just a matter of chance, I might have been able to live with it. But this was active malice. That's what put me where I am now."

Had she been able to see herself in a mirror as she made this utterance, would she have detected any conflict between her words, which sounded measured, and the wild insanity beaming out from her face?

"Anyway", she carried on at length. "There's no point in all this now. It's too late to rethink things."

The pistol came up, pointing at Ryan.

"You have to believe me when I say that I really don't want to do this, don't feel good at all about doing it."

At the time, but especially looking back, Ryan was amazed at how calm he felt just then. The possibility of suggesting a meeting between Brimley and Ryan's mother crossed his mind, a hopeless pipe dream, he knew, but at some earlier stage it could have offered a way back, a way out.

Not now.

There were a limited number of ways Ryan could protect himself during the few seconds he guessed remained. The pistol was as steady as a rock. Ryan was sure that she had finished talking. What was she thinking of? Her own delight at the first signs of Michaela's lifelong distress and regret? What would come next for her, in a life where the one burning objective had been achieved and no future beckoned? When she had killed Ryan, was she going to kill herself, here, in his flat? And miss the pleasure of seeing Michaela's grief? Unlikely.

Sometimes, the world can go topsy-turvy, lurch in an unexpected direction, either physically or metaphorically. And that's what happened just then.

Brimley suddenly collapsed sideways.

There was a cry of rage, the pistol was dislodged and skidded across the floor, and suddenly Ryan was seeing a grotesque wrestling match. The other wrestler was Rick.

Ryan moved toward the pistol, something that Brimley was also attempting to do. Ryan made it there first, kicked the pistol under the large armoire that sat in the corner. There was another shriek of rage and a bout of cursing. Ryan landed a kick on Brimley's thigh, but by then she was clawing herself free of Rick. She rose to her knees, stumbled to the low coffee table, grabbed the paring knife Ryan had used for his apple and cheese, turned, and springing to her full height she sank it into Rick's stomach, just as he had risen to his feet.

Rick froze, began to back away, and fell.

Brimley pulled the knife out of him and was closing in for another lunge. Looking back, it was all somehow just a piece of disembodied theatrical absurdity, a sequence clipped from someone else's nightmare that had somehow drifted into Ryan's life. He brought a chair down over Brimley's shoulder and arm, and the knife fell onto the sofa while Brimley's torrent of rage continued. Brimley and Ryan both dived toward the knife.

Brimley came up with it, but Ryan had an iron grip on her wrist. She fought like a demon. The knife swung back and forth before their eyes, at one point scoring a three-inch cut across Ryan's forehead. They continued to struggle and sway. Brimley was now shrieking continuously. The coffee table overturned, and the cheese and apple plate shattered.

The chair Ryan had used to strike her was behind her now, and Ryan pushed her backward against it. She began losing her balance, and her grip on the knife loosened as she sought a way to avoid falling over backwards. At that point, Ryan managed to rip the knife from her grasp.

"You evil bitch! Get out! Get away!"

He slashed the knife before her face. She ducked backwards but not before a large gash opened up on her right upper arm. More slashes of the knife and another deep cut appeared on her shoulder. She screamed and wailed. Blood was now running freely down her right arm, and she turned and ran from the flat still screaming. Ryan could hear her stumble down the stairs. There was the sound of the front door to the building closing, followed a few seconds later by the screech of tires.

Ryan was breathing heavily, shaking from adrenaline shock. He pulled out his cellphone and called for an ambulance and police, then dropped the phone onto the sofa and went to Rick.

Rick was rolling, moaning, holding his stomach. There was quite a lot of blood.

"Hang on, Rick! I'm here! Help is on the way! You're going to be all right!"

Rick nodded.

Ryan rushed to the bathroom for a clean towel, returned to Rick and applied it to the wound. The next few minutes were a blur. Ryan kept talking to Rick, but had no memory later of what he said. The ambulance siren, that slightly vibrato, two-toned, out-of-my-way warning sounded in the distance, rapidly approached, and was snuffed out just in front of the building. Two minutes later, the police arrived.

The paramedics were the picture of German calmness and efficiency. They snipped away Rick's shirt, spent only a few seconds examining the wound, exchanged a couple of sentences in German, then broke open their bag of tricks. The police entered, waved the paramedics to get Rick off to the hospital, then began taking photos.

The next forty minutes were taken up by a police interview in Ryan's flat. They walked Ryan through the events three times, took many pages of notes, snapped several dozen more photos, retrieved the pistol from beneath the armoire, bagged the knife and the towel, and asked if Ryan would mind coming back to the station with them to complete and sign a statement. Although phrased as a request, it was clear to Ryan that only one answer was acceptable.

At nine o'clock that evening, Ryan dragged himself back into his flat and collapsed in his easy chair. He was drained. The police had put a guard on his building.

Ryan made a couple of telephone calls, learned that Rick had been taken to the Städtisches Klinikum. He called the hospital, asked about Rick, and then waded through what seemed like an eternity filled by questions such as who Ryan was, what was his family relationship to Rick, and so on. In the end, the hospital gave out the minimal information that Ryan needed. Rick had had surgery and he would recover soon.

He now felt deflated, but on a sudden urge, he called Mitchell, who was clearly shocked and alarmed to hear what had occurred.

"Could we meet, Alan? Now? I'm hungry, and I really need an hour of friendly company."

Mitchell agreed instantly.

His door buzzer sounded, Ryan pressed the door release, but then locked his flat and started downstairs. He met Mitchell halfway and they carried on down together. The long bandage on Ryan's forehead brought an inquiring look.

"Let's get a drink and something to eat. I'll fill in the details."

They found a place quite close, and Ryan downed a quarter litre of beer practically at a single glug. They sat and talked for over two hours. Initially, the topic was the evening's events and their background and lead-up. But soon things moved on to Ryan's project report, Ryan's general experience in Karlsruhe, how Mitchell was finding his sabbatical thus far, and what lay ahead for both of them. Mitchell posed some questions on what Ryan planned to do next, but Ryan claimed still to be deciding and provided only vague replies.

Mitchell insisted on walking home with Ryan.

"Will you be all right? You're welcome to spend the night at my place. I have plenty of room. My wife won't arrive for another week."

"No. I'm fine thanks."

"Well, okay. But be sure to call me any time if you feel you need to."

"Yes. Thanks."

They shook hands at the door to Ryan's building, Ryan dragged himself back up to his flat, made sure the door was locked securely, and crashed.

His last thought before he drifted off was of turning a corner.

Thirty-Nine

Rick came out of the hospital four days after his injury. His parents were with him, and he introduced them to Ryan. Rick looked pale and strained, and his parents whisked him away. It was a week later before Rick contacted Ryan again.

Rick's parents had returned home, reassured that their son was well on the mend. Rick had moved back into his flat, and Ryan went there to meet him. Rick was leaning on a cane and looked a bit drawn, but his colour had returned and his smile was ready and spontaneous. Despite Rick's apparently lackadaisical approach to his studies, he was doing well, and KIT granted his request for an additional two weeks off to recover. This fit in well with what Ryan had in mind. Ryan asked about his recovery.

"They tell me I should be walking as much as I can, but gentle walking, and not too much at a time. No lifting, no stretching, no sit-ups, try not to sneeze."

"No sex", he added, through a gloomy expression.

Then a faint smile from Rick.

"And no straining on the toilet. But I can manage that."

"Have you been reduced to 0.3 litres of beer at a time?" Ryan asked, a question that brought just a rude gesture as reply.

Rick asked about Brimley. Ryan said that the police presence seemed to have scared her off. There hadn't been a sign of her. Then he laid out his plan for Rick.

"No! We can't do that!" Rick protested.

"Of course we can", Ryan said. "What else are you going to do? Sit in your room and mope?"

"But . . . the Ostsee? I mean, I've heard a lot about Germany's north coast. Never been there before. It's a long way."

"Haven't been there. Isn't that a decent reason for going?"

"Well, yes . . . but . . ."

"And I've never been there either. Lots of nice things are said about it. The beer's good. I like eating fish and there's lots of that up there."

"But, this business of you paying the whole shot. I don't think . . ."

"Seems that you've forgotten what happened in my flat not all that long ago. You saved my life, man! That's not nothing!"

This back and forth went on for another ten minutes, but it was clear that the idea of a week at the Ostsee really did appeal to Rick, a week away from Karlsruhe appealed even more, and he decided he could probably bring himself to accept Ryan's offer.

Once it was decided, it all unfolded quickly. Plans were made, and then they were off.

And it really was marvellous. There were a reasonable number of vacancies, it being still early in the season, and Ryan selected rooms at a premium rate in a lovely guesthouse, practically right on the beach, in the impossibly pretty town of Heringsdorf on the island of Usedom. Although the air was chilly, the weather co-operated, pouring down sunshine by the bucket, and the week was a dream. Ryan and Rick walked on long sandy beaches and flopped behind the guesthouse out of the wind, where they soaked up sun. Apart from spending some time chatting and a lot of time in companionable silence, they drank beer and ate fish every day.

While it was a means to promote Rick's convalescence, and the change in his colour and energy levels confirmed that he was indeed convalescing, it was also an escape for Ryan. *No*, he thought. *Let's be honest. It's a means of denial.* Because he could no longer hide from the immediate future and his need to decide what that future would hold. His report was finished. His project was ended. No more hiding there. The formal arrangement his father had set up with KIT was now being concluded. KIT had written their own report on the project, and both that and Ryan's monograph had now been delivered to James Chandler. No hiding there.

He would need to terminate the lease on his flat. And . . .

He would need to say goodbye to Rick.

These were barriers easier to ignore than to try to vault.

None of that got in the way of extracting every ounce of enjoyment from their stay in Heringsdorf. But all too soon, it seemed, they were back on the train to Karlsruhe. Rick was now the picture of radiant good health, sporting skin that had been bronzed by sun and wind, and hair that was slightly sun-bleached, and he seemed to smile all the way back to Karlsruhe.

The following two weeks were strange, deflating. Even worse, Ryan felt as though he was slowly unplugging a living thing. But something else was unfolding.

Ryan placed one more call to Di Biasi. They discussed possibilities. Di Biasi presented his persuasive case once more. He was clearly a man who had plans and would do everything he possibly could, within the realm of the gentlemanly, to see that his plans were carried out. Better informed, but telling himself he still had made no final decision, Ryan ended the call.

There was one important trip Ryan had to make. He had finally forced himself to do this. He made the arrangements and bought his tickets. He didn't know what to expect.

Heinrich and Erika Schröder, Angelika's parents, were both soft-spoken people, had ready smiles, kindly faces, and tried to conceal the air of grief that hung over them. Ryan knew that he had to explain to them his relationship with Angelika and why he had sat so shamefully in the background for so long.

To his astonishment, he was received like a lost son. Apparently, Angelika had spoken to them at length about him.

"She was such an intelligent young woman", her father said, looking toward some point in the misty distance. "And so forthright. One could have knocked us over with a feather the day she told us that she and you were going to be married."

Ryan had been in mid-sip on a glass of riesling and nearly choked. "Married? But ... I didn't ..."

"Yes. We know", Erika said. "She told us that you hadn't asked her yet. But she said it was obvious, and that in her mind she had already said yes."

An immense jagged shovel was hollowing Ryan out inside, his eyes began stinging, and before he knew what was happening tears began rolling down both cheeks. Erika Schröder teared up in sympathy right away, moved beside Ryan, and clasped him in a gentle motherly hug. The three of them talked for almost an hour, and Ryan's immediate pain, regret, and sadness dulled slightly, but he knew that the trek out of this vale was going to be a long one. When it was time for Ryan to catch his train back to Karlsruhe, they insisted on accompanying him to Stuttgart station, and Ryan caught sight of them as he boarded his carriage, two people who might have been his parents-in-law, waving goodbye down the platform.

On what turned out to be the third last night in his flat, a call came in on his cellphone.

"Mother! Hello! I wasn't expecting to hear from you. How is everything? Dad is okay?"

"Yes. He was when I saw him last. But he's back in Toronto. I'm in Karlsruhe."

"In Karlsruhe? Where are you staying? I'll come and meet you."

Arrangements were made, and Ryan set off for the *Hotel Kaiserhof*, wondering at what appeared to be impulsive behaviour by someone who wasn't impulsive at all.

Ryan and his mother always had soft spots for each other, and Ryan's absence for the best part of a year had only accentuated this. There was something else, and eventually Ryan put his finger on it. He was far from home, standing on his own feet. Apparently this mattered to Michaela.

They walked back to Ryan's flat, a distance that could be covered in less than half an hour. On the way, they stopped at a supermarket to pick up things for a nice dinner that Ryan insisted he would prepare for them. In the end, they both made the meal. Its consumption, along with a very nice bottle of wine, was something shared by two people who had just done the last bit of work on converting a parent-child bond to something deeper and more durable.

There was a long after-dinner discussion. Ryan's mother spoke about their family and how things had changed over the past year, how all three of them were making some fairly major adjustments at two different life stages, a young-adult change for Ryan, a mid-life change for his parents. Michaela spoke about their time at Porto Santo Stefano, and the long discussions they had both had with Di Biasi, then and since. And then Ryan told her about Angelika, how they had met, what she was like, how much he had loved her. Despite his efforts to avoid it, he broke down several times. His mother comforted him, was the same person of strength and compassion that he remembered so clearly from his boyhood.

She dried his tears.

"It's okay now", she said.

Ryan nodded mechanically, and smiled weakly at his mother, not thinking about these words.

They spoke about other things as well, things that astonished Ryan, things he would need to think about carefully. It was during that discussion that Ryan inched closer to his decision. It was all triggered by his mother's comments, reflecting on Ryan as a boy, as an adolescent, as a young man. Without saying so explicitly, her message was clear enough, that Ryan would have to forge his own path, for his own reasons, but that he could count on his parents' support every step of the way.

At eleven thirty, Ryan called a taxi for his mother, they had a long and almost tearful embrace at the entrance to Ryan's building, and then the taxi carried away a waving hand and a see-you-later smile.

Forty

It was April 14, Ryan's last night with Rick in Karlsruhe. Definitely something to be remembered. There was laughter, many great evenings recalled, practically every joke they had ever shared, beer by the gallon, and massive schnitzels. Ryan hedged about his plans for the future. But they both knew that this wasn't goodbye.

Ryan awoke late the next morning and faced a rough session with his Inner Voice.

So, Chandler. It's time to stop shagging the canine. Just what are you going to do?

The delay in replying was too long for the Voice.

I see. Okay. I guess then that you're just going let the clock run out, let the default decision be made, and scuttle ignominiously back across the Atlantic to the place you call "home". You're disgusting! You know that, don't you?

"What would you do?" Ryan wailed plaintively, speaking to an empty room.

It doesn't matter what I would do. It's your decision and you can't pass it off on me. I'm stuck with you, God help me, and I'm not impressed.

The Voice was right.

It really was decision time. And there was an activity that needed to precede that. Time to take stock.

His project at Karlsruhe had been a life-changer, and he was indeed a changed person now. His intellectual horizons had expanded massively, and he now knew what B.F. Skinner had meant about a mind that has been stretched to grasp a new idea never reverting to its original shape.

The before-and-after contrast was immense. In fact, he shuddered when he looked back. What he saw in the *before* frame was an immature being, an infant. He had grown during the past year. And although it would be a stretch to say that he was now mature, at least he was aware of his own immaturity and in a position to do something about it. *In the unlikely event that this story is ever documented*, Ryan thought, *it would probably be called a Bildungsroman.* Maybe. There was plenty of *Bildung* involved. But it had not been, was not in any way, a *Roman*.

He had met what probably was – could have been, should have been – the love of his life. And he had lost her. And he had to come to terms with that.

He had learned to live in a foreign country, but one that no longer felt foreign. He was now comfortable, if not fluent, in a new language. He felt that he understood a new culture. There was a range of people who made clear the stunted nature of the adolescent "friends" he had had in Toronto: Diana, Ted, and others, people who lived in a fog where they possessed only tactile knowledge of just a few objects, people whose reality was a space populated by canned reactions to those few objects, where the physical, emotional, and intellectual worlds barely intersected. A bit harsh? A year ago he would have thought so, been outraged had someone else painted this picture for him, of him. But now? Well . . .

Then there was Rick, the first new friend to people Ryan Chandler's European world. An oddly interesting person, someone who seemed to have a Peter Pan exterior, who liked to project an approach to the world that was picaresque, almost Rabelaisian, but who possessed a fine mind that knew where it was leading its body. Someone he now had the strong feeling would be a lifelong friend. Add to that Alan Mitchell, Nino di Biasi, and a few casual acquaintances.

The arresting thing about this before-and-after split-frame view was the quite sober judgment he was able to make on his pre-Karlsruhe life. It had been unformed, innocent, almost childish. The curious thing about reflecting on himself this way was that this wasn't a sneering or dismissive criticism. It was far more a realistic assessment, something that could be viewed for what it was, then placed back on the shelf holding all those things Ryan had left behind.

What was most astonishing however, and something that Ryan realized only gradually, was what he had learned as a sort of spin-off. This involved people. But all those people were dead. Furthermore, most of the details of those people's lives were peripheral to his reasons for coming to Karlsruhe in the first place.

Cannizzaro. Garibaldi. Nievo.

Of course, he *knew* none of these people, but he now knew *of* them, and he felt that he knew more about them than anyone else did, barring a relatively small handful of individuals attracted to various aspects of history. Okay. Maybe Nievo was an exception. Maybe every Italian had heard of Nievo.

He knew Cannizzaro's details. He could see him as a young man at the 1860 conference presenting information that would make at least one aspect of the conference a lasting success. He knew of Cannizzaro at Taormina, in Paris, and along his academic trail that led through Italy to la Sapienza and then to the Italian Senate. And he knew of Cannizzaro's death in Rome and his body's last trip home to Palermo, to his birth city and to his last refuge, a place that Ryan felt certain might well become one of his own personal refuges in the future, but a refuge of a very different sort. Perhaps a sort of anchor for the story documented in his project. Perhaps a vast background canvas for that intriguing individual, Cannizzaro, who provided one representation for Ryan on what the Risorgimento was all about. He knew of Cannizzaro's wife, the tough-minded Harriet Withers, Cannizzaro's partner in everything and part of the source of his excellent English. He knew of Cannizzaro being awarded the Royal Society's Copley Medal, a sign of high achievement. In many ways, he knew Cannizzaro, knew him well.

And then Garibaldi. Well, what can one say? A prodigious general. A true leader. Possibly the embodiment of charisma. A modern day Cincinnatus.

Finally, the mystery. Or rather, the mysteries. The Brimley connection was clear now, and even though she had made no appearance for a long time, he no longer worried that she was still out there, no longer still in the grip of her mad scheme. Ryan had also satisfied himself on how the Nievo connection had arisen. Early on, in Karlsruhe, he had been quite open about his interest in Nievo, once he had learned at least some of the story. It occurred to him that the very strangeness of this situation, a North American having no obvious connection to this very Italian story, was snooping around. He was now convinced that someone had noticed and decided to watch him. Then, his abrupt departure from Karlsruhe must also have been noticed. From the perspective of any watcher, this would raise questions. Where had he gone? Why? Had he noticed something? More than ample reason for someone to follow and observe. But then there were the spoilers. The note he had left at the hotel in Rome was as good as an open declaration that he had something important in his possession. Finally, the transfer of very clear information from Di Biasi to Faraci, entirely innocent on the part of Di Biasi, had been the clincher.

But none of that mattered now. It was done. Past. All this business regarding documents linked to Nievo was now history, as far as Ryan was concerned.

Putting this all together yielded what?

To his surprise, Ryan suddenly knew that he had made a new start on a new something. He himself had changed greatly. His unformed, innocent, almost childish past was now tucked away in that great photographic album that life assembles for you while you're not looking. This was the result of his project, which had been an academic success and a personal watershed. That project had generated new ideas, new paths, a new view of the world. Was he just going to ditch all that?

Clearly not. There was important unfinished business here. He had to carry on.

His decision had just been made. He would contact Di Biasi. About a week hence, sometime toward the end of May, or whenever the paperwork could be completed, Ryan knew that la Sapienza would be his new home for at least a few months.

And what about the "other stuff"?

There was family. Michaela's astute intuition had spoken to her long ago, saying that his project in Karlsruhe would take Ryan across an emotional and familial boundary. Ryan could see that the family he came from was reforming. He still had a place there but now as a free agent, while his parents were constructing for themselves a future mainly for two. Ryan was surprised at the heart stab that realization caused and could see that something similar was happening for his mother.

But his mother had explained other things. Sarah Brimley's hope was to deliver a lifetime of anguish to Michaela, all for slights that were imagined, products of a raving mind gradually becoming completely unhinged. There had been concern on the part of Ryan's parents because of all the things that happened around him in Karlsruhe and in Sicily, things they had learned of only after the fact. But this was all in the manner of looking-back, because Ryan had been careful to make sure that he revealed these things to them only later. There were fences to mend because of that.

Standing above it all, there was shock and the stunning depth and darkness of the intent that lay behind the hit-and-run in Rome.

And there was great and lasting pain for Ryan. His Angelika was gone. Had it involved an accident? Or was it Brimley tying off a loose end that might have reached out at some point and strangled her? Ryan had gone over that ground again and again.

The short time Ryan and his mother had spent together in Karlsruhe had been revealing. The things his mother had told him had written, closed, and sealed a book. There was nothing explicit, and it had taken Ryan some time to work through the subtleties of just what had happened. But eventually, he understood. And he remembered his mother's words in his flat: "It's okay now".

The book contained a story just for the two of them, and only for them, for a mother and her now adult son. And the story revealed that Ryan's mother had intuited, had guessed, and had discovered much more of the chain of events and Brimley's role in those events than Ryan had expected, that she had put it all together quite some time ago, and that she had acted on it decisively even before Ryan and Rick had set out for Usedom.

The story was stark but simple. It delivered and left behind a dark cloud that wasn't going to go away. It was the primeval story of a mother's protective instincts riled into action by a threat to her offspring.

Michaela Chandler's long explanation had come to Ryan through a veil that suggested nothing more than a vague pattern but delivered nevertheless a crystal clear message.

Sarah Brimley's body would never be found.

Author's Afterword

The central character in this book, Ryan Chandler, did what many young people should try to do. He lived abroad while he was still young.

In 1970, I (the author) was an IAESTE exchange student in Great Britain. IAESTE stands for International Association for the Exchange of Students for Technical Experience. I was assigned to work at the Atomic Energy Research Establishment at Harwell, where I was a "Vacation Student" for eight weeks.

My expectations prior to travelling to Britain were both modest and vague. I didn't really know what to expect, but it all looked different and interesting. That description – "different and interesting" – turned out to be a huge understatement. Although I combined this eight weeks at Harwell with another eight weeks travelling in continental Europe beforehand, it was the fact of having eight weeks to get to know another place in some detail that made the difference.

Having thus acquired a taste for living outside Canada, I subsequently spent three and a half years in Britain (Salisbury and London) and two years in Vienna.

Apart from a stimulating period of technical work, here are some of the impacts of my IAESTE work term:

- I discovered that, for those who remain open to new experience, "culture shock" is more than just "language shock", and for those who are willing to look for the positive side to this "shock", there is likely to be a strong jolt pushing them toward a wider cultural awareness.

- All around me, in southern England, I found a far greater collection of the physical markers of history than I had known to that point. This re-ignited for me an interest in history, one which had gone dormant since high school, but which today still burns brightly.

- One of the individuals I worked with at Harwell, Gordon Aitchison, inspired an interest in statistics that I still retain.

- During the eight weeks of my IAESTE work term, I lived in Oxford, and a lifelong interest in that city, its ambience, the literature it has spawned, and the countryside around it developed quite naturally.

- Within the first two weeks of my student exchange, I met the young woman who is my wife of 45 years and counting.

- Through the people who became my in-laws, I was given the best possible introduction to the complexities, the variety, the pleasant oddities, and the joys of English life and culture.

My IAESTE experience was overwhelmingly positive. Without any exaggeration, I can say that it was one of the major pivot points in my life.

Acknowledgements

My wife, Maggie, undertook the first review of what was then a ragged manuscript, badly out of focus. Her efforts helped greatly in bringing the text to its present state.

My thanks also to my superb editor, Paula Chiarcos, who applied both carrot and stick to help me complete the revision.

Dr. Trevor Levere, Emeritus Professor at the University of Toronto, and a friend and neighbour, read an early version of the entire manuscript. His advice and suggestions kept me on solid ground concerning technical details on Cannizzaro and the chemistry of his time.

Finally, my thanks to Walter Cimaschi for casting an Italian eye over the text.

www.ingramcontent.com/pod-product-compliance
Lightning Source LLC
Chambersburg PA
CBHW020553020726
47494CB00006B/2055